"Owen, are you all right?"

"Yes, they had hardly started on me—thanks to Hawc!" He settled his glasses—which were dangling from one ear but miraculously unbroken—back on his nose. "But how do you come to be here?"

"I asked Dada to come through by Pennygaff on purpose so that there would be a chance of seeing you, maybe. On our way to the fair at Devil's Leap—Nant Agerddau, we are. But how is it with you, Owen bach? Dear to goodness, how you've grown! Taller than me, now! Did you find your grandfather all right? Are you happy, with you? Who were those brutes?"

"Boys from my school."

"Fine sort of school! Why were they after you?"

"Oh, just because I am a stranger here."

Owen glanced down the hill. His enemies had dispersed. For the moment, at least, he was saved.

The Whispering Mountain

JOAN AIKEN

A TOM DOHERTY ASSOCIATES BOOK
NEW YORK

THE WHISPERING MOUNTAIN

A Starscape Book
Published by Tom Doherty Associates, LLC
175 Fifth Avenue
New York, NY 10010

www.starscapebooks.com

ISBN: 0-765-34241-3

First Starscape edition: May 2002

Printed in the United States of America

0 9 8 7 6 5 4 3 2 1

Contents

I wish to express my gratitude to Kitty Norris, who corrected my Welsh, and to the Head Librarian of Brecon Public Library, who let me rummage among his archives.

1

On a sharp autumn evening a boy stood waiting inside the high stone pillars which flanked the gateway of the Jones Academy for the Sons of Gentlemen and Respectable Tradesmen in the small town of Pennygaff.

School had finished for the day some time since, and all the other scholars had gladly streamed away into the windy dusk, but still the boy hesitated, shivering with cold and indecision. Once or twice he edged close against one of the soot-blackened pillars, so that his form was almost invisible, and, leaning forward, peered out through the close-set iron railings.

The street outside seemed empty. But was it really so? Very little daylight now remained. A thin yellow strip of light in the west made the shadows along the narrow cobbled way even blacker; there were too many doorways, porches, passages, and flights of steps in or behind which any number of enemies could lurk unseen. And a great bank of purple-black cloud was advancing steadily westward across the sky, blotting out what little light yet lingered. In a minute, torrents of rain would fall.

The sound of quick footsteps behind him rang in the paved yard and the boy swung round sharply, but it was only the schoolmaster, Mr. Price, on his way home to tea.

"Owen Hughes!" the teacher said with displeasure. "What are you doing here? Run along, boy, run along; you should not be loitering in the grounds after school has ended. Where are your books? And why have you no coat? It will rain directly. Your good grandfather will be wondering where you have got to. Hurry along now."

Mr. Price said all this as he passed the boy at a rapid pace, without pausing, meanwhile buttoning his own greatcoat against the huge drops of rain which were beginning to strike heavily on the flagged pavement. Owen's "Yes, sir," followed him, but he did not turn his head to see whether he had been obeyed, and Owen did not move from his position by the gate despite the downpour, which, now commencing in good earnest, soon drenched his thin nankeen jacket.

Intent on his scrutiny of the empty street, Owen did not even notice that he had begun to shiver with wet and cold, and that the scrap of paper which he rolled between his fingers had become sodden and indecipherable. Its short message was printed on his memory.

WE SHALL BE WAITING
FOR YOU AFTER SCHOOL

The message, written in large, uneven capitals, was unsigned, but Owen was in no doubt as to where it had come from: only one of his seven persecutors could write.

"Dove Thurbey," he said to himself. "Dove Thurbey, Dick Abrystowe, Luggins Cadwallader, Mog Glendower, Follentine Hylles, Soth Gard, and Hwfa Morgan. They'll all be waiting, and they'll have stones and stakes and broken bottles. What had I better do?"

He simply did not know.

He could probably run faster than any of the seven, but he could not escape from a hail of cobblestones, and his chief dread was that his spectacles should be broken, for he possessed only one pair, and there was no means of repairing them. He was not a coward but he knew, too, that once Dove, Dick, Luggins, Mog, Follentine, Soth and Hwfa had him down there would be little hope for him. They wore metal-tipped clogs and they were all twice his size—Hwfa was nearly six foot—and big and brawny. Mog was going to work next month, Dick, Dove, and Luggins played in the town football team. The seven of them sat together at the back of the school and paid no heed to Mr. Price, who had long ago given up trying to teach them.

Nor was there much chance of aid. The citizens of Pennygaff were all snug in their kitchens by now, with doors and windows shut; if they heard a sound of fighting they were more likely to pull the curtains tighter than to leave their firesides in defence of an outsider. Wild boars from the forest were known to come into the streets after dark, and wild men too, on occasion; it was very seldom that the townspeople left their homes after nightfall except in compact groups.

While he was thinking these gloomy thoughts Owen heard, with surprise, the sound of running footsteps. His heart jolted with anxiety, hope, suspense. Could the runner be a possible ally? He could tell that it was not one of his enemies—the steps were too light and much too fast.

A man came into view, bolting at top speed down the mountain road. As he approached Owen saw, first, that he wore some sort of livery; next, that he was a stranger. He grasped a staff in his right hand. But here was no ally, Owen realized with sinking hope—this man was in the last extremity of haste and exhaustion. His legs would hardly have carried him had not the way lain downhill. As it was, they fled weakly along and he followed them, only half aware, it seemed, of where they were taking him.

As he neared Owen, words fell from him in a clot:

"SisplacePennygaff?"

"Yes!" Owen called back. "—Sir!"

But already the runner was past, careering down the hill into the darkness below, as if all the wolves of the Black Mountains were at his heels.

Down in the valley the town clock tolled six times.

Owen knew that in the next few moments he must come to a decision.

He had left his schoolbooks and coat under a loose board in the classroom—a hiding-place which, fortunately, had so far gone undiscovered. A coat would only hinder flight and give his pursuers something to catch hold of, while the books belonged to his grandfather and were precious with age and use. Owen could hardly imagine what his punishment would be if any harm came to them. Besides, he loved books for their own sake, and hated the thought of their being torn apart and dashed on the muddy cobbles.

What was that sound?

He turned quickly, just in time to see a black shadow dart from one point of concealment to another. He caught a whisper, and a brutal chuckle.

They were closing in.

There was no second way out of the school, which stood enclosed by iron railings, higher up the mountain than any other building on that side of Pennygaff. To reach home, Owen was obliged to descend the steep winding hill through the town, cross the single bridge over the river Gaff, and climb an equally steep hill on the other side. Even supposing he could outdistance his enemies as far as the bridge, he could hardly keep ahead of them up the farther hill; some of them would almost certainly be posted on the bridge, waiting for him.

Now a second figure dashed across the road, apelike and crouching; he recognized Mog. And to his left Owen heard the sound of a throat being cleared, deliberately, mocking and shrill; that was Hwfa, who, despite his size, still sang treble in the chapel choir.

"Well now, boys," whispered another voice—that was Luggins—"if the snivelling little dummer won't come out, go in and get him we must!"

Searching his pockets for anything that might serve as a weapon, Owen found a small heavy worsted bag. He ran his fingers over it in bewilderment; what could it be? Then he recollected that his grandfather had bidden him go during his dinner hour and collect a couple of items that had been omitted from the weekly order sent up by old Mrs. Evans the grocery. Soap and something else—perhaps whatever it was would serve to delay his attackers for a moment—

Just then both parties were checked by a new sound, the clipclop of hoofs and carriage wheels rattling over the uneven roadway. Next moment a chaise came briskly round the corner above the school and drew to a halt beside the gates, its single lamp shining on Owen's face.

"Hey, you—you there, you boy!" The driver's voice startled Owen by its loud, harsh, resonant tones. A tall man, swathed in many capes, waved a whip at him commandingly. The deep brim of his beaver hat shaded his face from Owen's view.

"Y-yes, sir," he stammered. "Can I help you?"

"Is this dismal place the town of Pennygaff?"

"Yes, sir."

"Thank God for that, at least. I've been traversing these hideous black hills for the best part of three hours—I wish to heaven I may never have to set foot here again! Well then, can you direct me to the museum—though, by Beelzebub, if ever there was a piece of arrant impudence, it is for a pre-historic settlement like this to possess such a thing? Place should be on show itself as a savage relic."

"Down the hill, sir, across the bridge, and up the other side. You'll see it on your right, above the Habakkuk chapel," said Owen, rather indignant at this slight on the town of his ancestors, and surprised, too. What could this stranger want with the museum, at such an hour?

"Any decent inns here?" the man demanded.

"There's one inn, sir—the Dragon of Gwaun, by the bridge."

"*One*—is that all? How far is this desolate spot from Caer Malyn?"

"A matter of twenty mile, sir."

"Perdition! The mare'll never do it, she's dead lame. I fear I must resign myself to pass the night at the inn." The driver was about to touch up his horses when he paused again, and said in a careless, offhand manner,

"Do you know, boy, if a pair of ruffianly rogues of English peddlers have come to this hamlet recently—a tall man and a short one? Bilk and Prigman, I believe they call themselves."

"Why—why, yes, sir," Owen said, pondering, "I do believe such a pair has been about. You might hear tell of them at the inn."

"Humph! Very probably! Come up, then, mare!"

The chaise clattered on without a word of thanks from its driver, leaving Owen ready to curse himself for his folly at letting slip such a chance of escape. Why had he not offered to accompany the man and show him the way to the museum? Nothing could have been more natural. But there had been something about the stranger's harsh voice and cold, half-angry bearing that made Owen discard the notion as soon as it entered his head; this was not a man likely to grant favours.

Almost before the sound of hoofs had faded down the hill, Owen's attackers were closing in once more. Only three of them, though. It seemed that he had guessed right; Soth, Dick, Follentine, and Dove were waiting down at the bridge to cut off his escape.

Well, he would sell his life dear.

He pulled the cloth bag from his pocket and, delving inside, extracted a twist of paper.

"Go on, Hwfa, man! Pound the little flamer!" whispered Mog.

As the three of them edged towards him Owen, suddenly taking the initiative, darted forward and shot the contents of the packet full into Hwfa's face.

It was snuff. Nothing could have been more unexpected, or more successful. Stopping short with a gasp of pain, Hwfa rubbed and rubbed at his eyes, cursing and blubbering.

"Wait till I get at you, will you! Oh dammo, my eyes. Have the head off him, Mog!"

But Owen had not waited. Darting past Hwfa he doubled round Luggins and Mog while they were still taken by surprise, and was off like lightning down the hill. In a moment, though, he heard them coming after him. A cobblestone whistled past his ears. He had very little start.

Halfway down, the road from Hereford came in on the left. As he crossed the turning, Owen was obliged to swerve in order to avoid a hooded wagon which swung out of the side road and turned downhill towards the bridge. Grabbing, to steady himself, at the shaft, which had passed within six inches of his shoulder, Owen glanced up at the driver in apology.

"I'm sorry, sir," he panted, and then, in utter astonishment, "Why—*Mr. Dando!*"

"Eh? What's that? Who? Where?" The man on the box peered down at him absently. "Dando's my name sure enough, but do I know you? Face seems familiar, certainly—but then, so many faces do—all faces much alike,

I am thinking? Still, yours—yes, seen it before somewhere, I do feel I have. But where, now?"

"Don't you remember? You took me up in the port of Southampton last summer when I was starting out to walk to Wales and carried me as far as Gloucester—surely you recall?"

Mr. Dando was still rubbing a hand through his long dark locks, making them stand on end, while he muttered, "Perhaps—perhaps—" when he was interrupted by the three pursuers, who arrived with a clatter of clogs and hurled themselves on Owen. For a moment, all was confusion. Owen fought desperately, but his feet were knocked from under him and he was being borne to the ground when a girl in a red dress put her head out at the back of the wagon.

"What is it, Father? What is happening? Why—*Owen*!"

Big clumsy Mog, hindered temporarily from his assault by the bodies of his two allies, looked up at the girl on the wagon and gaped in astonishment at what he saw. Her dark hair was piled on top of her head in a knob, or coronet, and perched upon this, as if it were the most natural thing in the world, was a large black-and-white bird, with a curved roman bill.

When the girl saw what was happening she exclaimed, "Scatter them, Hawc!" in a voice that carried like a bell.

Instantly the great bird launched himself off her head, rose, circled a couple of times high over the combatants, and then hurtled down on them in a whistling dive. He landed with a thump, striking his razor-sharp talons into the jacket of Hwfa, who gave a shrill yell and ran for his life. The falcon loosed him, at another command from the girl, and returned to pounce on Luggins, scoring a set of deep parallel tracks through his tow-coloured hair. Completely terrified at this unexpected pain and the fierce clutching weight on his head, Luggins let go of Owen, whom he was slowly throttling, and tried to shake off the falcon. Mog, seeing the battle was lost, had already made his escape.

Luggins stumbled after him, calling out desperately,

"Mog! Mog! Don't leave me! Get this brute off me, boy!

Mog made not the slightest effort to help, but at another whistle from his mistress Hawc released the punishing grip on Luggins's scalp and came oaring back through the rainy night, to take up his perch once more on the girl's crown of hair.

She had jumped off the wagon and was hugging Owen, who could hardly believe his eyes.

"Arabis! What are you and your father doing in these parts?"

"Owen, are you all right?"

"Yes, they had hardly started on me—thanks to Hawc!" He settled his glasses—which were dangling from one ear but miraculously unbroken—back on his nose. "But how do you come to be here?"

"I asked Dada to come through by Pennygaff on purpose so that there would be a chance of seeing you, maybe. On our way to the fair at Devil's Leap—Nant Agerddau, we are. But how is it with you, Owen bach? Dear to goodness, how you've grown! Taller than me, now! Did you find your grandfather all right? Are you happy, with you? Who were those brutes?"

"Boys from my school."

"Fine sort of school! Why were they after you?"

"Oh, just because I am a stranger here."

Owen glanced down the hill. His enemies had dispersed. For the moment, at least, he was saved.

"There's silly, and your father and granda born here. Gracious, how it rains! Come inside the wagon, Galahad won't mind another in the load, will he, Dada? I'm sure Owen doesn't weigh any more than he did last summer—thin as a withy he is, still."

"Galahad? He could haul half the mountain and never notice. Fresh as a daisy, aren't you, my little one?" Mr. Dando clucked to the horse—who was indeed of massive build—and shook up the reins; the wagon began to rumble slowly on down the cobbled hill while Arabis and Owen scrambled up the steps, under a bilingual notice which said, "Barbwr a Moddion. Barber & Medicine. Prydydd. Poet."

Once inside, Owen looked round with indescribable pleasure at the place which had been his happy home for two months as they travelled leisurely across southern England. And a snug, delightful home it made: the roof and sides were cunningly woven of latticed withies, which had a canvas facing within and without; a coat of pitch had rendered this weather-proof on the outside: inside it was whitewashed and Arabis, who had a decided talent for painting, had decorated it with a design of roses, cabbages, and daffodils. Red drugget covered the floor, and a fire burned in an iron stove. An aromatic smell came from the many bunches of herbs which hung overhead drying in the warmth, and on a high shelf stood pillboxes, medicine bottles, jars of ointment and papers of powder. Two shelf-beds were neatly made up and covered by patchwork quilts, while two more, strewn with cushions, were used as seats. A red baize curtain could divide the room in half but was at this moment drawn back. A table, fastened to the floor, had a kind of wicker fence to prevent dishes sliding off it if the wagon tilted. An oil lamp swung on a chain from the ceiling, throwing warm golden light and a never-ending procession of shadows. Pots, pans and some Bristol ware shone on a slatted shelf: everything there sparkled with cleanliness. From a hook on the wall dangled a gaily ribboned instrument, something between a violin and a mandolin; it was called a crwth.

"I'm glad you still have Hawc," Owen said, as the falcon, excited and roused from his foray, continued to hiss and heckle, raising and lowering his wings.

"Yes, indeed!" Arabis slipped a hood over Hawc's head to quiet him, and placed him on a perch ingeniously contrived from an old broom. "If we hadn't, hard it would be indeed to keep the stockpot filled; Dada is writing a long poem about King Arthur now, just, and there is absent-minded it makes him! he only speaks on Wednesdays, Fridays, and Sundays at present, so lucky you are that today is Wednesday."

She laughed, nodding towards a great heap of books and sheets of paper scrawled across and across with handwriting, which covered one of the beds. Owen, screwing his head round, read a title on the sheet nearest him: "The King at Caerleon: An Epic Poem in CCC Cantos by Tom Dando. Canto CCLXXXVIII."

"I still think it must be odd to have a father who speaks only every other day," he remarked involuntarily.

"Oh well—" Arabis was philosophical. "Not so bad, he is, old Tom. Better it is than having no father at all." Then she blushed and exclaimed anxiously, "There's sorry I am, Owen dear! Where were the wits in me? Have you any news of your father yet?"

He shook his head. "No. But that means little. Grandfather thinks he may still be alive; a prisoner, perhaps, in the Chinese wars, or cut off somewhere so that he cannot send a letter. And letters take so long to come."

"Tell me about your granda, then, is it? Found him all right, did you, after we parted that day at Gloucester?"

"Yes," Owen said, remembering the sad day last summer when he had been obliged to say goodbye to the kind friends who had carried him so far. "Yes, I had a lift in a carrier's cart along to Monmouth, and from there I walked; it took a week but I was lucky with the weather."

"And your granda? Was he pleased to see you? Fond of him, are you?"

Owen had to look away from Arabis. There was too much of a contrast between the warmth of her voice, the kindness in her dark eyes, between the whole friendly comfort of the little home on wheels and the other home he was so soon to re-enter. He stared hard at the falcon, biting his lip. After a moment he was able to say,

"It took a little time for Grandfather to—to believe that I was his grandson."

"But you had the papers—the certificate of your birth, and your father's letter?"

"He said anybody might have stolen them—that my having them proved nothing."

"There's silly! Who'd do such a thing, pray? And so?"

"Well, so in the end he took me in. He still says, though, that—that I must take after my mother's family, that I'm not like a Hughes. But he's a just man. He—he said he was prepared to give me a home and pay for my education."

"So I should think indeed!" cried Arabis. "His only son's son! And your poor mama dead of typhus fever on the voyage home from China, and the captain's letter—There, there, never mind me, bach, I didn't mean to grieve you by reminding you. Here, have a mug of soup, is it?"

Owen smiled, remembering how Arabis always administered hot soup to anyone in trouble.

"Good soup it is too," she said, "Hawc caught a hare as we came over Midnight Hill. And I put in a drop of the mead a sailor gave Dada in Cardiff. So drink up."

Owen kept his eyes on Arabis over the rim of the mug. He had never for a moment forgotten her during the time spent at his grandfather's, but the picture of her had set firm in his mind and become less alive. Now it was almost a shock to see her again—her real self—talking and laughing. He found that he had grown so that he was very slightly the taller of the two.

"You haven't changed a bit, Arabis," he said.

She had long, soft hair, black as coaldust, which she wore in the knot on top for Hawc's benefit. Her eyes looked almost black too, because the pupils were so big, but they were really a very dark grey. Although she spent most of her days out of doors, scouring the hills and woods for medicinal plants while her father, with Galahad and the cart, plodded along the road, her skin never tanned, but remained pale and clear. When she smiled a three-cornered dimple appeared under her left cheekbone.

Owen and she were not unalike, both being thin and dark, but his eyes, behind the glasses, were brown, not grey. On the journey from Southampton to Gloucester people had sometimes taken them for brother and sister. Owen knew that Arabis had once had a younger brother but he and her mother had both died of an inflammation in the hard winter ten years before.

"So you go to school now?" Arabis said. "Lucky boy! You can learn history and astronomy and all the languages that they speak in foreign lands. It makes me sad to think that if I met my mother now she might be speaking and maybe I'd not understand her."

"You'd pick it up fast enough," Owen said, remembering Arabis had told him her mother came from the island of Melita. "You are such a clever girl, Arabis! I believe you know all there is to know about herbs and wild creatures—and younger than me, too!"

"There's wonderful!" she laughed at him. "How would I help it? But to learn in school! I'd go, if it didn't mean leaving Tom. Don't you love learning?"

"Yes," Owen said truly. He did not speak again of his difficulties with Mog and the others who hated him because he was a stranger. Why whine about his troubles to Arabis? Nothing seemed to perturb her; he had seen her quiet and unafraid before a bullying magistrate, accused of witchcraft; and equally calm, facing the charge of an angry bull, maddened by the pain of a broken horn. She would probably think he was making a fuss over a trifle.

But, he suddenly thought, he could tell her about his

other worry. Arabis was the only person he could think of who might have sensible advice to offer.

"Arabis," he said on this impulse, "have you ever heard of the Harp of Teirtu?"

"Telyn Teirtu? Indeed yes. Tom would be telling us stories about it when we were little: that it was made of gold, and had three rows of strings, one for men, and one for kings, and a row that would burst out playing all on its own if a strange hand tried to steal the harp; and a lot more beside."

"Yes, that is it," he said. "My father told me the story too. Kilhwch, son of Prince Kelyddon, got his cousin King Arthur to help him steal it for a bride-gift for the Princess Olwen. It was taken from Castell Teirtud to the king's castle at Caerleon, and then to the castle of Yspaddaden Penkawr. But then it was lost, some say St. Dunstan had it and gave it to St. Ennodawg, some that it found its own way home to Castell Teirtud."

"There was a prophecy about it made by one of the old bards," Arabis said.

"When the Whispering Mountain shall scream aloud
And the castle of Malyn ride on a cloud,
Then Malyn's lord shall have and hold
The lost that is found, the harp of gold.
Then Fig-hat Ben shall wear a shroud,
Then shall the despoiler, that was so proud,
Plunge headlong down from the Devil's Leap;
Then shall the Children from darkness creep,
And the men of the glen avoid disaster,
And the Harp of Teirtu find her master."

"But it is a very confusing prophecy, indeed, for how could the castle of Malyn ride on a cloud? And who is the despoiler? Anyway, what about the harp, boy?"

"Well, that's it," Owen said. "My grandfather thinks he has found it."

"No!" said Arabis, and her eyes went wide. "Well, there is a piece of news, indeed! But you look as glum as if you had lost a guinea and found a groat. Where did he pick up the old harp?"

"He was taking stones from the ruined monastery on the island in the river Gaff, to build another room on to the museum. He pulled down a bit of wall and found a little closet hollowed out in it. In the closet was an old chest lined with copper, and in the chest was the harp."

"No nonsense?" said Arabis, much interested. "Will it play?" She glanced up at the crwth hanging on the wall. "Dearly would I like to get my fingers on it!

"No, it won't play. It is old and black and all the strings but one have gone. But the frame is made of gold, Grandfather thinks, and there is ancient writing on it."

"Valuable, then, it will be?"

"Yes," said Owen gloomily, "and that is one of the reasons why there is trouble in the town."

"Why, in the name of ffiloreg?"

"Nobody can agree about what should be done with the harp. Some say, sell it, and let the money go to build a new school. There's a foreign Ottoman gentleman in the town, and it's believed he wants to buy it. But some say the harp should stay here because it was found on town land and belongs to the people of Pennygaff. And everybody seems to be angry with Grandfather."

"What does your granda say?"

Owen looked troubled. "He says it isn't clear yet who has a right to the harp. He says the island where it was found isn't town land."

"Whose is it, then?"

"Grandfather thinks it probably belongs to the Marquess of Malyn. He owns most of the land round here."

"Ach y fi! That bad man!"

"Is he so bad?"

"When my mam was ill," Arabis said, "we'd halted the wagon in a patch of bushes up by the lodge of Castle Malyn. The lodgekeeper's wife, who was a decent sort of woman, had Mama in her cottage, with my little brother, and was nursing them. His lordship got word of it and said he'd have no gypsies and vagabonds squatting in his cottage, or tinker' wagons standing by his park gates. My dada asked to see him and told him she was ill, and it was only for a little time, till she took a turn for the better. But the lord said if she was ill she had better go to the workhouse, rather than infect his people. So he sent three of his men to carry her out of the lodge. Out in the snow they carried her, and put her in the cart. So we went on, over the hills, but that night was the worst storm of the winter, and the horse died in the shafts, halfway over, and Mama and my little brother died too."

There was silence for a minute. Then Arabis went on,

"I've heard other tales of him too. They say the rents he charges his tenants are the highest in the country, and if they can't pay, out they go that same day. And that he treats his servants like slaves—hundreds of them are at work, day and night, polishing the hoofs of his horses, blowing between the leaves of his books, cleaning his collection of gold things. He keeps a footman who must run before his carriage wherever he drives. Imagine having to run faster than a carriage all day long!"

With a start, Owen remembered the man who had rushed panting down the hill. So many things had happened since then that, until this moment, the strange event had vanished from his mind.

Arabis went on, "If the Harp of Teirtu really belongs to him, it could hardly have a worse owner."

"Nobody knows for sure yet," Owen said. "But Grandfather is determined to act fairly in the matter."

Looking out (while they talked the horse Galahad had been slowly but stoutly breasting the steep hill from the river Gaff) he added, "We are almost at my home now. I should so much like Grandfather to meet you—won't you please come in and—and take some refreshment? I think—I'm sure he'd like you."

As he said the words he felt a faint qualm. But surely old Mr. Hughes would like Arabis and her father? Who could fail to do so?

"My word!" Arabis exclaimed, looking out. "Do you live in a museum, then, boy?"

"Why yes," he said, "my grandfather is the curator, you see, ever since he retired from being a sea-captain like my father."

The little town now lay below them, slate roofs shining with rain in the gloom, and only a dim street lamp here and there to throw a few dismal patches of light. In front of them a pair of gates, not unlike the school ones, led to a cobbled yard. A notice on the gates bore the words

"YR AMGUEDDFA."

"O Dewi Sant!" breathed Arabis enviously. "To live in a museum! There's lucky! Whenever we stop in a town, if Tom is busy with the hair-cutting, I always look for the museum. Full of wonders, they are. And your granda is the ceidwad? He must be a wise man, Owen, and greatly respected in the town!"

"Well," Owen said, "yes." A troubled frown creased his brow. "But this trouble of the harp, and the sleepers' tickets—'

"Sleepers' tickets?"

"Here we are, though," he said. "I'll tell you about that later. You can stay the night here? The wagon will go in the courtyard."

"Hey, Da!" Arabis jumped out and ran round to take the reins from Tom Dando, who was in his usual dream and would have driven on over the mountain westwards towards the coast. She turned the horse and led him in through the gateway. "Wake up, Dada! Owen lives here in the museum, lucky boy! And he's invited us in to meet his grandfather. Where shall I tie Galahad, Owen? To this stone pineapple on the gatepost?"

She kicked a loose rock under the rear wheel of the wagon so that it should not run away backwards downhill into the river Gaff.

The museum was housed in a brick hall that had once belonged to the Detached Baptists, until they had merged with the Separated Rogationists, who owned a larger chapel, built of granite, with an organ. The courtyard in front of the hall was a pool of dark, split by feeble rays from a small lamp over the door. Here another notice, fresh-painted, announced that the museum was open from 10 am to 5 pm every day except for the Sabbath, St. David's Day, St. Ennodawg's Day, Christmas, Easter, and various other public holidays. It was signed O. Hughes, Custodian. The light above was just bright enough also to reveal some words chalked on the wall under the sign. They said:

GIVE US BACK OUR SABBATH OPENING!
DOWN WITH SLEEPERS' TICKETS!

Looking desperately worried, Owen began wiping this message off the wall with his handkerchief, while Arabis exhorted her father,

"Come you now, Tom! Don't you want to meet Owen's Granda?"

"Oh, well, now, I don't know," Mr. Dando said doubtfully, struggling out of his dream. "Meet his grandfather? What for? Do we really want to do that? Eh? More to the purpose, does he want to meet us?"

"Of course!" Arabis gave him an impatient shake and pulled him down, straightening his cloak and putting him to rights. Dislodged from his box he was revealed as an unusually tall, thin man, with wild dark locks beginning to turn grey, and deep-set eyes in a long, vague, preoccupied face.

Owen by this time had opened the heavy outer doors of the museum and stepped into a large porch. Here he found another damp sheet of paper lying on the floor which, when he held it towards the light, proved to bear the message:

LEAVE THIS TOWN, OWEN HUGHES,
WE DON'T WANT YOU

Without a word he folded it small and thrust it into his jacket pocket. Arabis and her father, who came up at this moment, had noticed nothing. Owen pulled on a bell-rope, which hung by the locked inner door, and they all waited, shivering in the damp darkness.

Owen's qualm was growing inside him faster than a thundercloud. How would his grandfather receive the visitors?

He was to discover soon enough.

The inner door flew open as if it had been jerked by a wire. His grandfather stood just inside, peering angrily out into the gloom.

"Is that you, boy?" he said sharply. "You are over an hour late from school. What kept you, pray? You knew that I particularly required you to be on time today. I will not have such unpunctuality—I have told you before!"

"I—I am sorry," Owen stammered, "but, you see—'

"Call me sir, or Grandfather! Well! What explanation have you to offer? I suppose you have been idling and playing and wasting time with your classmates."

Captain Owen Hughes—or Mr. Hughes, as he preferred to be called, saying there was no sense in using bygone titles—was a smallish, spare, dried-up old gentleman with pepper-and-salt grey hair, worn in a short peruke and tied with a black velvet bow. He had on a jacket and pantaloons of grey alpaca, exceedingly neat, but shabby. His linen, however, was white as frost, and the buckles on his old-fashioned shoes and his eyes behind his rimless pincenez were needle-bright.

"Sir, I m-met the kind friends who carried me all the way to Gloucester last summer. I have brought them to see you—" Owen began again.

"*Friends!*" exclaimed his grandfather harshly. "I thought you said they were a travelling tinker, or bonesetter, and his gypsy daughter? How can such lower-deck sort of folk be friends?"

"Grandfather—please!" Owen was in agony. "You must not speak of them so! Here they are, Mr. Dando and Arabis—'

"Tush, boy, I have no time for them now, or ever. I have an important appointment at the inn and must delay no longer. But I can tell you this: when I return you shall be punished for your tardiness—soundly punished." He shook himself impatiently into a frieze greatcoat and picked up a shovel-hat and cane, muttering, "Arabis, forsooth! What kind of an unchristian name is that?"

"But sir, they are here now, in the porch!"

"Then they will just have to take themselves off again—I've no intention of receiving them." Mr. Hughes cast an angry glance at the cloaked figures of Mr. Dando and Arabis standing quietly in the shadows. "Bustle along now—make haste, pray!" he snapped at them. "I must go out, and I've no wish to leave the museum while there are strangers loitering outside it. Let me see you take your cart out of the yard, if you please!"

"Certainly, sir," Tom Dando replied with dignity. "We

have not the least wish to remain where our presence causes inconvenience."

Owen, half choked with grief and indignation, could say nothing. He stood speechless while Arabis turned the horse and led him out of the gate. Her father climbed back to his perch on the box. Then, realizing that unless he moved they would depart without another word, Owen flew after them and caught Arabis by the hand.

"Arabis, I am sorry, oh, I am sorry!"

Her grave face broke into the smile with the three-cornered dimple.

"Proper old tartar your granda, isn't he?" she whispered. "Poor Owen, there's sorry I am that we came to bring trouble on you. Never mind, boy, we'll take ourselves off quick."

"I wish I were going with you. I hate him!"

"There's silly! When he's giving you a home, and a fine education too? You make the most of it, boy!"

"But when shall I see you and Mr. Dando again?" he said forlornly.

"Does he ever let you out for a bit of pleasuring? We'll be stopping over by Devil's Leap for a week while the fair lasts—it's only half a day's ride. Would he let you go?"

"Not while I'm in such disgrace, for sure."

"Welladay!" she said laughing.

"Owen!" called his grandfather. "Come here directly!"

"Never mind," Arabis whispered. "We're sure to meet again." She gave his hand a hurried squeeze and jumped nimbly back into the wagon as it rolled away.

Dumb with suppressed feeling, Owen moved back towards his grandfather.

"Now sir, what have you to say for yourself?" barked Mr. Hughes. "Rogues and gypsies off the road, indeed! Never let such a thing occur again, I beg! And *now*, just *now*, too, when we are housing such a treasure in the museum. Thoughtless, reckless lad! I trust you did not speak of the Harp of Teirtu while you were hobnobbing with that shady pair?"

"I—yes, I did, Grandfather."

Mr. Hughes raised his hands to heaven. "May all the saints give me patience! Why was I ever saddled with such a millstone round my neck? And now I must go off to see his grace and leave you—*you*—alone in charge of the harp! I've a good mind to take it with me, inclement though the weather be. But no," he added, half to himself, "in the circumstances that would hardly be wise, until it is certain how matters stand. However, let me be sure that all doors and windows are double-locked, barred, and chained. I have enough to contend with, dear knows, in this town of cockatrices, without risking the loss of my good name. Boy! follow me."

In sullen silence Owen accompanied his grandfather as they made the rounds of the windows and the front and back doors. All were securely fastened.

"Very well," Mr. Hughes said at last. "Now—while I am gone, unbar to no one—*no one* at all, do you understand me, boy? No respectable person should be abroad at this hour, in any case. If there should be a knock, open the slot in the outer door, ask the business of whomever it be, and tell them to return in the morning. Do you understand?"

"Yes, sir."

"And don't show me that sulky face! While I am gone you may occupy yourself usefully by dusting the glass cases and polishing the Roman, Saxon, and Danish weapons. You will find your supper in a bowl. Do not neglect to stoke the brazier. There will be no occasion for you to enter the library—I do not wish to come back and find you with your nose in a book and no work done! Do not retire to bed until I return—I shall not be late."

"No, sir."

"No, sir, yes, sir!" snapped his grandfather. "I would wish to have less of your yes, sir, and a more obliging, open manner and honest will to please. But it is no matter. We cannot, I suppose, fabricate a silk purse out of a sow's ear.—I will take my departure, then. Let me hear you make fast the front door behind me. I have the key of the rear."

He stepped out into the night and Owen shot home the heavy bolts.

When his grandfather's brisk footsteps had died away across the yard, Owen picked up a feather duster and began listlessly passing it over the glass cases which held Roman pottery, geological specimens, birds' eggs, and old coins. These, with a stuffed sheep, a crossbow, and some iron tools, use unknown but probably instruments of torture, occupied the two main rooms. The library, a smaller room, shelved from floor to ceiling, housed volumes of sermons and reference books. A sign on its door said: "Sleepers' Tickets 5/—. Not transferable. No sleeping in the Library without a Ticket."

At the rear of the museum a series of small offices had been adapted by Owen's grandfather, with the minimum of alteration, to serve as kitchen, washroom, and broom closet. Owen slept in the broom closet, his grandfather in the main hall on a truckle bed, erected at night beside the helmet of Owen Glendower, which, up till now, had been their most valuable exhibit.

The place was bleak and cheerless enough, its sole source of warmth being the small charcoal brazier which served Owen and his grandfather as a cooking-stove. Some rush dips gave a flickering uncertain light and threw odd-shaped shadows.

In general Owen did not object to being left alone at night in the museum—his grandfather's occasional absences on town business gave him indeed a welcome sense of freedom—but this evening he felt a strange anxiety and uneasiness. He tried to tell himself that this was merely because of the encounter with Hwfa's gang, or the second unhappy parting from Arabis and her father. But there was something more to it than that.

Taking a rush dip he once again made the rounds of all doors and windows listening at each. But there was nothing to be heard save the moaning of the gale outside, as it swept over the bare grassy mountain and licked round the corners of the museum. The wind itself did not penetrate, but the stout little building quivered with each new blast, so that the air inside was agiatated and the candle flames were never steady.

Having satisfied himself that all was secure, Owen wandered back to the kitchen, where his supper, a bowl of flummery—cold, sour, jellied oatmeal—was set out for him. He had no appetite for it, and covered it with a dish, to wait for breakfast. His heart ached at the thought of Arabis and her father, out on the windy mountainside.

Would Galahad still be plodding on his way towards Devil's Leap, or would they have decided to stop and camp somewhere for the night? He imagined them, snug by their stove, Galahad, good easy horse, turned out to grass, a blanket which Arabis had embroidered with his name, Gwalchafed, strapped round his barrel sides. Tom and Arabis would be telling stories—since it was one of Tom's talking days—or playing verse games, swapping rhymes. Or they would be singing together, treble and tenor, accompanied by Arabis on the crwth, hymns, probably, for Tom dearly loved a good hymn. Many a time had Owen heard him booming out the strains of "Llanfair," or "Hyfrydol," or some other favourite, conducting himself so vigorously that he swayed about like a tree in a hurricane, and seemed likely to lift himself clean off the ground.

Plucking his thoughts away from this picture, which presented such a contrast to the chill, silent museum, Owen busied himself with stoking the brazier and polishing the weapons. But his thoughts would not be checked; they raced away from him like a pack of hounds, and their cry was that he would be happier anywhere else, working as a clerk, as a labourer, in the fields, in the mines, anywhere rather than this cheerless place, where he was barely tolerated by his grandfather, and treated as an interloper by the boys of Pennygaff.

Suddenly, almost without being aware of it, Owen found that he had come to a decision.

He would stay here no longer; he would go to Port Malyn and try to find employment on a ship.

He would have liked, above everything else in the world, to join Arabis and her father in their roving life, but he was much too proud to run after them begging to be taken up. What could he offer them? Nothing. Of what use was he? None at all. He was unhandy, short-sighted, timid, and the only subject on which he could claim to be well-informed was navigation, since he had been born and brought up on His Majesty's sloop *Thrush*.

No, a ship was the only answer.

With neat dispatch, he packed his possessions in a bundle: two new shirts, some hose, a comb, a lock of his dead mother's hair, and his greatest treasure, a little book which had been given him by his father. It was called *Arithmetic, Grammar, Botany & c; these Pleafing Sciences made Familiar to the Capacities of Youth.* His other treasure, a compass, always hung round his neck on a cord.

It would be needful to leave a note for his grandfather: no easy task. Owen wasted five or six sheets of paper in false starts before achieving a message that satisfied him.

Dear Grandfather:

I feel I do not truely belong here & can only add to your Troubles. So I fhall not give you the Burden of my Prefence any longer, but fhall try to find Employment on a fhip fo as to follow my Father's Calling. I am forry to be obliged to carry fome of your Property with me [he meant the shirts] but will fend Money to Repay as foon as I am in a Pofition to do fo. That you may long continue to enjoy the blefsings of Health is my Sincere Wifh. Pray reft afsured that I am very Senfible of the many Kindnefses you have fhewn me & though I feel I am undeferving of them I am & fhall always Remain

Your moft dutiful Grandfon

Now, where to leave the note so that his grandfather would be sure to discover it in due course, but not too soon? After some consideration Owen decided to put it under the Harp of Teirtu; his grandfather's first act in the morning was always to lift the cover off this treasure, but on his return late at night he was unlikely to do more than glance in and make sure that it was still in its place.

At this moment Owen was startled by a single loud bang on the front door. His heart shot into his mouth. Could Hwfa and the others, discovering that Mr. Hughes (whom the town boys disliked but held in considerable respect) was from home, have agreed that this would be a good time to raid the museum? Or could Arabis and her father have returned? No, sadly Owen dismissed that idea. Full of apprehension for his trust, he made his way to the porch, opened the peephole in the outer door, and looked out.

He found his face two inches from another—a broad, olive-coloured countenance with two splendid black moustachios and two enormous chestnut-coloured eyes.

"My dear sir, friend, mister," said this face, "I beg pardon exceedingly if I have disturbed your repose, but could I speak with the custodian, curator, guardian of your museum?"

"I am afraid the museum is shut," Owen said. He did not want, if he could help it, to disclose the fact that his grandfather was not there.

"Heigh-ho, alack, yes, I have already ascertained as much from your notice," agreed the visitor. "But the gentleman whom I wish to interrogate, catechize, moot, frisk, reconnoitre—Mr. Hughes—is he within?"

"He can't see you," Owen said stoutly, "He is engaged at present."

"O lud, lud! And will he never be at liberty, scot free, out of harness?"

"I do not think he will be free tonight, sir. May I take your name and make an appointment for you to see him tomorrow?"

"There would be no chance of a peep, just one glimpse, glance, espial, at all your beautiful treasures and antiquities while I am here?"

"Oh, not a chance at all, I am afraid, sir. Mr. Hughes is very strict about opening hours."

"Lackadaisy! Of this I have been apprised, advised, tipped the wink. In that case, as I would not wish to do anything obreptitious, please to tell him that the Seljuk of Rum will do himself the honour of waiting on Mr. Hughes tomorrow at ten precisely."

"The Seljuk of Rum?"

"If you please! And until then I will wish you the top of the night, my dear sir."

The black moustachios parted to reveal a brilliant flash of white teeth, the large face nodded (bringing into view a section of a high cap made of black, tightly curled fur) and then the visitor turned on his heel and was gone.

Owen, puzzled, anxious, and very much wondering if this mysterious caller had believed him when he said that Mr. Hughes was engaged, shut the peephole again and made his way back to the library.

The harp stood, for the present, on the big table in this room which, since Mr. Hughes's unwelcome introduction of sleepers' tickets, was little used. Regardless of his grandfather's prohibitions, Owen carefully removed the canvas cover from the harp and stood for a few moments admiring it. It was not the full-sized modern instrument, tall as a man, but a travelling harp, the sort used by Henry VIII, about two foot six inches high, which was intended to be balanced on the player's knee.

Owen, who loved mathematics, thought of it as a triangle which had been blown by the wind so that one side had bellied out and up, giving a line like that of a ship's prow. The maker had evidently seen this likeness, too, because the frame, which was richly carved with leaves and fruit, had a kind of figurehead at the top corner, staring up and ahead, away from the player. The metal of the frame was tarnished with age and dirt to a bronzed dark green, nearly black, and the snapped strings hung curled in fantastic twists and tendrils. But although the harp was dirty and broken, Owen thought it one of the most beautiful things he had ever seen, and he could not forbear passing his hand round the graceful flowing lines of the frame, and then plucking with the tip of his finger at the last remaining string. The sound it gave out was low but piercingly clear; it seemed to fill the whole room with echoes. Glancing nervously over his shoulder—but no one was there—Owen lifted the pillar of the harp and tucked his letter underneath so that one corner showed, then replaced the cover which protected the harp from dust and damp.

He had no intention of violating his trust by going off and leaving the museum unguarded; he meant to slip away as soon as Mr. Hughes had retired to bed. Meanwhile, as he was very weary, he crouched on the floor; he thought there would be less chance of his dropping off to sleep on the ice-cold flags than if he sat on a chair. Reading was forbidden, so he recited to himself all the poems his mother had taught him.

When he had gone through all his stock he tried to recall the prophecy that Arabis had quoted that afternoon:

When the Whispering Mountain shall scream aloud
And the Castle of Malyn ride on a cloud,
Then Malyn's lord shall have and hold
The . . . something . . . harp of gold . . .
. . . Then shall the despoiler, that was so proud
Fall headlong down from the Devil's Leap . . .

What could the lines mean? The Whispering Mountain was another name for Fig-hat Ben, the mountain that lay between Pennygaff and the next town, Nant Agerddau. Owen knew that it was called *whispering*—y mynydd sibrwd—because inside the mountain, in the cave known as Devil's Leap, there was a hot spring which constantly gave off steam and made a bubbling, or whispering sound. In bygone days the place was thought to be haunted by ellyllion—ghosts who stretched long skinny arms out of the water and pulled you in—if not by Y bwci-bo, Old Horny himself. But now people went there to take the waters for their rheumatism, and the little town, Nant Agerddau, had sprung up in the rocky glen below the cave. But how could a mountain scream aloud? And who was the despoiler who would fall from the Devil's Leap? The Leap itself was a great gulf, boiling with steam, inside the cave, whose depths no man had ever dared to plumb. And the Castle of Malyn was of course at Port Malyn, on the coast, ten miles away. How could it ride on a cloud? Puzzling over these mysteries, Owen tried to remember the last lines. Something about the Harp of Teirtu . . .

Then shall the Children from darkness creep

(what children? what darkness?) and something or other about disaster?

And the Harp of Teirtu find her master.

It did sound as if the harp were in some way definitely connected with the Marquess of Malyn. Which was a pity, as by Arabis's account he certainly did not deserve to possess such a treasure.

Owen gave a deep unconscious sigh, that was half a yawn. His eyes closed. With a guilty start he forced them open and sat upright, but in a few minutes his head was nodding forward again.

"Arabis," he murmured, nine-tenths asleep. "Arabis . . . no use waiting at . . . Devil's Leap . . ."

Then, gently and silently as sand falls in an hour-glass, he toppled sideways on to the floor and lay curled up, fast asleep, underneath the table. One slow tear trickled from his cheek to the dusty flagstone on which it was pillowed.

His slumber was so profound that he never heard the crunch of footsteps outside, nor the cautious creak of the back door as it slowly began to open.

2

The Dragon of Gwaun was a small, glum-looking inn which stood just below the bridge, on a narrow piece of flat land rather too close for comfort to the foaming Gaff. Heavy drinking was beyond the means of the people of Pennygaff, and anyway discouraged by Mr. Morgan the landlord, and this was just as well: a man whose legs were led astray by mead or cider so that they carried him into the river could easily be swept into a pothole and never be seen again until his body floated past the wharves of Port Malyn and out round the Shambles Lighthouse on its rock. For more than half its course the river Gaff ran underground.

From the centre of the bridge it was possible to look down into the coffee-room window. Old Mr. Hughes did so, pausing in his brisk march; the room was much more brightly lit than usual, which was what had caught his attention; clusters of candles burned everywhere. A man stood at the window looking out; he could not have seen much for all outside would have appeared dark to him, but Mr. Hughes had a clear view of his face, which was illuminated by the candle he held. It was a handsome face, though singularly lacking in expression; the well-formed eyebrows curved upwards like the markings on a tiger's forehead. The nose was straight and the mouth somewhat thin. Due to the candle-light, a sort of halo seemed to encircle the man's head because of the fairness of his hair, which appeared either white or yellow. He wore a loose gown of saffron velvet and stood looking out, or listening to the voice of the river as it rushed by in the dark. Then, with an impatient movement, he rattled the curtain across, and old Mr. Hughes went on into the crowded public room of the inn.

This was not a place he would ever have entered from choice; he stood distastefully eyeing the clumsy wooden tables, marked with wet circles from beer-mugs, and the sawdust floor.

"Fancy now!" said Dai potman, a little sad-faced red-eyed man with a glassy drop hanging permanently at the end of his nose. "Mr. Owen Hughes the museum, isn't it? Honoured we are, indeed. And what can I do for you, Mr. Hughes? A drop of mead, will it be, to keep out the chill?"

"Nothing to drink," snapped Mr. Hughes. "I have an appointment with his grace the Marquess of Malyn at half past seven."

"Indeed to be sure now, is that so? Wait, you, then, Mr. Hughes bach, be so good, while I find out if his lordship is ready to receive you."

Looking much more respectful, Dai potman disappeared through an inner door, while Mr. Hughes tucked his hands under his coat-tails and turned his thoughts inwards, ignoring the people round him.

A hush had fallen when he entered. The men who were sitting there did not look at him; they pointedly stared into their mugs, but at length one voice muttered,

"What's *he* want to come here for?"

And another suggested,

"Come to sell us some sleepers' tickets, maybe!"

There was a rumble of laughter. "Wake up, Dada!" they told one grey-bearded old man who was nodding over his pint of osey. "Have to pay to sleep these days, man!"

At this moment Dai potman returned. Through the open door behind him a high, weary voice could be heard saying,

"Let him kick his heels for half an hour or so, then. Tell him, fellow, that I do not choose to see him yet." And the voice added in a lower tone, but still audibly, to someone else in the other room, "Persons of that insolent, hotheaded kidney sometimes cool off if they are left to reflect for a period."

"Indeed, indeed, that may well be so," agreed another voice, rich, treacly, and rather foreign in its intonation.

Dai closed the door behind him and said shortly to Mr. Hughes's, "His lordship's having his dinner now, just, and can't be disturbed yet awhile."

A snigger ran round the room at Mr. Hughes's discomfiture. Just then Mr. Morgan the landlord (father of Hwfa) came in. He was a burly, cheerful, independent man, much surprised and not altogether pleased at all the high-class custom which had suddenly favoured his inn.

"Well now, if it isn't Mr. Owen Hughes the museum!"

he said. "And what can we offer you this wet evening, Mr. Hughes, my little one?"

"Nothing to drink, Mr. Morgan, thank you," old Mr. Hughes replied, somewhat put out. "I am waiting till his grace the Marquess is free to see me."

"Take a little something indeed you should, though! A drop of osey, now, or a drop of perwy? Licensed premises these are, fair play! Poor dealing it is, by my way of thinking, to use up space in a man's house and bring him no custom, look you."

Broad grins spread over the faces in the bar. Somebody called out, "Sell him a sleeper's ticket, Davy!"

"Oh, very well, if that is how you feel, I will wait outside!" snapped the goaded Mr. Hughes, and he stomped off into the rain, amid roars of derision.

"Hwchw!" said Mr. Morgan, pretending surprise. "Touchy, he is."

"No loss, him," one of the customers said. "Small need to grieve over such a dried-up bit of old lemonrind. What with his worship the Marquess and all that great tribe of servants he have brought, not to speak of the Ottoman gentleman and *his* servant, there's a fortune you must be making this night, Davy man."

"Thankful I'd be without the whole pack of them," Mr. Morgan grumbled. "Reckon they are all like hounds on the trail of our holy harp."

"Hush, man!" Dai said, and made a warning gesture towards the corner where a thin, white-faced young man, who seemed utterly exhausted, was slumped across a table sleeping with his head on his arms.

"Gŵr drwg," Mr. Morgan said. "*He* wouldn't waken for

the trump of doom, and who's to wonder, forced to run like a stag in front of his lordship's carriage all the livelong day? Black shame it is, indeed."

There was a general murmur of agreement.

"Say one thing for the Ottoman gentleman, I will," Mr. Morgan went on. "Treats his servant very civil, and all here too. 'His lordship's compliments,' I say to him, 'and will you be so kind as to let him have the coffee-room to himself after dinner for a couple of hours?' 'O, no inconvenience at all,' says he, ' 'tis the time for my evening prayer, now, just, and after, I'll take a stroll round to see the sights of your fine town, Mr. Morgan, bach.' "

"And what sights will those be, I am wondering?" Dai said. "The stocks and the gallows and the new Habakkuk chapel?"

"Monastery, he was asking about. 'Can you tell me,' he says, 'where I can find the monks of the Order of St. Ennodawg?' 'All dead and gone these many years,' I tell him, 'and their bones and their monastery crumbled to dust down there on the island.' 'O, wbwb,' says he, very sad, 'and there was I hoping to have talk with their Reverences!' "

'Hoping to have our harp out of here, more like," growled Dai. "Vultures, the pair of them. There's his lordship, with a whole castleful of gold treasures, they say—why should he think himself entitled to our harp, pa herwydd?"

"Always the way with rich folk, that is," Mr. Morgan said gloomily. "Everything he do want in the whole world, Lord Malyn has; all that's left now is something to want, and *that* is the fiercest kind of wanting; no wonder he have such a desperate hunger for our harp."

"Get it he will, for sure," said the old greybeard, finishing his osey and standing up. "Had his will from birth, that one, and nobody in this town able to stand up to him, I am thinking. Only one ever took courage to say no to him, and that was a woman, at Pontyprydd, and they do tell that he's never spoken to another since, because of the hate and spite that was in him from her refusal. Not a maidservant will he have at Caer Malyn, and quick with his whiplash at any child that comes near him, but extra quick if that child is a girl. Eh well. Bad times we have now, indeed. Back home, me."

The street door swung to behind him.

"Never spoke to a woman since, maybe" said a new voice, "but there was a woman once spoke to him." Everybody started, because it was the young footman, who had half woken, raised his head from the table, and looked drowsily about him. "Dying, she was, see, and he had her carried from the lodge where the gatekeeper's wife was tending her. Out into the snow, and came down himself to see he was obeyed. 'Woe to you, Malyn,' she says, lifting her weak hand. 'Woe to the rooftree and those beneath it, woe to the platter and the food on it, woe to the stock in the barn (both live and dead), woe to the hands that wrought this deed and the mind that planned it, may they frizzle in hell for ever!' A fine, rousing curse it was. And he not a groat the worse, from that day to this."

"Never mind, boy," said Mr. Morgan. "His time will come."

The young footman's head dropped back on his arms,

and the talk, in lowered voices, went elsewhere.

In half an hour's time the Marquess signified that he was ready to receive his visitor, and Mr. Hughes was shown in, considerably wetter, shaking the rain off his shovel hat.

He found the coffee-room almost transformed by brilliant carpets and cushions. Numerous little gold ornaments were strewn about and a table set with a handsome gold dinner service had been pushed back against the wall. A huge fire burned in the hearth, and a gold-brocaded sofa stood before it. On this reclined the Marquess, who had finished supper some time since, and was now brooding over wine and nuts and a dish of quinces and peaches—brought, like the furniture, in the baggage coach that had followed his chaise.

He looked up, yawning, at Mr. Hughes's entrance, as if this were an irksome interruption to an evening's pleasure, and not the interview for which he had travelled three hundred miles from his town house, through mountains and bad weather.

He was a tall man, not yet much past middle age. Seen close to, almost everything about him appeared pale—his fine thin lips were colourless, so was his skin. His hair looked as if it had been bleached by weather or ill-health. His long delicate hands were whiter than the lace ruffles which fell over them. Only his eyes had colour—they were a deep, clear, burning yellow, like the eyes of a tiger, dark-rimmed, with pupils as small as peppercorns. He held a long, slender but heavy piece of gold chain, and played with it, pouring it from one hand to the other.

Mr. Hughes met the strange eyes unflinchingly, and made a small, stiff bow.

"Ah yes," his lordship murmured in a high, fatigued voice, stirring with a careless hand among two or three papers which lay on a small table beside him. "You are the curator of the museum here, I believe? Mr.—Humphries?"

"Hughes."

"I have your letter here, somewhere," said the Marquess, yawning again. "I cannot imagine why you did not send me the harp as I requested. You have put me to a deal of trouble, Mr. Hughes; I have been obliged to come all the way from London on this errand, and I greatly dislike visiting Wales in the winter."

Mr. Hughes stood silent.

Then, in quite another tone, astonishingly different, much deeper, harsh, and resonant, the Marquess suddenly demanded,

"Well? Have you brought it with you now? Where is the harp?"

"I have not brought it," Mr. Hughes said stiffly.

"Why not?" The Marquess was quiet again, he stared at Mr. Hughes with narrowed eyes, and his hands stirred gently among the folds of his velvet robe, the gold chain sparkling between them. "Why have you not brought it when I explicitly instructed you to do so? Pray understand: I *want* that harp. It will form the key-piece in my collection of gold articles."

"I have not brought it because—excuse me, sir—I am not yet fully convinced of your lordship's title to it."

His lordship's tigerish eyebrows flew up. He stood,

overtopping the small, spare Mr. Hughes by some six inches.

"You say that to *me*?" He began to pace to and fro. It was an odd characteristic of Lord Malyn that, although he always appeared fatigued, he never seemed able to keep still, but was in continual, languid, restless motion; whereas Mr. Hughes, with a sailor's economy of effort, moved only when it was needful and then in a brisk, neat, finished manner.

"I do, sir." Mr. Hughes looked the Marquess firmly in the eye.

"You are aware that I own all the land hereabouts and anything found on it?"

"Excuse me again, sir—not the island in the river Gaff. That, I have discovered, was made over to the monks of the Order of St. Ennodawg two hundred years ago, by a grant from your ancestor the first marquess. The grant was made in perpetuity."

The Marquess paused in his pacing and suddenly swung round, the gold chain dangling from one hand. Mr. Hughes noticed that its clasp was fashioned in the form of a snake's head with tiny onyx eyes.

"Ah no—my dear Mr. Hughes," Lord Malyn said softly. "*Not* in perpetuity. That is where you mistake."

Mr. Hughes stood his ground. "The town records have it so, your lordship."

"The town records err. In my possession at Caer Malyn is the original deed by which the island was made over."

"Would your lordship perhaps be so kind as to let me cast my eyes over the document?"

Lord Malyn drew himself up. His yellow eyes flashed.

"Do you doubt my word, sir?"

"Naturally not, my lord," Mr. Hughes said drily. "But in a legal document there may be differences of interpretation—'

"—which you think *I* am not competent to judge? And, pray, what were *you* before you took to dusting fossils at the Pennygaff Museum?"

"Sir, I had the honour to command for many years one of His Majesty's sloops in the Eastern Seas—during which time I was frequently obliged to explain ships articles, treaties, cease-fire agreements, and many other legal documents."

"I am sure your legal knowledge is of the highest excellence," said the Marquess with a disdainful smile. "But in this instance it will not be needed. The deed says, in the plainest manner, that the grant of the island is made, not in perpetuity, but merely 'so long as the Order of Ennodawg shall continue'. But where is the Order now, Mr. Hughes? I think you will not dispute that the monastery is in ruins and has been so for the last fifty years? What has become of its gardens, its cattle, its furnishings? Gone, burned, stolen, decayed. Where are its monks, pray?"

"In China," said Mr. Hughes unexpectedly.

"What?"

The Marquess, for once, was quite taken aback.

"In China?" he repeated. "What do you mean?"

"Shortly after the monastery was established, sir, half a dozen monks from the Order departed on missionary work in China. The fact is plainly stated, both in the diary of my great-great-grandfather, who was resident here at the time, acting as bailiff to the community, and also in the town records."

"Oh—two hundred years ago," said the Marquess contemptuously. "And you expect me to believe that they are still alive? Stop trifling with me, I beg. This tedious dispute has lasted quite long enough and is wearying me to death. I do not like you very much Mr. Hughes, I do not like this countryside, or this inn, and I detest this miserable, poverty-stricken little town. Everything about the place is repulsive—the smell, the buildings, the people. There was a boy I saw earlier this evening who reminded me most disagreeably—however that is no concern of yours.—Kindly send up to your place for the harp, Mr. Hughes, before I become impatient."

"Permit me, your lordship—one moment." Ignoring the Marquess's gathering rage, Mr. Hughes put up a hand. "It is certainly possible that the original monks who went to China are no longer alive, but they must have recruited others to their number."

"What gives you cause to think so?" snapped Lord Malyn.

"I had a letter from my son—like myself a captain in the China seas—dated no longer than ten years ago, from the port of Yngling, in which he clearly reported having met two monks of the Order of St. Ennodawg, Brother Twm and Brother Ianto."

The Marquess started and became even paler than usual, but then said silkily,

"I do not suppose that you have kept this important letter, Mr. Hughes?"

"On the contrary, sir, I have it here." Mr. Hughes handed over several sheets of paper embossed with the heading "H.M.S. *Thrush*."

The Marquess took them in hands that trembled. Observing that his lordship's eyes turned to the roaring fire behind him, Mr. Hughes added with a slight cough,

"And I have also, sir, back at the museum, a sworn copy of the letter and an affidavit, signed by two deacons and the Reverend Mr. Thomas Edwards, vouching for the original's being in my son's handwriting. So you see, my lord, that until the death of Brother Twm and Brother Ianto is established, your lordship has no shadow of a legal claim to the Harp of Teirtu."

There was a longish pause.

Then the Marquess said coldly, "You appear to have worsted me for the moment, Mr. Hughes. Accept my congratulations. However I have no doubt that your triumph will be short-lived—I see from this letter that Brother Twm and Brother Ianto were both reported to be elderly men even then. They may already be dead.—Where is your son now, by the way?"

"He is missing, my lord. No word has been heard of him or his ship since the Poohoo Province uprising two years ago, in which many whites were slaughtered."

"I regret to hear it," said the Marquess, but he did not sound regretful. "Now, before your departure, Mr. Hughes, you must take a glass of metheglin with me. No, no, I insist—I will accept no refusal. You are wet, I can see—a glass of this cordial will keep the rheums at bay." He tinkled a small golden handbell. Immediately a door (not that by which Mr. Hughes had entered) flew open, and a man dressed from head to foot in black velvet made his appearance. "Ah, Garble," the Marquess said carelessly, "bring a glass of your metheglin for Mr. Hughes here, be so good. And tell those two men in the kitchen, Bilk and Prigman, that I shall be wanting them to do an errand for me later this evening. Do you understand me?"

"Perfectly, my lord," Garble said coolly. He left the room.

"My secretary," the Marquess explained. "A most versatile fellow. He brews this metheglin himself, from sweetbriar, cowslips, primroses, rosemary, sage, borage, bugloss, betony, agrimony, scabious, thyme, sweet marjoram, mustard, and honey. It is a most sovereign remedy against gout, chill, or phlegm.—Thank you, Garble, give the glass to Mr. Hughes."

Mr. Hughes sipped and choked.

"Powerful, is it not?" the Marquess said smoothly. "You should drain it at one draught to experience the full benefit."

Mr. Hughes drained the glass and staggered.

"The old gentleman is not used to strong liquors, I am thinking," said Garble the secretary, and he caught the half-conscious Mr. Hughes and lowered him to the floor.

"Well, do not leave him lying in here, man," Lord Malyn said coldly. "I have no wish to listen to his snores. Get those two men to help you shift him before they leave."

Garble stepped to the half-open door.

"Psst! You there!" he called in an undertone.

Two men shouldered their way in awkwardly, with a promptness that suggested they had been listening outside, and pulled their forelocks to the Marquess. One was short, stout, and red-faced, with gaps in his teeth, sandy, greasy hair that fell across his forehead in streaks, and a bland, smiling expression. The other, who might have been planned as a contrast, was tall and pale, black-haired, with a mouth like a letter-box and eyes as inexpressive as black beans.

"Get this tipsy fellow out of here," Garble ordered them in the same low tone.

"Where'll we put him, gaffer? In the street?" the small man asked quietly.

Garble looked for directions to the Marquess, who had sunk down in a fatigued manner on the sofa.

"Eh? The street? Certainly not, man. If he were found lying in the street one or another of his fellow-citizens might feel pity for the cross-grained, obstinate old fool and drag him home; in the inn I daresay he can snore all night in some corner. Carry him into one of the public rooms and then be on your way."

"Yes, your lordship," said the smaller man in a submissive tone, but the taller, sour-faced one lingered a moment and demanded truculently,

"What about the bung, then?"

"Don't come your thieves can't with me, fellow," said the Marquess sharply.

"You knows what I means, gaffer. The ready, the lour, the mint, when does we get it? No use to stand on your pantofles with me, or I won't do the prig."

A white line appeared round Lord Malyn's mouth at this insolence, but he only said icily,

"Not a penny do either of you receive until the end of your task. I shall expect you at Caer Malyn by Wednesday. Then you shall be paid, not beforc. Now, begone."

With a resentful scowl the tall man stooped to grasp Mr. Hughes's feet. By accident, or design, he brushed against the yellow folds of Lord Malyn's velvet robe in doing so. Quick as an adder, the Marquess swung the doubled length of his gold chain and dealt the man a savage cut across the face.

"Don't do that again, dog," he said, breathing a little fast. "Or I shall quite lose my temper."

The secretary, Garble, moved one smooth step forward.

But his intervention was not needed. The tall man dropped his eyes sullenly before Lord Malyn's yellow stare, and shuffled out of the room, carrying his share of the unconscious Mr. Hughes. A mottled red weal was beginning to come up on his cheek.

The smaller man, holding Mr. Hughes's head, found it difficult to close the door behind him; finally he managed by jamming the head between his knees and pushing the door to with his hip.

"Now, perhaps," said the Marquess, fanning the air as if to eliminate a disagreeable odour, "now perhaps we can have a little civilized peace and quiet." He drew towards him the dish of fruit, made a leisurely selection of the largest peach and began to peel off its furry skin, adding, "You may tell our swarthy-skinned Ottoman friend—what title does he give himself?"

"The Seljuk of Rum."

"—Just so. The Seljuk of Rum. You may tell him that the coffee-room is quite at his disposal should he wish to return. I will even challenge him to a game of chess."

But, unlikely though it seemed, considering the rain and dark, the Seljuk of Rum must still have been out inspecting the sights of Pennygaff, for he was nowhere to be found.

3

Owen suddenly realized that he was awake, and listening to low voices. In fact he had been vaguely aware of them for some minutes, but had thought they were part of a dream.

"Blow my glaziers!" somebody whispered. "Here's a rummy set-out! I never in all my days saw a ken so full of halfpenny stuff—not a thing here worth prigging."

All in a moment three words jerked Owen into full wakefulness.

"Keep your fambles in your pockets, cully!" another voice muttered warningly. "We're not suppose to prig anything except this blessed bandore—this Harp of Teirtu. Or as likely as not we'll end up in the queerken."

"All right, all right," complained the first voice, "stop grutching at me! I can look about, I suppose? Anyway, where *is* this here sanitary harp?"

Owen felt a cold draught on his legs. Someone had pushed open the library door. He saw two pairs of feet approaching—feet whose clumsy leather boots had been bound with strips of rag to muffle their noise. Somebody carried a lantern: a circle of dim light swam across the floor.

"Naught in here but books," whispered the first voice.

"Stow your crash, doddypol! What's that on the table covered with a caster? I'll lay a brace of demies that's the harp."

The feet were right beside Owen now; he lay under the table, paralysed with indecision and sheer surprise. How had these men managed to enter? Who were they? And where was his grandfather?

"Soho! What did I say?" the first voice whispered with satisfaction. "This is the bandore all right."

"*That* pitiful kickshaw? The Harp of Teirtu there's all this rumpus about? Why, it's as black as my brogue, and has but one catling left."

"That's it, just the same, no question. There's the letters on it that his worship said to look for."

"Give it here, then. I'll carry it and you dup the jigger."

In a flash Owen understood that he must act, and at once.

"Hey! Don't you dare touch that harp!" he shouted, rolling out from under the table.

The two thieves were startled almost out of their wits. One of them let out a yelp, and dropped his lantern, which went out. The other, who had been about to pick up the harp, jumped towards the door. But there he paused. The room was still dimly lit by Owen's rush dip, flickering on the table.

"Why," he said in relief and disgust. "What mugs we

are! He's naught but a kinchin, no bigger than a sparrow. Clobber him, Bilk!"

"Hell's bellikins, I will!" growled the other. A large black shape approached Owen, who, shaking with fright and determination, had taken up his position in front of the harp. Ducking, he evaded a blow which whistled past his head, and dodged away, yelling loudly,

"Grandfather! Grandfather! Wake up! Bring the blunderbuss! Thieves! Call the watch! *Thieves!*" in hopes of scaring off the intruders.

"Stow your maundering, you little caffler! It's no manner of use roaring for the old gager, anyways; *he* won't come, I can tell you. Wake up? Lucky if he wakes up afore Turpentine Sunday."

Desperately, Owen shook a heavy hand from his arm, seized one of the burglars by his coat, and butted him with all his strength in the stomach; the man let out a ghastly crowing yell and staggered backward against the wall, completely winded. Owen's triumph did not last, however; the other man clutched him round the throat, exclaiming,

"Would you, then, you little whipper-snapper? Stall down, or I'll trine you with your galleyslops!"

His grip tightened till the room whirled round in green and black flashes; with a frantic effort Owen broke free and, snatching up a volume of sermons that must have weighed fifteen pounds, thumped his assailant with it. Gaspingly, he continued to shout,

"Thieves! Help! Thieves!"

"Blow the varmint! He'll have the macemongers on us yet! Here, Bilk, for pittacock's sake, give us a hand, don't just stand there mammering."

The other man, having recovered his breath, came back into the fight and dispatched Owen by one conclusive blow that knocked him half across the room; as he went down both men flung themselves on him, pummelling and belabouring; his glasses fell off when he was thrown on his face and, with a sick feeling of despair, he heard them crunch under somebody's foot on the stone floor.

"Right, then," said the man called Bilk, breathing heavily. "Tie his fambles with summat—tear a strip off his shirt, that's the dandy—and shove a clout in his gan so he can't yammer any more." Owen's hands were dragged behind him and tied violently tight; somebody's cheese-smelling neckerchief was stuffed into his mouth.

"Got your shiv, Prigman? Spit him, then, like a partridge; we don't want him telling our names to the constables; you'd no call to go shouting *Bilk* like that, you fool!"

"Must I spit him?" Prigman objected, sounding uneasy. "*You* do it. I never relishes spitting a cove in cold blood."

"Dang it, man, go on, spike him!"

"Hold up," Prigman said quickly, "here's a bit of writing stowed under the harp."

"What's it say, then? You're sharper at reading gybe than I am, spell it out. But spit him first."

However Prigman read the letter aloud first, with a good many fumblings and stumblings.

"Well, by'r Ladybird!" he said when he had come to the end. "If that ain't providentickal! Here's our young sprout just about ready to run off his very own self with this here tinkleplunk! 'Dear Granda, I be sorry to be obliged to carry off some of your property!' he says. Cool, I calls that, cool as a cowsleycumber!"

The other man, Bilk, gave a short, deep chuckle.

"Cool or no, it serves our turn," he said. "Here, stow the paper back where he left it, and we'll mizzle, and take young Tantony with us. Then we can scrag him and leave him in a hugger somewhere out on the mountain; everyone'll think he done the prig."

"That's it, Bilk, that's it!" Prigman was skipping about as the full beauty of the situation dawned on him. "And I'll tell you summat else—'

"Stow your whids now, for mussy's sake, let's get clear from here afore we pollyvow. You carry the boy, I'll take the bandore. Is all straight? We don't want anyone to suspicion as there's been a mill here."

The two men hastily put the room to rights, returning the volume of sermons to a shelf and kicking Owen's broken spectacles under the table. Prigman, who seemed enormously strong in spite of his short stature, slung Owen on to his shoulder, Bilk put the harp in a large canvas bag together with Owen's bundle, and the two men left the museum by the back door, locking it behind them and tossing the key into a little brook which ran down the mountain to join the river Gaff.

The gale had blown itself out, and a watery moon was struggling from behind ragged clouds. The two men picked their way over the rough hillside to a gully in which a couple of ponies were tethered, and Owen was hoisted on to one of them. Prigman mounted behind him, Bilk threw a leg over the other pony, and they trotted away round the mountain.

For a long time Owen was hardly conscious of where they were going. Several hours went by, and at last, by degrees, daylight began to filter into the sky. A cool, fresh wind, smelling of leaves and water, blew into their faces and presently helped to revive Owen, who slowly raised his head and looked about him.

They were travelling along the side of a small, deep valley, not far above the tree-line. Above them the grassy mountainside ran up to scree, and then to crags; below lay thick oak woods. When they reached the head of the valley they crossed the stream which had cut it so deep, at a point where it was only a brooklet, easily fordable by the sure-footed ponies; presently they turned a corner of hill into a second valley, threaded that, and so into a third, sometimes riding close beside the rushing streams in the valley bottoms, more often hundreds of feet above.

Great birds, buzzards or eagles, soared above: sometimes they heard the grunt and thump of a wild boar digging for roots in the woods below.

To Owen, without his glasses, everything seemed a confused, dazzling blur; the trees in their autumn colours of rust and gold, the greener hillsides above them streaked with white threads which were waterfalls, all swam together into a vague but beautiful tapestry.

Prigman felt Owen's restless movement.

"Hallow, my gamecock, are you rousting a bit, then?" he said in a low voice. "Best not clapper about overmuch, or old Bilk will call you to mind, and he's rare and handy with a shiv. You don't want five inches of cold steel in your breadbasket, I'll lay. Best hold your whids till we get to the stalling-ken."

Bilk, who was riding ahead spying out the way, heard his companion's voice and reined in.

"I'm stamashed," he growled. "How about a bit o' peck, and finish off the young co? We can hugger him away in one o' the caves round here, and not a soul the wiser for the next ten-twenty years."

This was true, Owen guessed. The country was wild and empty of human inhabitants owing to the wolves and wild boars which thronged the woods. Caves—narrow, deep cracks in the hillsides—were numerous, and there were, too, potholes of an unknown depth, into which streams sometimes disappeared. Disposing of a body would present no problem at all.

"Right, let's nibble," Prigman said, and, dismounting, pulled Owen down, roughly enough, on to the ground. "Bide there," he warned, "and don't go trying to mizzle, or you'll have a taste of *her*." He flourished a long and wicked-looking knife, which, however, as Owen lay half-dazed on the grass, he proceeded to use in a more domestic manner, cutting slices off a loaf and a hunk of bacon. He laid a slice of bacon on a lump of bread, took a huge bite of both, and then prepared a similar slab for Owen.

"Here, young co, I daresay you can peck a bit." He held it handy and Owen, suddenly realizing how ravenous he was, made a clumsy bite at it, which amused Prigman greatly.

"Dang it, man, don't waste pannam on him!" Bilk said, scandalized. "Why, soon's we've done I'm agoing to slit his tripes and drop him in the lage yonder."

"No, hearken, friend, I've a better lay than that! You go to gybing-ken, don't you, young co? School?"—as Owen looked bewildered. "We knows you can scribe, acos of that paper you left for the old gager, your granda."

"Yes, I can write," Owen said, puzzled. "Though I don't know how clear it would be—my glasses got broken in the fight and I can't see far without them."

"Oh, I'll lay you could do it naffy enough for us," Prigman said, and then, with a meaning glance at Bilk, "Reckon if you're so sand-eyed without your glazing-cheats, you can't see me and Bilk very clear, eh, boy? Not to know us by our nabs?"

"No, I wouldn't recognize you if I saw you across the street," Owen said truly. Prigman gave another triumphant glance at Bilk, who, however, remained suspicious.

"So, so?" he growled. "That's not agoing to put any mint-sauce in our pockets as I can see."

"Oh, don't you gammon, slow-top," Prigman exclaimed impatiently. "The young co can scribe a letter saying as how *he* took the harp and he wants a deal of mint, a thousand guineas, say, afore he'll hand it back. And *we* can tell Old Stigmatical as how the harp had been prigged afore we ever got to the ken. *Now* do you glimmer?"

"Ha, hum," Bilk said, pondering this. "Who does the young co send his letter to?"

"Why, to his granda, you Banbury cheese!"

"*That* old gager hasn't got a thousand guineas! Odds if he has a thousand groats."

"Oh, give over pribbling and prabbling! He'll pass the letter on to his lordship."

"Not he," said Bilk, shaking his head. "The old gager's as proud and stiff-stomached as a porcupig. Look how he wouldn't hand over the harp last cockshut. 'Not fully convinced of your ludship's title to it,' says he, calm as a whelk, and my lord's glaziers fair flaming with passion, and his crashers a-gnashing."

"That's true," muttered Prigman. "You've got a rare pig-headed granfer, young co. Didn't it been for him refusing to hand over the bandore, you'd be snug asleep in your libbege now, instead of a-rambling out in the dews-a-vill with us."

In spite of the trouble he was in, Owen felt proud to think that his grandfather had refused to give up the harp. Pity the people of Pennygaff didn't know that, he thought.

"Are you taking the harp to Lord Malyn, then?" he asked incautiously.

"Ask no cattakicks, you'll hear no peevy whids," growled Bilk, moving his knife from side to side in a very disagreeable way. Owen took the hint and asked no more.

The two men went on with their discussion.

"Why not send the letter straight to my lord, then?" Prigman suggested. "*He'd* pay up and plenty. Special if he thought some other cove might get his fambles on the bandore first."

"By gar, I have it, my bully-cove!" Bilk gave a shout of laughter; it came oddly from his bad-tempered face. "We'll send letters to *all* the worships—ay, to his highness the Prince of Wales, too! Old Morgan at the bousing-ken said his highness is a-coming to stay with his lordship at Malyn for to hunt the wild grunters. Then the first of 'em to pass over his thousand mint clinkers gets the bandore."

"Whoa! That's none so bad," Prigman said admiringly. He began to count on his fingers. "A letter for Prince David—and a letter for the whiskered sir at the jumble-ken,"—Owen supposed that by this he meant Mr.

Hughes—"and a letter for old Stigmatical, that's three, and t'other lordship is four. Can you scribe four letters, boy?"

Owen had not the least intention of writing any letters demanding money for the harp, particularly if they purported to come from him, but Prigman gave him a warning kick, so he nodded cautiously.

"Odds chitlings, then," Bilk said, "let's be on our way to the stalling-ken. There's no ink or paper hereabouts. Then, when the young sprig's done the scribing, we can slit his weasand and drop him over Devil's Leap."

They bolted their last bits of bread and bacon, untied the ponies, remounted, and continued on their journey, taking a circuitous route through more and yet more uninhabited valleys.

By now the day was well advanced, and presently the sun dropped behind a craggy hill ahead of them which bore, as they proceeded, a strong resemblance to a man wearing a large, flat hat. There could be no doubt that it was Fig-hat Ben, the Whispering Mountain. Owen had once accompanied his grandfather to Nant Agerddau in order to help him carry home some volumes of sermons for the museum library, and had been greatly struck by this unusual peak.

By now they had abandoned the valleys and were crossing a wide, barren, shelving upland, covered with loose stones. Ahead of them the great summit showed black against a pale yellow sky.

"In all my born days I never did glim such a dismal, frampold part o' the country," Prigman muttered with a shiver. "They say old Bogey-Boo lives up here in this nook-shotten place—well, I say, if he does, he's welcome to it."

Bilk, on the faster pony, and carrying less weight, had again drawn some distance ahead, so Owen risked another question.

"What part do you come from then?"

"Bless your nab, me and my cully comes from London town, where the streets is paved with mint sauce and the birds has diamond plumes! And shan't I be joyful when I'm a-posting back there," Prigman said in heartfelt tones. "Mind you I *knows* this country, oh yes, I knows it; time was, I was a kitchen boy at Castle Malyn, scouring the pots and basting the cracklers, till I got turned off for prigging a gold chafer and sent to the queer-ken."

Prison, Owen guessed.

"But then, why did you come down here again? It's a long way from London."

"Hang me, it is! But a certain worshipful gent bespoke me and my cully to do a bit o' work for him, said he'd line our pockets with white money."

"Lord Malyn?"

"Ah, never mind, my clever young co! There's others besides his ludship, remember."

For the first time Owen remembered the odd conversation he had held through the peephole. What had the foreign gentleman called himself? The Bey, the Dey, No, the Seljuk, that was it.

"The Seljuk of Rum," he said to himself.

"You hold your whids, my twiggy young cull, and don't be so free with your prattle." Prigman advised him. "If my mate was to hear you going on so, he'd tickle your ribs for sure."

As Bilk was now waiting for them, Owen fell silent again, pondering over what information he had. He was fairly certain that the man in the carriage who had asked about the museum must have been Lord Malyn himself, who had presumably then summoned Mr. Hughes for an interview. The Marquess had asked about Bilk and Prigman too. So was he Prigman's "worshipful gent"—or was he merely trying to discover if the two men were working for the Seljuk? Would Lord Malyn be likely to employ a man who had stolen a gold dish from his own kitchen?

"Cut out the canting now," grunted Bilk as they came up with him, "We don't want any row or we'll start the whole hill a-sliding."

Very slowly and gingerly the ponies made their cautious way down a little narrow slippery path which crossed a whole hillside of loose scree. As they descended, high shoulders of hill rose about them; at length a winding track by a stream led them into a narrow, gorge-like valley, so deep that it was almost dark at the bottom, although high overhead and in front the last pink rays of the sun still gilded the crown of Fig-hat Ben.

There was a drear, dank feel about the glen; yet it was not cold but unnaturally, steamily warm, and became warmer as they made their way along it, following a tolerably well-surfaced track.

Far ahead of them some lights twinkled in the gloom.

"It's a drodsome place, if you ask me," Prigman muttered, "I'd as soon live in a cameleopard's den."

Even the ponies seemed subdued by the atmosphere of

the gorge; they snorted and twitched their skins, and set their hoofs down with exaggerated care.

Owen did not dare ask Prigman if the lights were those of Nant Agerddau, though he felt certain they must be. A dazzling thought had just flown, like a comet, into his mind: somewhere, not too far away, Arabis and Tom Dando would be established in their wagon, cutting hair and selling herbal remedies, for they had planned to stay in Nant Agerddau during the week of the fair. If only, somehow, he could get in touch with them!

" 'Tis a doomid outistical sort o' place to hold a fair, by my way o' thinking," Prigman muttered.

"Where is the fair held?" Owen asked hopefully.

"Up at the top end o' the town; we shan't pass up that-ways, cully, so it's not a bit o' use you readying yourself to roar out for help," Prigman replied. "Our stalling-ken is just here-along."

In fact almost at once the ponies turned aside towards a little dark row of five houses, set right underneath a great overhang of cliff that shelved out above them, cutting a black wedge against the twilit sky.

Not a light showed in any of the windows, not a thread of smoke issued from any chimney. It was plain that the whole row had been deserted, though the houses seemed in reasonably good repair; what could be the matter with them? Owen puzzled vaguely over this but could not arrive at the reason; stupid with weariness after a day and most of a night in the saddle, all he really wanted was to throw himself on the ground and go to sleep.

"Right," said Bilk. "You take the young co into the ken and hobble him up good and tight; I'll go on and get some ink and paper. Shan't be long; back afore darkmans."

"Get a bit o' prog while you're at it," Prigman called after him softly as he rode away, "And a drop o' bouse!"

Then he propelled Owen before him towards the middle house of the row, gave the front door, which was not fastened, a kick to open it, and entered a dark room which smelt strongly of hens. Owen stumbled on the rough dirt floor and was kept from falling only by Prigman's grip on his bound hands.

"Through here," said Prigman, who appeared familiar with the house, and guided Owen into what seemed to be a back kitchen. "Us doesn't want anybody a-spotting our glim. Now, you stall there while I make things trig." He dealt Owen a sharp clip on the ear, taking him by surprise and knocking him over. While he struggled in vain to get up, Prigman calmly struck a light, revealing a small empty room in which generations of hens had certainly roosted. Its furniture consisted of two beams crossing the room at knee-height, which had evidently served as perches. A piece of sacking hung over the one small window. There was a pile of straw against the back wall.

"Snug, eh?" Prigman said cheerfully. "No one won't live here nowadays, acos there was a bit of a landfall last Michaelmas and they reckon some day the rest o' the mountain will come ploudering down on the roof, but *I* say that won't happen till Turpentine Sunday, and meanwhile it makes a famous ken, dunnit?" Intercepting Owen's longing glance at the straw he added, "Tired, are you, cully?" Owen nodded. "Well, soon's you done scribing those papers for us you can snooze all you've a mind to."

Owen summoned all his resolution.

"Mr. Prigman," he said firmly, "I'm not going to write any letters for you."

"Ah, now, mate, don't you be so twitty," Prigman said earnestly. "Acos I tell you straight, my cully Bilk can't abide to be crossed. If you cuts up rusty, it'll be the last thing you ever does."

Owen felt he hardly cared. His eyes were closing, all he longed for was sleep. Death seemed just as harmless.

"Hey! roust there, cully!" Prigman said sharply. "You'd best get up on your stamps; no shut-eye for you till the scribing's done." He drew his knife and prodded Owen with it to make him stagger to his feet, helping him with a jerk of the arm.

"Right; you hold up like that against the wall—here, by the beam—and I'll lay old Biter up against your ribs *so*—she's mortal sharp, ain't she?—and you just keep your glaziers open till Bilk gets back!"

Nobody wants a knife between the ribs. Owen dragged his eyes open and stood as straight as he could, leaning away from the point of Biter, back against the wall. Prigman, always keeping the knife steady with one hand, contrived with the other hand to drape a truss of straw across the beam and sat on it at his ease facing Owen. He then observed that he couldn't abide the smell of cackling-cheats, which Owen took to be hens.

An hour went by. Several times Owen nearly toppled forward and Prigman roused him by a sharp cuff or a jab with the point of Biter. Meanwhile he kept up a stream of talk to which Owen hardly listened—something about Lord Malyn's house in London where even the door-knobs were made of gold—something about his highness the

Prince of Wales who was mortal fond of hunting the wild boar—something about the Ottoman gentleman who had travelled all the way from the Costa Fraucasus to Pennygaff—why? what could he want in such an out-of-the-way little place?—something about old Mr. Hughes, stubborn and foolhardy in refusing to hand over an object that was no possible use to him.

At last the door flew open and Bilk lurched in, accompanied by a strong odour of metheglin.

"You been in the bousing-ken!" Prigman said indignantly. "And never brought me a dram, I'll lay a barred cinque-deuce."

"I have, then." Bilk produced a leather bottle.

"And the scribing-gear?"

"Ay. But see here, we ain't staying in this ken. Why, the whole miching, impasted hillside's due to come colloping down any day now. They was on about it in the ale-house."

"Old stuff!" Prigman said scornfully. "We knowed that afore. Don't ferret your head about it."

"No, but they reckon it'll be any cockcrow now—the whole cliff's been diddering and doddering hereabouts and great nuggins of rock keeps a-tumbling down. That's why no one won't even keep their grunters and cackling-cheats in these houses now. Hark!"

In fact, even as Bilk spoke, they could hear a rumbling fall of rock not far away, and several stones bounced on the slates overhead.

"I'm gasted," Bilk said. He was pale and sweating. "Let's get out o' here."

"Ay, tol-lol, all in good time," said Prigman, less convinced of danger. "Let's make the young woodcock do his scribing first. That won't take but a wag of a lamb's tail."

"Why?" Bilk was itching to be off.

"Why, you abram, then we can leave him here, it'll save dropping him off Devil's Leap. The cliff'll come down and that's the end of him, no fault of ourn."

Bilk nodded once or twice in acknowledgement of this. "Ah, that's probal. So, let's press on then. Does he hear us? He seems half aswame."

"Wake up, drumble-head!" Prigman said, poking Owen with Biter. "Fetch a board, Bilk, for him to scribe on, while I unties his fambles." He took the cloth bindings from Owen's wrists and tied them instead round his ankles.

Owen, so weary by this time that he was only half conscious of what was happening, found a pen thrust into his hand and a paper presented to him.

"Now, scribe what we say or I'll slit your gorge," Bilk ordered, pressing a knife against his throat.

"No!" Owen said faintly. The knife pressed deeper and he felt a trickle of blood start down his neck.

"Easy, mate; don't go at it too skimble-skamble and mar all! Try him with a drop o' bouse," Prigman suggested hastily. "He's still dozey as a dormouse."

Owen's teeth were pried open and the neck of the bottle forced between them—half a cupful of fierily strong sweet liquor was jerked down his gullet.

"Now," Prigman said optimistically, "with all that inside him, I'll lay he'll scribe as nimbly as the Veritable Bede himself. Off you go, my young spragster—and don't act tricksy and make a slubber of it a-purpose, acos I can read, don't forget that, even if I can't scribe. 'My lord'—set it down, that's the dandy—'my lord, I have the harp what you wot of and will part with same on consideration of one hundred gold guineas, same to be left in Devil's Leap cave atwixt cockshut and cockcrow afore St. Lucie's day or harp will never be seen more.' Got that? And sign it 'Owen Hughes'."

Half fainting, stupefied by strong drink, with a knife pressing on either side of his throat, Owen mechanically wrote down the words Prigman dictated. The only way in which he attempted resistance was by making his spelling and handwriting as bad as possible; this was not difficult to contrive, for his fingers were cramped and swollen from having been tied up all day. Prigman shook his head over the clumsy script, but said it would have to serve. He did not notice the spelling errors. "Now another, cully—the same words, but this one begins 'Your Royal Highness'." 'Yor roil Hynuce,' Owen wrote, while the two men leaned over him, breathing fumes of metheglin into his face. A third letter was addressed to 'Dere Granphadder', and a fourth to 'Yor Warshipp'.

"There! Ain't that gratulous!" Prigman said buoyantly when the last letter was signed "Owainn Huwes'. "Now you can sleep, my young co, just as long as you like. Lay him on the strummel, Bilk, while I fold these and put 'em in my prig-bag. Ah, and here's the young co's bundle—best leave that beside him. Now I'll loose the prancers while you dowse the glim and we'll be on our way."

"I'll just make sartin sure he doesn't mizzle out o' here," said Bilk, and he retied Owen's hands and made various other arrangements while Prigman, having folded the letters and put them carefully in his satchel, went to untether the horses.

"All rug?" said Prigman, meeting Bilk outside.

"*He* won't stir from there in a hurry," Bilk replied grimly. Then, as another shower of stones rattled down on the roof from the hillside above, the two men hastily mounted and rode away into the dark, Bilk, as before, carrying the harp slung over his shoulder.

4

Arabis was sitting in an oak tree, munching a piece of oat bread and waiting for the sun to rise.

She had come out in search of medicinal ferns, which she liked to pick with the dew on them, but it was still a little too dark to tell one plant from another, and so she leaned back contentedly, cradled in a fork of the tree, and listened to the voice of Fighat Ben, the whispering mountain. Up here the whisper was clearly audible, a sort of sighing murmur, like that of a sleeper disturbed by dreams. The tree in which Arabis sat grew on the side of a quarry situated above the little town of Nant Agerddau, where the road came to an end and the sides of the gorge drew together to meet in a semicircle of rugged cliff.

Long ago, before the town grew up, the road through the gorge led only to this quarry, where men had once mined for gold, until the day came when the last sparkle of gold had been scraped from the mountain's veins. The sloping cliffs, now all grown over with a tangle of trees and bushes, were pocked with little eye-shaped mine entrances. Some of these openings were screened by ferns and briars; cascades of reddish water poured from others. One of the biggest openings was halfway up the cliff, right under the gnarled roots of the oak into which Arabis had climbed. Ferns half concealed the cave and had taken root, also, in the tree's mossy bark, sprouting on trunk and branches like a green mane; Arabis had established herself in a sort of nest, almost hidden among their feathery thickness.

Presently she was surprised by the sound of voices uplifted in a rude chant.

"The harp that once in Tara's pad
—Yo ho ho and a bottle of perry—
Did hang, is now upon the gad!
Hey diddle diddle and derry down derry!"

In the dim, pre-dawn twilight Arabis could just see two men lurching clumsily up the steep slope.

"Watch out, Bilk, you silly cullion! Don't raise such a garboil, or we'll have half the macemongers of the town on our tail."

"Garboil! I like that! You're the one as is making the most of the whoobub. If you hadn't swigged so much tickle-brain down there at the Boar's Head, we'd ha" been here long since. Look at the sky! It'll be lightmans in twenty minutes. Anyone might twig us."

"Tush—hic!—who's abroad? All snug in their libbeges. Anyways, here we be—let's stow the bandore under this big rufftree, nobody'll come prying here-away."

"I'm willing," said the other man. "Poop it in plenty deep, so no one won't lay their glaziers on it."

There was a grunting, rustling and shuffling in the ferns directly underneath Arabis. She longed to see what was going on, but did not dare move in case they heard her; plainly they were up to no good.

"All rug?" said one of the voices at length.

"I reckon she could lay there till Doomiesday, no one would twig. Back to the bousing-ken, eh? Us could do with a dram of hot stingo."

"You go on, then, cully, and lay on a dram for me; I'm agoing to give my napper a rinsing in yonder freshet."

"Tol-lol; I'll meet you at the bousing-ken then."

The two men fumbled their way down again; Arabis heard them slipping and cursing among the rocks and brambles. Though dying of curiosity she judged it prudent not to move from her hiding-place until they were some distance off, and it was a good thing she waited, for after about five minutes she heard one of the men returning, much more quietly, though he panted a good deal and sometimes let out a bad word.

"Where the deuce *is* the miching thing, then?" she heard him mutter. "I made sure we laid it hereabouts. Aha! There she be! Now, let's fool old Bilk, let's lay her in another o' these here vaultages, down there-along."

Arabis, craning out warily from her nest of fern, saw him withdraw a large sacking-wrapped bundle from the cave-mouth underneath, and transfer it to another hole in the cliff some twenty yards distant. In the still morning air she distinctly heard him chuckle to himself as he retreated through the bushes:

"Oh, won't old Bilk-o be set back on his pantofles when he finds the bandore's not there any more. Ho, ho, I can't wait to see his nab!"

He disappeared in the direction of the town. Five minutes went by, and still Arabis, with her habitual caution, remained crouched in the fern. Then a dark figure rose up from behind a curtain of ivy on her left, and made its way towards the bundle's new resting-place.

"Thought you'd diddle me, eh, Prigman, my sprag young co? Think yourself tricksy as a weasel, eh? But old Bilk knows a prank worth two o' that. Just you wait, my woodcock!"

He withdrew the bundle once more, and moved it to yet another cave mouth. Arabis heard him grunt to himself:

"You lay there, my pretty, and old Bilk'll be back for you afore Turpentine Sunday. Then us'll turn you over to the highest bidder. And *then* it'll be velvet gaskins and satin galleyslops for Sir Toby Bilk, ah, and a cloth o' gold weskit and frumenty every night!"

Chuckling deeply, he, too, made off in the direction of the town.

"Well!" Arabis said to herself. "There goes a fine pair of rapscallions, each one cheating the other! But I'd dearly like to know what this treasure is they've been so careful to hide away."

The sky was now quite light; indeed the first rays of the sun were beginning to gild the tops of the distant Black Mountains, though the gorge of Nant Agerddau still lay in shadow under the great peak of Fig-hat Ben. Looking down towards the little grey stone town Arabis could see a few threads of smoke beginning to trail upwards from the chimneys. Between her and the houses stretched the flat quarry floor, now overgrown with a thick carpet of moss and lichen. Here the gypsies and fair people had pitched their tents and halted their gaily-coloured caravans, but as near to the town and as far from the quarry-face as possible, for there was a general belief that the caves and cliffs hereabouts were haunted by little black, furry, elvish people who came out at night, and who had a thieving and malicious disposition. It was said that strange lights shone at midnight in the caves, that weird wailing sounds could sometimes be heard; anybody who saw the lights or heard the sounds was supposed to be in danger of becoming deaf and blind. These beings were referred to politely as the Tylwyth Teg, the Fair People, but some townsfolk asserted that the name should really be Fur People, or Fur Niskies, and many believed that they were the black imps of Old Bogey-Boo himself. Arabis, however, did not worry about such tales; she had never met anybody who could truly say they had seen the little people, nor had she herself, but if she did, she felt sure she would not fear them.

Having now made sure that both men had really gone, she slipped down from her oak tree and gathered an apronful of ferns. Then, stooping to pick more as she went, taking care not to let her course appear too particular, she began to move towards the spot where Bilk had finally stowed the mysterious bundle.

Much to her annoyance, just as she judged she must have reached the point where Bilk had been standing when he made his remark about a gold waistcoat and frumenty, she heard a loud hail from below her, on the floor of the quarry:

"Aha, there, good morning, good morning to you, my dear young person, maiden, female! Can you inform me, I pray, whether the cavern containing the famous Devil's Leap is in this region, area, location, vicinity?"

This new voice, deep and fruity, was certainly neither of the two she had heard before. Looking down the bushy slope Arabis perceived a strange figure: a tall, fat man, rather dark-skinned, and most oddly dressed in tight-fitting pantaloons and a sort of tunic, over which he wore a dazzlingly striped satin sash and a fur coat. He had a fur cap on his head and a pair of moustachios which curved upwards like terriers' tails.

Fixing his large earnest brown eyes on Arabis he scrambled up towards her, puffing heavily.

"Can you give me this information, my esteemed young damsel? I shall be most greatly obliged."

"The Devil's Leap cave is nowhere near here, sir, indeed," Arabis said quickly. "Down in the middle of the town you will find the way to it, right by the Town Hall, if you do know where that is?"

"I recall, I remember, yes, yes, I bear in mind. A large most hideous building, the colour of camel's liver, is it not?"

Arabis gave him directions how to find it, but he did not seem to be paying very close attention; all the while she spoke, his eyes were roaming up and down the side of the quarry.

"These holes, now, these gaps, these apertures? The ancient goldmines, yes? There is no gold-mining now, I believe?"

"No sir, not for many a year," Arabis replied, wishing he would go away.

At this moment the sun popped into view over a shoulder of the mountain, making all the dewdrops in the ferny quarry sparkle like diamonds. Immediately the stranger flung back his head and let out an amazingly piercing yell—"Aie, walla, wella, willa, aie, walla wo!" until the echoes, dashing across the quarry and bumping into each other, sounded like the shouts of an advancing army. Birds flew squawking from bushes. Heads were poked in sleepy, startled inquiry from caravans and tents.

"A religious observance, my dear young lady," the stranger explained urbanely, panting a little.

Arabis, seeing that for the moment she had lost her chance of investigating the men's bundle, tried to memorize the spot where she stood and began to move casually downhill.

The stranger accompanied her, making polite remarks about the beauty of the countryside, all the while keeping up a sharp scrutiny of their surroundings and of Arabis herself.

"You are a native, resident, denizen of this charming spot, my dear person?" he was inquiring, when there came another interruption. A large black-and-white bird, which had been hovering in an undecided way high above the quarry, now sighted Arabis and dropped like a plummet on to her head, cushioning his landing with a skilful last-minute brake action of the wings.

"Hey-day! Lackadaisy! My stars!" exclaimed the foreign gentleman. "Madam, I fear you have been assaulted by a songster, one of the feathered tribe! Allow me to assist you!"

"No danger, sir, I thank you," Arabis answered, laughing. "This is my tame falcon, Hawc."

"Aha, indeed, verily? For sure," the man said, his muddy brown eyes studying Hawc with their usual keenness, "how foolish I am. I now observe that he brings you a letter, missive, epistle."

"I—I beg your parson, sir?" Arabis said, very much surprised. What could he mean? But when she pulled on a glove, which she always carried hanging at her belt, and gently dislodged Hawc on to her wrist, she saw that the stranger seemed to be right: impaled on one of the falcon's long, talons was a small piece of paper.

"A well-trained fowl, bless me!" the man remarked, trying very hard to see what was written on the paper. Arabis slipped it quickly into her glove but not before she had had time to read the printed words:

> The Infatiable gluttony of the Peacock tends to alienate our attachment from it, while the harfh fcream of its voice diminifhes the pleafure received from its Brilliancy.

A page from Owen's precious little book! But how curious! How had Hawc come by it? And where could Owen be?

"Er—excuse me, sir," she murmured hastily. "Leave you I must, now, I am afraid. No trouble at all to find the Devil's Leap you will have; anyone in the town will be telling you. My dada is wanting his breakfast now, just, see."

In fact, as she well knew, this last was hardly true. She reached the caravan to find Tom Dando wreathed in paper and streaked with ink, scribbling away at his poem; verses poured out of him like water from a spring. One or two people were waiting to buy medicine or have their hair cut; luckily they seemed in no hurry and kept respectfully silent, sitting in the sun on the steps outside the van as the sheets of paper piled up higher and higher inside. Arabis glanced in, to make sure Owen was not there—which he was not—and then whispered,

"Down the town I am going, Dada. Back home in time to make your dinner!"

Her father nodded abstractedly; his right hand with the quill never for a moment stopped its gallop across the paper. Arabis left him and threaded her way through the fair; a number of people were stirring now, fetching water, blowing on the ashes of last night's fire, grilling bacon. Before entering the town she made sure that the foreign gentleman was not following her.

Just before she reached the first houses, Arabis loosened a long tress of her fine black hair and held it up for the falcon to take in his beak.

"Easy now with the pulling, Hawc, my little one," she said. "Remember hair will come clean out if you will be tugging too hard."

Keeping his beak firmly clenched on the strand, Hawc flew slowly off, with long easy flaps of his wings, and Arabis followed him at her swiftest walking pace, sometimes breaking into a run.

Right down the cobbled street and through the little town of Nant Agerddau they went—bakers, butchers, and grocers were still shuttered, and the whisper of Fig-hat Ben, up above the rooftops, was the only sound to be heard. Midway along stood the new town hall, backed against the cliff, and by it, with pillars and a portico, very grand, was the entrance to the big cave, a long, high tunnel leading into the mountain. Arabis thought, as she sped past, that she caught a glimpse of a fat, fur-coated figure standing a short way inside the tunnel. He had his back turned and did not seem to notice her.

Hawc, eager to reach his objective, flapped along faster and faster, giving Arabis some terrible tweaks; she could run like a deer but there was no possible hope of keeping pace with him when he flew at top speed.

"Wait you now, you old mule of a bird, os gwelwch yn dda!" she panted. "Will you be having the scalp off me?"

He gave an apologetic croak, "Hek, hek, hek!" and slowed down a little, but soon forgot and began going faster again.

"Wchw!" Arabis gasped. "I have a stitch on me that could have been made by Cleopatra's Needle, indeed!"

But catching Hawc's anxiety she ran as fast as she could; in little more than ten minutes they had left the town behind them and entered the stretch of narrower gorge below.

"Taking me to those empty houses, are you?" Arabis said, much puzzled. "Are you sure the sense is not clean gone from you, you old gwalch?"

But the falcon drew her on steadily, though now more slowly; it was plain he disliked the neighbourhood, and

Arabis could see why, for the whole overhang of cliff above seemed likely to topple down and bury them at any time.

"Hai how!" Arabis muttered. "Men will be fools, I am thinking, to build houses in such a place."

Tiptoeing near, she looked up and down the deserted row and softly called,

"Owen! Owen! Are you by here, boy, or is my old he-bog making a fool of me?"

She wondered if Owen could have run away from his grandfather and be sheltering in one of the houses, though she would have expected him to choose a less dangerous refuge. But there was no answer to her call.

Then, as she went slowly down the row, a slight movement attracted her attention; she peered through one of the glassless window-holes. For a moment she thought she had been mistaken; she was looking into an empty front room with a door leading to an inner room beyond. The door stood half open. Then she saw what had caught her eye: a foot extended from behind the doorpost and was moving up and down, as if somebody in the back room were lying on the floor doing keep-fit exercises.

Greatly startled, anxious, but unhesitating, Arabis pushed open the front door and went quietly in. Hawc, with a harsh croak of disapproval, let go of her hair and went to sit on a little spindly ash tree a hundred yards off.

"Owen?" Arabis said in a low voice, and then, a little louder, "Is anyone by here?"

No answer, but a faint muffled grunt from the next room. Arabis ran through, and what she saw there made her eyes go round as saucers.

"Owen!" she whispered on an indrawn breath. "Achos dybryd, who have done this to you, boy?"

Owen's right hand had been tied to his left foot, and his right foot to his left hand. The ropes fastening them together had been passed over the hen-roost beam that crossed the room at knee-height, so that he hung suspended from it. He could have rested, if he chose, on the straw-heap which was piled under the beam at one point, but he had preferred to work his way along to the door so that, by dragging the upper part of his body painfully half over the beam, he might be able to make that faint, desperate signal with one foot. A thick cloth was tied over his mouth, which was stuffed with hay.

"Wait, you, a little half-minute and I will have those things off you," said Arabis through her teeth, and with shaking hands she pulled out the small knife that she carried always for cutting witch hazel and wild liquorice. In a moment she had the cords cut and lowered Owen gently to the floor. He made an inarticulate sound behind his gag, and rolled his eyes towards the roof warningly.

"Easy, then, boy!" She sawed through the cloth and flung it in a corner; Owen spat out the dusty hay that had been half choking him.

"Danger!" he croaked. "Mustn't stay here, Arabis—house may be buried—any minute!"

"Hwt, boy, will I be leaving without you? Stir your old stumps and come along with you, then!"

It took Owen three tries before he could stand upright, so numb from lack of blood were his hands and feet; but at last he managed it, leaning on Arabis, and staggered out of the house.

"Best leave me now, Arabis," he muttered. "If those men came back—if they caught you—'

"What men? No, never mind for now! Leave you? Ffiloreg! As if I should do such a thing! But where can I take you that is not too far?" she muttered, her brows creased. She could see that he was feverish; plainly it was out of the question that he should walk a mile uphill, right through the town, and back to the Dandos' caravan.

Besides, whoever it was that had tied him up so brutally—could that strange man with the moustaches have had something to do with it?—might come back, or be in the town and see them go by.

"I have it!" she exclaimed at length. "I will take you to Brother Ianto! Do you think you can walk a quarter of a mile, Owen bach?"

He nodded faintly. She tucked her arm through his and led him up the gorge, away from the dangerous overhang to a point where the cliffs on either side of the track were sheer vertical rock.

"Only a few more steps now, cariad! There's brave you have been. Wait you now, by here, while I call the good brother."

Owen, dizzy and only half conscious, was not particularly surprised when she disappeared into a cleft in the rock. Hawc, who had been flapping along uneasily behind them, planed down and settled with a croak on Owen's shoulder.

In a moment Arabis was back with a small, brown, wizened man in a monk's habit who took one look at Owen and remarked,

"Bed, him! Bit of fever there is on him, nothing much. Come you this way, my man."

And when Owen, taking a faltering step, began to slip towards the ground, Brother Ianto, with arms thin and wiry as steel cables, picked him up bodily and carried him into a warm, steamy cave at the end of a short passage. There he was laid on a bed of moss and obliged to swallow a mug of hot water. It had a strong and disagreeable taste of rotten eggs, but went gratefully down his dusty and aching throat.

"He will do," Brother Ianto said. "A long sleep, that is all he needs."

"I will be gone from you, now, then," Arabis said, "and I will be bringing back some of my good broth and herb tea by and by. And I am grateful to you, indeed, Brother Ianto!"

"No matter for that, child! I have had a fine pot of ointment from you for my rheumatic old leg-bones, that have made me lively as a young colt. And your worthy father have cut my beard with not a penny to pay, and loosed a noble gale of poetry on me while he did it. No thanks needed among such friends!"

Arabis left the cave, and the sound of her footsteps echoing in the rock passage was the last thing Owen heard before he sank into a heavy, dreamless sleep.

When he woke up again he lay gazing about him in bewilderment. The little cave was dim, lit only by two tapers that stood in front of a rude statue of St. Ennodawg, and misty from the steam of a little hot spring that ceaselessly bubbled and sank in one corner. Brother Ianto sat working away at something in another corner; presently he took his work, whatever it was, outside into the daylight to have a look at it. Owen, roused a little more by the movement, now began to remember where he was and what had happened to him; involuntarily, he let out a groan of anguish.

Brother Ianto came back quickly.

"Are you in pain, with you, boy?" he said.

"The harp!" Owen muttered. "They took the harp, I couldn't stop them. But that's not the worst—'

He was unable to go on just then. At the thought of the letters he had been made to write, a great lump of despair and misery came up into his throat and nearly suffocated him. His grandfather would think—everybody would think—

"Oh, what shall I do?" he muttered hopelessly.

"Humph," said Brother Ianto. "When did you last have to eat, boy?"

Owen tried to remember. He had eaten a little with the thieves, Prigman putting morsels into his mouth. Was that one day ago, or two? How long had he been in the empty house? He shook his head.

"As I thought," Brother Ianto said. "Weak from lack of food. But in a good hour here comes someone to put that right. Split peas I have by here, but I am thinking they would be a bit hard for you."

Arabis came into the cave. Her hair and the red cloak she wore shone with raindrops. She carried a covered basket in one hand, and a covered can in the other.

"Herb tea first," she said, pulling a little flask from the basket, "then broth."

Owen would have preferred the broth first; the herb tea

tasted even nastier than the mineral water from the cave spring, but both Arabis and Brother Ianto assured him that it would do him good, and when it was drunk he did feel strong enough to sit up and swallow two mugfuls of delicious broth.

"And I brought you some picws, and a loaf of bara brith for your supper, Brother Ianto," Arabis said, taking them out and putting them on a ledge of rock. The spicy scent of plums and cloves and cinnamon filled the cave.

"Too good for me, they are," Brother Ianto objected, busy at his work, whatever it was. "Dried peas are enough."

"Oh, pooh, pooh," Arabis said. She surveyed Owen anxiously and asked him, "The sleep have done you good, is it?"

He nodded. He did feel better, almost well in body, but his mind was so sore and wretched that he hardly knew how to bear it.

"Right, then," Arabis said. "If I don't have your story out of you this minute, I am afraid my ears will grow tongues on them and be grumbling away at you like a pair of old ravens."

So Owen told his story.

"And then they left me in the cottage," he concluded. "Bilk tied me up the way you saw, and put the gag on me; I thought I was done for."

"How did old Hawc come to find you?" Arabis demanded.

"I heard him outside; at least I heard the whistling sound of a hawk's dive and I thought there was just a chance, as you were staying in Nant Agerddau, that it might be Hawc."

"But how could you call him?"

"Do you remember when I was travelling with you in the wagon, how I trained Hawc to come if I whistled 'The Ash Grove'?"

"No danger I'd forget," Arabis said laughing, "when Dada made us walk a hundred yards behind the wagon because he said that if he heard that tune one more time he would go wild mad and take the shovel to us. But, Owen bach, you had that great gag stuffed in your mouth. How to make the old hebog hear you?"

"Oh," said Owen, rather embarrassed, "I whistled through my nose."

"Through your *nose*, boy? What kind of a tale is that? Tell to the crows!"

"True, though," Owen said, and produced a strange droning tune through his nose that might just be recognized as "The Ash Grove." Hawc, who was perched near by on a knob of rock, turned his head alertly and was across the cave with one flip of his wings to sit on Owen's shoulder. "I learned it on the boat coming home from China; the bo'sun taught me," he added awkwardly.

"Well! There is useful!" Brother Ianto said in his quiet way. "Otherwise there would not have been too much chance for you, I am thinking.

"Just let me get my hands on that pair," Arabis muttered vengefully. "Hard put to it their own wives will be to recognize them! And taking your granda's precious harp—*oh!*"

Her hand flew to her mouth. She stared at Owen and Brother Ianto.

"What did you say their names were?"

"Bilk," Owen said. "Bilk and Prigman."

"That was it, then! Where are the wits in me? *That* was what those two men were stowing away so tidy! And each of the wretches meaning to rob the other!"

"What are you talking about, girl?" But there was a little more colour in Owen's pale cheeks.

Arabis told of her morning's watch and the two men hiding their booty.

"Keeping an eye on the quarry all day, I have been," she said. "But no chance to go back and take a peep—always someone about down below. Hurry back now, though, I must, or maybe that one called Bilk may go and shift it again."

"I'll come with you," Owen said, struggling to his feet, wonderfully restored by the news. "Those men are dangerous. If they caught you, gracious knows what they mightn't do—really you shouldn't go near at all."

"There's silly! Go I must, boy, if the place is to be found."

Owen realized the truth of this. "Let us hurry, then," he said. "If I can only get the harp back to grandfather, then the letters will not matter so much—perhaps I can explain—'

He was nearly dragging Arabis from the cave.

"Wait, you, my young hotheads," Brother Ianto said. He rummaged in a crevice, and produced another monk's robe. "Put this on you, boy, it will fit you well enough. It was poor Brother Twm's, who was so glad to get home to his native land that he died and went to heavenly rest the very next day. Pull the cowl over your head, see, and if those two men should be roaming the town they will not know you from Merlin the Magician."

He then put on a pair of spectacles, at which Owen gazed enviously, pulled his own cowl over his head, and added, "Go with you, I will. No harm to have another along, and eager I am, indeed, to see this Harp of Teirtu."

Outside the rainy, misty afternoon was rapidly turning to evening.

"Wbwb!" shivered Brother Ianto. "Homely it is to be back in this curs—this curiously damp climate. Doubled up like an old man I'd be with the rheumatics if it were not for your wintergreen ointment, Arabis my child."

They set off, Arabis in the lead, Brother Ianto hobbling as fast as he could with a stick, Owen bringing up the rear. Even after the rest and hot food, he was still stiff from his long painful hours of captivity, and purblind without his glasses; however he gritted his teeth and stumbled along, just managing to keep up. The thought of recovering the harp was a powerful spur.

The fair, when they reached it, was in full activity: stalls, brightly lit, offered everything from gingerbread men to the Water of Perpetual Youth; hawkers called their wares, children screamed and laughed and raced about on painted hobby-horses, clog-dancers stamped on wooden platforms, and the music of harps, flutes, and dulcimers tinkled and lilted in the rainy air. But beyond the circumference of the fair, up in the back of the quarry, all was dark and silent.

"Light, we need," Arabis muttered, and she slipped off to her own caravan and returned with a horn lantern which threw a small golden flickering shine on to the wet brambles and oak leaves and ferns. Then she led the way, slow but sure, in among the bushes, following in reverse the course she had taken that morning.

At last she whispered, "This was the place. Marked it careful, I did, by that old stump like a mother hen with chickens. Up there, not twelve feet above, should be the hole where he laid the bundle."

They moved carefully up the hillside, noting traces where Bilk had passed; here a footprint in a tussock of moss, there a broken sapling. The slope they were climbing ended in a short vertical cliff and soon, among the bushes at its base, they found the cave, a gaping black hole about the size of a chair-seat.

"That's it, that must be it!" Arabis breathed. "Look, you can see the marks in the mould and leaves where he pushed the bundle into the hole."

Forgetting his weariness Owen hurled himself up the hill to the opening and thrust his arm inside. He could feel nothing except earth and sand, which had silted up on the floor.

"I'll go in," he whispered. "Then you pass me the lantern and I'll look round."

Ducking his head and compressing his shoulders he crawled through the small opening and then reached back with an arm for the light. His two companions waited anxiously in the dark.

Once right inside the little cave he found the ceiling was higher, and he was able to hold up the lantern and survey the whole place. His hopes, which had been feverishly high, came down with a sickening rush. For the harp was not there. A depression in the soft sand, just inside the entrance on one side, showed where something had lain, but marks also showed where it had been dragged out again.

The blow was crushing. To have come so near where it had been hidden, and to miss it by so short a time!

"Bilk must have come back for it while Arabis was rescuing me," Owen thought wretchedly. For a moment he almost wished that she had not found him; that he had been left in the cottage until the cliff came down and buried him. Turning to edge his way out of the cave—for it led nowhere, merely ending in a blank wall—he hit his head a violent crack against the low roof; two red-hot tears of pain spurted out of his eyes. Angrily rubbing them away with an earthy fist he passed the lantern out to Arabis.

"It's not here. Bilk must have come back for it," he whispered, trying to keep his voice from wavering.

"Diafol fly away with that Bilk," said Arabis, very cross. "Are you sure?"

He wriggled out before answering, then merely nodded to her anxious, questioning look. She saw that he was speechless from disappointment, and gave him a hug.

"There's sorry I am to have brought you all this way for nothing, Owen dear," she said quietly. Brother Ianto took the lantern from her, and observed,

"Let us hope the men can still be caught."

"Come back to our caravan, now, is it?" Arabis said. "Maybe Dada will have finished with his poetry for the day. Good sense he do often have, when the poetry's not too thick in him for the sense to find a way out."

But when they reached the wagon they heard the sound

of voices coming from inside. Arabis stood on tip toe and peered through the window.

"That strange man I met this morning, it is!" she whispered, rather astonished. "Talking away to Dada as if his tongue ran on wheels! Better, maybe, if he do not lay eyes on Owen—not sure I am if I trust that fat stranger."

"Right," Brother Ianto agreed. "Back to the cave, us, and a bit more sleep for this young man. On the way I will inquire a bit as to the whereabouts of those two wicked crwydadiau. Then in the morning we will see what is to be done."

He turned towards the town.

Owen had a desperate longing to creep into the warm, cosy wagon—no matter who was inside—curl up on his old bunk, and fall asleep. But another part of him forbade this idea. What right, after all, had he to expect a welcome there? His grandfather had snubbed and insulted Arabis and her father; besides he, Owen, had lost the harp, behaved like a coward, and disgraced himself; if Arabis had known all that before, she would probably have thought him not worth rescuing.

Without a word, without even saying goodnight, he turned and stumbled shortsightedly after Brother Ianto.

Arabis, puzzled and a little hurt, was on the point of calling after him when the door of the caravan opened and Tom Dando appeared, seeing the stranger out.

"Goodnight, a thousand goodnights, my dear sir, esquire, mister! It has been a most respectable pleasure to chat, natter, chew the rag with you! We shall meet again soon for another instructive palaver, I trust. Aha! Here comes the helpful young person who set me on my way this ack emma!"

The foreign gentleman made such a low bow to Arabis that his moustaches brushed the steps. She curtseyed in return, first glancing back warily to make sure that the stranger had not been able to catch a glimpse of Owen and Brother Ianto. But they were both safely out of sight in the darkness.

5

Another disappointment awaited Owen in the town: Mr. Thomas, landlord of the Boar's Head Inn, told Brother Ianto that the two English peddlers Bilk and Prigman had sold their ponies, bought provisions enough for several days, and left the town well before noon.

"Miles off they'll be, by now," he said, "and not sorry to see the backs of such a pair!"

Back at the cave, Owen and Brother Ianto ate the picws that Arabis had left—it was oatcake crumbled in warm buttermilk, but the buttermilk had grown cold—then Brother Ianto said evening prayers and they went to bed. Brother Ianto, lying on the rock floor, was peacefully asleep within two minutes. But Owen could not sleep; for what seemed hours on end he tossed unhappily on his mossy couch, staring with hot unseeing eyes into the dark.

At last Brother Ianto's quiet voice said,

"Try to get some sleep, boy, is it? Worrying will do no good with you."

All Owen's misery burst out.

"I'm nothing but a useless coward! I couldn't even guard the harp—any of the other boys in Pennygaff would probably have been able to fight the thieves or raise the alarm, but what did I do? Get myself captured like a fool—like a baby! *Arabis* had to rescue me—and that's the second time she's done it! I daresay if those men had captured her, *she* would have found some way of escaping with the harp. And I'm sure she would never have let herself be forced to write those shameful letters—she would have died sooner."

"No use to grieve over what is done," Brother Ianto said calmly. "All you must think of now is how to right the harm. You are free, and that is good—after all it was not the action of a fool to summon the hawk and send a message—nor that of a coward to fight with the thieves when you knew you were bound to lose."

"All it did was get my glasses smashed," Owen said bitterly. "Now I couldn't recognise the men if I met them in the street! And heaven knows how I'll ever get another pair of glasses. And without them I'm even more useless—I couldn't even get w-work . . ."

He broke off, biting his lip, but Brother Ianto exclaimed, "Glasses, are you needing glasses, with you, boy?"

"They got broken—'

"Fool I was, not to have noticed for myself the short-sighted way you were peering about," Brother Ianto went on, ignoring Owen. "Bit of a concussion, I thought you had. But glasses, now! I can have you fixed right before you can say haihwchw."

"You m-mean"—Owen was stammering with excitement—"you know someone who can make them?"

"Make them myself, boy—maybe I even have a lens to suit you now, just." He struck flint and steel, lit a rush dip, and showed Owen his working materials in a velvet-lined wooden case—flat glass discs waiting to be ground into lenses, some lenses already shaped, wires for making spectacle frames, and a variety of fine little tools and polishing materials.

"Came to the right place you did, indeed," he said cheerfully. "Always interested in the optics, I was, but in China I learnt a whole lot more. Wonderful clever spectacle makers those old Chinese boys—seems they have had the trick of it for thousands of years. Taught me a thing or two, they did. Now the old sun is not far off poking his head up. Say my morning prayer I will, then we'll get some breakfast down us, and then I'll fit you up with a pair of glasses you'd be proud to nod to his majesty King James in."

The instant breakfast was done (they ate the bara brith that Arabis had brought; it was delicious: a juicy, spicy raisin loaf), Brother Ianto set to work. First he tested Owen's sight by making him hold his little Book of Knowledge at different distances and say when he could see to read. But since Owen, who knew the book almost by heart, found it hard not to cheat unconsciously, Brother Ianto wrote letters of varying sizes on the cliff with a bit of chalk, and made Owen read those. Then he brought out different lenses from his collection and looked at Owen's eyes through them. Finally he fell to reshaping two which he said would need only slight alterations to suit Owen perfectly.

"See like an eryr, like an old eagle, you will."

"But how shall I ever pay you for them?" Owen worried.

"One thing at a time, is it?" Brother Ianto said. "The Harp of Teirtu is more important than paying for a pair of glasses, I am thinking."

But the prospect of being able to see again seemed to Owen worth almost anything he could offer. Feeling so blind and helpless had been half his trouble. A new hope filled him now and he sat deep in plans, while Brother Ianto carefully ground the lenses and polished them to a fine brilliance. Then he twisted wires into a frame and adjusted it to fit Owen's face.

"Brother Ianto," said Owen, while the monk was inserting the lenses into the frames.

"Well, boy?"

"You said you had been in China?"

"Lived there fifty years," Brother Ianto said. "Fine and hot for my rheumatism, see. And then Brother Twm and I began to pine for a sight of the old country, so we made up our minds to walk home. Came right across Asia, and very hard going, but interesting, mind you, and the people most obliging.

"Didn't it take quite a long time?"

"Ten years we were at it. Eh dear. There was a walk. But we had a lift at the finish. Saved the life of a gentleman whose coach had fallen in a crevasse in the Caucasus mountains, we did, Brother Twm being a handy man with a rope. Very grateful and civil, the gentleman, and asked a friend of his, captain of a ship at the port of Smyrna, to bring us as far as Cardiff. So that saved us to walk up through Europe, besides a couple of swims across the Bosphorus and the English channel. Bit troublesome those might have proved, Brother Twm being no swimmer."

"I suppose you didn't happen to meet with my father while you were in China?" Owen said wistfully. "Captain Hughes, of his majesty's sloop *Thrush*?"

"Indeed we did, and a fine man!" Brother Ianto said warmly. Owen's face lit up. "Met him at the port of Yngling, we did, when he was bringing supplies to relieve the pink-eye epidemic ten years ago." Owen's face fell again.

"You haven't seen him since then?"

"No, my boy," the monk said kindly. "But doing his duty I am sure he is, wherever in the world, so take comfort you have a worthy man for a father."

"Yes," Owen said in a small voice.

"Come now to try these glasses, is it?"

Brother Ianto fitted the hooks over Owen's ears and the bridge across his nose, setting the lenses straight. Instantly the candlelit walls leapt into focus so sharply that they seemed pressing on Owen's face and he took a step back.

"Why," he said in a dazed voice, "it's all so clear! Far better than with my other glasses!"

"How long had you worn them?"

"Five years," Owen said, joyfully turning his head about to see the cave from all angles.

"Grown out of them, most likely. Now, boy, if you should have the bad luck to break those, not to worry, is it? but come you back to Brother Ianto. Couple of weeks more I shall stay here, for half the folk in Nant Agerddau seem to be needing glasses with them. And the steam in this cave have helped my stiff bones, indeed."

"Where will you go then?"

"Back to the old monastery at Pennygaff, where else?"

"Not much left of it now," Owen said doubtfully. "Nothing but a ruin, it is."

"All the more reason to start building again, then, and quick too."

Owen took a step forward, and the walls of the cave rushed to meet him, and the floor seemed ready to come up and bump his chin. He walked outside, and felt as if he could put up a hand to touch the highest crags of the black cliff frowning above.

"Not so fast, boy!" Brother Ianto called, hobbling out. "Where are you off to now, then?"

"I must go back to my grandfather," Owen said, for this was the resolve that he had reached while Brother Ianto had been at work. "I must go back right away and tell him how the harp came to be stolen."

"Good," Brother Ianto said, nodding, "Straight thinking, that is. Up to my friend Davy Thomas at the Boar's Head we will go again, to find out is anyone travelling to Pennygaff this day. Quicker if you can get a ride than to walk over Fig-hat Ben on your two legs, or maybe get eaten by wolves in the forest."

Owen saw the sense of this, though he was longing to start that instant. But at the Boar's Head he had a piece of luck. An Englishman on a lathered horse had just stopped in the middle of the street and was shouting out a public announcement.

"Oyez! Oyez! Oyez! If any of the loyal citizens of this town do know of the whereabouts of His Royal Highness Prince David James Charles Edward George Henry Richard Tudor-Stuart, Prince of Wales, ye are instantly to declare it!"

Nobody spoke at all; the crowd remained hushed in wonder while the man (who was dressed in the uniform of a king's messenger, with a short staff, a three-cornered hat, and gold lace, very mud-splashed) repeated his proclamation. Then whispers broke out.

"Gracious to goodness, now! O dear, dear. Lost, can he be? Only fancy if his royal highness do be fallen down a pot-hole! They do say the old king is ill, with him, on his deathbed, and calling for his son! There's pitiful, poor old James Three! Terrible, it is, and not a soul can say where by Prince Deio is at! Shocking, shocking!"

When the Englishman had called out his message three times, he rode across to the inn, to exchange his tired horse for a fresh one, and inquire the shortest way to Pennygaff. At this moment a chaise and pair which had been pausing outside the inn, evidently for its passenger to listen to the announcement, started up, and rolled briskly on its way towards Caer Malyn.

"Here's a young man will go along with you to show the way to Pennygaff, and never charge a farthing for his trouble," said Mr. Davy Thomas the landlord, with a wink for Owen.

"King's Regulations don't allow for passengers," the messenger snapped. "Besides, two riders would slow up the nag."

"Weigh no more than a feather, this boy do! Help to you he will be, too. Who's to warn you of the wild boar when he do come after you in the Fforest? Have you in mincemeat he will, the old twrch trwyth, before you can so much as turn round and lay a bolt in your crossbow. Through the Fforest is the quickest way, indeed, but dangerous with it, and a few do vanish there every year, what with the wild boars and the wolves, the ravening blaiddiau!"

This argument seemed to strike the messenger; he turned round and considered Owen with care.

"Are you a good shot with a crossbow, eh, boy?"

Owen was about to shake his head doubtfully when Brother Ianto gave him a poke in the ribs.

"Never know what you can do till you try, boy. Wearing new glasses you are now, don't forget."

"Try a shot," invited the messenger, and handed his arbalest to Owen with a short metal arrow ready fitted in it.

"What shall I shoot?" Owen asked nervously.

"Shoot my hat," suggested the landlord. In front of the inn was an ash tree, scrawny and tall as if it were trying its hardest to reach up out of the dark gorge in which it grew. On the topmost twig hung a steeple-hat.

"Y diawl knows how the little scaff put it up there," Mr. Thomas said. "One of them from the fair; good whacking he'll get if ever I catch him! Shoot it down, boy."

So with trembling hands Owen took aim and let fly at the hat; much to his surprise it came sailing down, neatly transfixed by his bolt.

"Da iawn, not bad at all!" exclaimed Mr. Thomas, tenderly picking up his hat and removing the arrow, while the messenger said to Owen, "You're the boy for me!"

Smiling like a wrinkled brown old gnome, Brother Ianto patted Owen on the shoulder.

"Go you on your way, then, boy, and remember, things

are never so bad but they may take a turn for the better. A safe journey to you!"

"Look lively, then," said the messenger. "There's no time to waste," and he mounted the wiry dun pony the ostler had just brought out.

Owen hesitated; he would have liked to say goodbye to Arabis and thank her. But very likely she despised him so much that she would rather not be embarrassed by another meeting; and in any case the messenger was waiting impatiently for him to mount. He sprang up on the pillion, but called to Brother Ianto.

"I'll be back to pay for the glasses. Or I'll see you in Pennygaff!"

And, "I'll keep a look-out for those thieves," promised Brother Ianto.

"If you should see Arabis—" Owen shouted, but the clatter of the pony's hoofs on the rock pathway drowned his words.

"How far is it to this Pennygaff?" asked the messenger as they rode down the gorge.

"Forty miles if you go through the Fforest," Owen said. "About twice as long over the mountain."

They were passing the row of little abandoned houses; the cliff had not fallen yet; instinctively the dun pony skirted well over to the other side of the gorge. Owen shivered at the recollection of his imprisonment.

"Through the Fforest's our way, then," said the man. "Maybe we'll have the luck to chance on his highness in there. Seems he came down to stay with Lord Malyn and go boar-hunting, but I've been to Castle Malyn already, and nobody's there but servants. His lordship expected any minute from London, Prince David any day, but neither of them there yet. So I left an urgent message and came hunting this dod-gasted countryside; trouble is, his pesky highness don't like to be bothered with a whole procession of grooms and lackeys when he goes hunting; he'd given them all the slip at Gloucester and gone off on his own."

"Is it really true that King James III is dying in London?" Owen asked timidly.

"Bless your gaiters, no! Tooth-ache, that's all the old boy has! It made him fretful and low-spirited; then he began to worry that Prince David would be eaten by a wolf or pronged by a wild boar. And on top of that he lost the key of his writing-desk and took a fancy into his head that the prince had gone off with it, so nothing would please him but to send for his highness to come home again. Lot of garboil over nothing, if you ask me."

But Owen thought his highness the Prince of Wales was lucky to have a father who worried about him when he was in danger and pined for him when he was away.

Soon they had left the narrow gorge behind and, instead of striking up over the stone shoulder of Fighat Ben on the route taken by Bilk and Prigman, the king's messenger, guided by Owen, followed a track that led them down rolling, grass-grown slopes, and at length into the great oak forest, the Fforest Mwyaf, which lay like a border of fur round the feet of the mountains, and stretched far away, eastwards to England, westwards to Caer Malyn and the coast.

"Keep a sharp lookout now, my boy," warned the messenger, "for I've no fancy to be guzzled up by a wolf or spitted on the tusks of one o they fustilarian wild boars that run ramping and champing in these dern woods you have hereabouts."

Owen pulled the little book of knowledge from his bundle. "The wild Boar, *sus scrofa*," he quoted from it, "has a thick undercoat of long, curly hair through which bristles pass to form an outer covering of dark brown or greyish black. Tusks may be eight to ten inches long. The young have brown fur with spots and stripes of white. The adult, very savage, has been known to kill a tiger."

"A *tiger*?"

"Not in Wales, I think." Owen turned over several leaves. "No, that would be in Africa or Tartary. The Boar is naturally stupid and of a sluggish disposition, but he is Restless at every change of the weather, and greatly Agitated when the Wind is high."

"D'ye reckon there's much chance of a breeze at present?" inquired the messenger, glancing uneasily at the last of the golden autumnal leaves gently stirring above them. "I'd as lief not brabble with one o' they agitated hog-pigs. You keep a sharp watch, young 'un; if you lets a tusker creep up on us unexpected, I'll lamback you, or my name's not Smith!"

"*Is* it Smith?" asked Owen, whose spirits had risen amazingly since his decision to return to the museum and tell all to his grandfather. Being able to read his dear little book again cheered him still more.

"O' course it's Smith," growled the messenger, kicking his pony into a canter down a long ride between mighty oak trees.

"Well, Mr. Smith, did you know that the Lard of the

Boar is used for Plaisters and Pomatums, and the Bristles for Brushes?"

"No I didn't, and what's more I don't care a fig," replied Mr. Smith. "I just hope we shan't be needing any plaisters, that's all. Here, you put that book away and tend to business."

"We are going too far south," Owen said, obeying, "you should turn eastwards."

"How do you reckon that out, boy?"

"With my compass," Owen said, and showed it at the end of its cord.

"That's a handy little article!" Mr. Smith exclaimed in tones of respect. "Pity his majesty wouldn't issue us messengers with the likes o' that, special when we're obliged to leave the highway and roam about in this sort o' nookshotten wilderness. How much farther would you say it was now, lad?"

"Thirty-seven miles," Owen said after a little calculation.

"And how d'you work *that* so pat?"

"The pony's steps are a yard long, and every five hundred steps I've made a chalk mark on your leather jerkin."

"Ho, so you have, have you? Well, just you wipe 'em off afore we get to Pennygaff, I don't wish to ride in looking like a horn-book. Thirty-seven miles," said Mr. Smith, and did a little calculation on his own account. Then he kicked the pony's slab-sides. "Here! Shake your shaggy shanks, Dobbin-ap-dobbin, or we'll not be there till cockshut time. And spending a night in these woods is something I'd not fancy above half."

The pony, however, was obstinate and would go at his

own pace and no faster; if kicked more than he considered reasonable he stood stock still with legs apart and head down until such time as he chose to move on again.

"The devil fly away with the perishing nag and the scoundrel who fobbed him off on me," grumbled Mr. Smith, vainly jerking at the reins on one of these occasions.

Owen consulted his book.

"The Horse," he read out, "is generous, docile, fpirited, I mean spirited, and very tractable."

"Oh, to be sure! Certainly!" snarled Mr. Smith. "About as tractable as Windsor Castle!"

"The Horse distinguishes his Companion, and neighs to him, and will remember any place at which he has once ftopped."

"He'll remember *this* spot, I'll lay. Counting the blades of grass, he is, I daresay, to tell his stablemates. I don't suppose that there chap-book of yourn tells how to *start* a horse when he's stopped, do it?"

Owen was obliged to admit that it did not. "I wish my friend Arabis were here. She knows how to whisper in the ears of horses when they give trouble."

"If I were to whisper in the ear 'o this here Turk, what I said 'ud make him blush to the end of his tail."

"Shall *I* try whispering to him?" Owen suggested diffidently.

"Whisper if you've a mind to, boy; no harm I reckon; only look sharp about it."

Owen accordingly slipped from the pony's rump and going forward, took hold of one furry ear and whispered into it. Having no notion of what sort of soothing spells Arabis used to charm refractory horses, he decided to try the Table of Corn measures from his Book of Knowledge:

2 lasts 1 wey
10 weys 1 quarter
20 quarters 1 comb
80 combs 1 bushel
320 bushels 1 peck

This had an electrifying effect. On the word *peck* the pony bounded forward as if he saw a manger full of corn ahead of him under the trees. Mr. Smith, violently dislodged from the saddle, fell sprawling.

"*Dang* it!" he cried furiously and, leaping to his feet, made after the pony, who kept evading him and remained tantalizingly just out of reach. Owen ran round to the pony's other side and tried to grab his reins, but the wayward animal kicked up his heels and cantered to the end of the glade.

"This is all on account o' *your* parlous notions!" Mr. Smith said to Owen. "A right slubber you made o' the business. Now what are you agoing to do about it?"

"I don't suppose you have any Carrots, Sugar, or other delicacies of which horses are Inordinately fond?"

"No I have not; and anyways if I had I wouldn't offer them to that son of Beelzebub."

Owen reflected. "My grandfather considers that mushrooms are a delicacy; I wonder if the pony would do so too?"

"No knowing what whim that rug-headed prancer might take into his noddle," remarked the messenger. "Try him if you like. Only don't poison the brute! I daresay half these toadystools is sudden death."

However Owen, aided by his useful book, was able to pick out a cluster of wood mushrooms from the various kinds of fungi which grew profusely in the vicinity. He pulled a few and broke them in pieces, then approached the pony, who watched him come with suspicion, but pricked his ears interestedly as the scent of the mushrooms reached him, borne on the rising wind.

"Stap me!" muttered Mr. Smith. "I do believe the unnatural animal's agoing to swallow the bait."

The pony stuck out his neck and then lifted a lip to nibble at one of the portions of mushroom.

Matters were in this delicate state when they were all startled by the sound of a low, fierce series of grunts, alarmingly near at hand. With a shrill whinny the pony flung up his head and bounded aside; Owen looked swiftly round and, to his horror, saw an immense wild boar emerge from a clump of hazel bushes midway between him and Mr. Smith. Its bristles were a dark mahogany-brown in colour, its curved tusks were fully ten inches long, and its tiny red eyes gleamed with ferocity.

"The bow! The crossbow!" Mr. Smith called frantically. "You've got it, boy! Shoot the monster, don't just stand there gawping!"

Owen had slung the bow on his back when he dismounted. Hurriedly he wiped his glasses, unslung it, and fitted a bolt. The boar, roused and irritated by Mr. Smith's shout, was moving in his direction, pawing the ground menacingly and shaking its huge head so that a spray of saliva flew about, while keeping its little eyes fixed on the terrified messenger.

"Shoot!" Smith croaked again. The boar made a rush at him and he dodged round a massive oak. "What ails you, boy? *Do* something!" he cried to Owen, who looked quickly about, picked up a stone, and hurled it at the boar. Uttering a high-pitched squeal of rage it spun round and made for him, ramping and frothing, and covering the distance at fearful speed on its short powerful legs.

Shaking but resolute, Owen knelt down and took aim; at the last possible moment he launched a bolt right into the boar's open gullet. Still it came on; desperately he pulled out another arrow and fitted it into the crossbow. Then suddenly, with a last screaming grunt, the old king-boar pitched over heavily and fell dead not half a yard from where Owen crouched.

"Phew!" Mr. Smith emerged from behind the oak tree, fanning himself with his three-cornered hat. "I thought we were properly lugged that time! Hey, boy, what made you take such a tarnal long time to shoot?"

"Because my book says the Boar is insensible to Blows on account of the Thickness of his Hide; so shooting him in the mouth seemed our only hope."

"Humph; well, you're certainly a cool customer," was all Mr. Smith said to that.

Owen would have liked to stay and make a careful examination of the dead animal, but Mr. Smith was anxious to get on; by great good fortune their pony, panic-stricken at the sight of the boar, had run blindly into a hazel thicket where it had been obliged to remain, sweating and shivering, with its reins hopelessly tangled among the boughs.

Docile now, and subdued, it allowed itself to be mounted and made no objections to cantering off at top speed.

"Likely we'll have no more trouble with the nag now, at least," Mr. Smith remarked. "If I'd ha" thought, though, I'd ha" cut off one of the boar's pettitoes to tirrit him with if he should get resty again."

However Owen had prudently stowed some of the mushrooms in his pockets; he felt sure they might prove more efficacious than frightening their mount with a boar's trotter.

As it proved, though, they had no need to cajole or threaten the pony, who behaved in a meek and biddable manner for the rest of the journey. They met no more wild boars face to face, and if they chanced to hear the distant grunts of one, rooting for truffles or chestnuts farther off in the forest, the very sound was enough to start the pony into a gallop, so they were able to cover the remaining distance to Pennygaff in record time, and arrived at the outskirts of the town just as a windy dusk was falling.

"Is this Pennygaff, then?" Mr. Smith inquired as they threaded their way down a narrow, empty street between little slate-roofed dwellings. "It's a doleful sort o' borough, isn't it? Where's all the folk?"

"They are indoors, I suppose," Owen said doubtfully.

The town did seem unusually deserted. Not a step echoed on the cobbles, apart from their own; not a light showed in the windows.

Mr. Smith shouted his message about the lost prince in front of the stocks, and the gallows, and the new Habakkuk chapel. Nobody appeared to take the slightest interest.

"Is it much use making the announcement if no one hears you?" Owen ventured to ask.

"I'm not paid to swabber out the folk from their houses if they don't choose to come, am I?" Mr. Smith replied. "I've let it be known three times in a public place that the prince is missing, that's all I'm required to do. *I* shan't weep millstones if he never turns up.—Is this a decent inn, boy?" he added as they approached the Dragon of Gwaun.

"It's the only one in the town," Owen told him.

"Humph! Better than a bed of prickles in the Fforest Mwyaf, I suppose. Well, boy, thanks for your company; if anyone asks, you can tell them that Ebenezer Smith said you had a good stomach in a trammelsome corner."

"Thank you, sir," Owen said, as this seemed high praise from the tetchy Mr. Smith. "And thank you for letting me ride with you."

He returned the crossbow to Mr. Smith, who tied his pony to a staple and entered the inn; Owen went on towards the museum with a fast-beating heart.

As he neared the top of the hill he began to hear the murmur of voices, and to see the light of numerous lanterns ahead; soon, to his astonishment, he perceived what appeared to be most of the inhabitants of Pennygaff assembled outside the museum. As many as could had entered the courtyard; the rest were beyond the wall, thronged as close as they could get.

Owen, being thin and light on his feet, managed to wriggle and work his way towards the front of the crowd without anybody remarking him. On his way he caught scraps of conversation.

"Down with sleepers' tickets, *I* say!"

"Give us back our holy harp!"

"They say the old ystraffaldiach have sold the harp to buy more flint arrowheads and stuffed birds!"

"Sold it to Lord Malyn, *I* heard, in return for a pension and a house in Pontypool!"

"His grandson took the harp over to Caer Malyn five nights ago, Cyfartha Jones told me."

"Achos dybryd! Foul crime it is!"

"Thief! Gŵr drwg! Thief!"

Horrified by these unjust accusations Owen, who by now had reached the middle of the courtyard, lifted up his voice and shouted,

"That's a lie! My granda is not a thief! He has not stolen the harp!"

A thunderous silence fell. The people who were standing close around Owen drew away from him in a semi-circle so that he was left alone, midway between the crowd and the museum entrance.

"Young Owen Hughes, that is," he heard somebody whisper, "the old rheibiwr's grandson. Come back, maybe, from disposing of the harp at Caer Malyn!"

Then the silence about him changed its quality and became steely-cold; although he had caught no sound from the museum Owen turned instinctively, sensing that the people in the crowd had shifted their attention to something behind him.

Old Mr. Hughes had come out and was standing in front of the door, staring at the crowd. He seemed quite calm, totally unmoved by their accusations. But when he saw Owen his face set like granite.

"Oh," he said. "It's you, is it? Well? What have *you* come back for?"

6

Arabis very much wished to ask her father what the foreign gentleman had been talking about so earnestly. But by the time the latter had ambled off into the darkness, turning to bow again every few steps, one or two customers had appeared outside the wagon; for half an hour or so Arabis was busy fetching down boxes of cough pastilles, phials of ointment, bottles of lotions and potions, and discussing their ailments with the people of Nant Agerddau.

"Pains in the night after too many slices of bara brith, ma'am? Then it is tincture of rhywbarb you will be needing, I am thinking."

"A sore throat when you do sing in the Maccabeus Choir for nine hours on end, sir? Our syrup of synamon will make you clear as a lark in no time."

"Chilblains with you, is it, my little lass? Here's some ointment of marchruddygl and marchalan, horseradish and elecampane, that will soothe them better in a twinkling."

"Runny nose and the sneezes, boy? Nasty old cold you have got, isn't it, and here's a dose will do you good—persli, perwraidd a perfagl, parsley, liquorice and periwinkle, oh, most delicious indeed!"

"A love potion you are asking, sir, a diod huolus, because your young lady won't speak to you? Indeed I am afraid we have no such thing with us, but one piece of counsel I can be giving you—eat no more wynwyn, no more onions in your lobscows, for, not to tell you a lie, sir, the angel Gabriel would hold his nose to be near you; sure I am then you will find your young lady quite civil and sociable again!"

"Can't sleep at night, is that the trouble with you, and nasty dreams when you do drop off? Certainly to goodness that is a grievous trouble, and here is some juice of llysiau cwsg, llysiau dryw, poppy and agrimony, that will lull you off before you can blow out the candle. And here, to turn your thoughts in a smiling direction, here is one of my father's beautiful poems: The Dream of the Emperor Maxen, it is called, and tells how he saw the Princess Helen in a vision, and sought her over land and sea; how much? One hatling, half a farthing for the medicine, sir, and one gini, twenty-one shillings, for the poem; and never again will you be in the way of buying a whole lifetime's pleasure for so little!"

Right at the end of the queue, lurking outside the wagon door in the darkness, was a curious little person, not much over three foot in height, and so covered with bushy black beard and whiskers that it was not possible to see anything of his face but a pair of sorrowful dark eyes which he fixed steadily on Arabis when, the last of the other patients being out of sight, he ventured into the van. He was wrapped in a black blanket-like robe which came over his head in a hood and covered all but his face.

"And how can I help you, sir?" Arabis inquired in her kind, warm voice. "Oh, there's silly I am"—as a fearful cough and spell of shivering shook him—"Indeed I can hear what troubles you, and a bad old cough that is! But wait you a little minute now . . ." and she mixed him a hot, soothing potion of aconite, belladonna, bryony, and ipecacuanha, beaten up in honey, lemon, cinnamon, and steaming metheglin. "There, sir, now we shall soon see you better. Indeed, my da says that dram would make Julius Caesar jump up out of his grave and invade Britain all over again! And I will give you this powder of herbs, mustard, tansy, and dandelion—put one-third in a bath of hot water before to go to bed every night for three nights, is it, and have a good old soak; that will soon stop the shivers."

All this time her small patient had not spoken one word. Pushing back the blanket, and revealing a sort of black knitted stocking-cap on his head, he drank the potion, and seemed greatly astonished by its flavour (nevertheless it appeared to do him good); he received the powdered herbs and instructions with a puzzled expression, but stowed the paper obediently under his blanket; then Arabis perceived that he was holding out to her something that glittered; a small lump of gold it proved to be.

"Dear to goodness, sir, that is far too much payment indeed, far and away too much! One shilling for the powder and one for the dram, one ffloring altogether, if you please! No more at all."

But the little patient did not seem to understand her; he still held out the lump of gold.

It was no use appealing to Tom Dando for advice; he had suddenly been struck by a new verse for his poem and was frantically scribbling it down before he forgot again. All Arabis could do was to compare the size of the gold lump with a gold guinea-piece, decide that it was three times as heavy, and so give her patient two guineas, nine silver florins, and a shilling, in exchange, which he regarded in a baffled manner. For a moment she feared he was going to swallow the shilling.

"No, no, sir, it is your change from the gold you gave me—too much it was, see? Please to put in your pocket."

Did he understand? It was hard to discover his expression, since so much of his face was concealed by the tangle of beard and whisker. But at length he put the coins away and made a sort of bow, pressing her hand for a moment against his cheek. Then he was gone swiftly into the dark outside.

"Well!" said Arabis. "There is curious for you! Didn't seem to follow what I said too well, though very civil to be sure. Hey, Da! Are you listening to me, Dada?"

"Eh? What is that, my little one? Did you speak?" Tom Dando put down his quill, having come to the end of a canto, and rubbed his eyes, blinking, like someone who has just woken from a deep sleep. His shirt collar was rumpled and his long curly dark hair was standing on end; his forehead was splashed with ink.

"Did you see that strange little fellow that was in by here, with a nasty cough on him? Look what he has given me in payment!"

Tom Dando examined the lump of gold, smelt it, felt it, and bit it.

"Pure, new-minted gold, that is," he pronounced. "Not often is it that you see the like, these days."

"But how could he have come on it, Dada?"

"Maybe he do have a goldmine by him," Tom Dando said vaguely, his mind and eyes once more straying back to his poem.

Arabis seized the chance before he was lost again. "Dada! The man who was in here before—the foreign gentleman in the fur hat. What did *he* want, with him?"

"Foreign gentleman?"

To prevent her father beginning to write again, Arabis gently removed the quill which he had picked up, and swept his pages of poetry into a neat heap.

"The man with the moustaches like rams' horns and the great flow of polite talk on his tongue."

"Oh, the Seljuk of Rum, is it? Kind of a foreign prince he is, down in those parts where they have a lot of sandy deserts, and eat dates. Telling me about his country, he was, while I gave his moustaches a bit of a trim, and then we got to talking of poetry; a fine clever man he is, indeed, and not at all proud with it."

Arabis breathed a breath of relief. Talk of poetry was harmless enough.

"You didn't tell him how I found Owen in that empty house this morning?"

"Found Owen in a house? What for should Owen not be in a house?"

Tom Dando looked round absently, picked up his pen, and, for lack of paper, began to write on a large flat Caerphilly cheese which Arabis had just put out for his supper. She moved it beyond his reach.

"Oh, Dada!" she said patiently. "You know I told you about finding Owen."

"Did you so? But what should the Seljuk of Rum care about that? He have never even met Owen! Have sense, girl! Talking poetry, we were—and he was asking questions about the parts round here; interested in the old gold mines, he is, and who used to work them."

"Why?" Arabis asked suspiciously. "None of his affair, surely?"

"Some reason he had, I am forgetting what. One or two lines of my poem burst sparkling into my mind then, just, so I am not remembering very clearly what he said. Something about somebody he was looking for was it? Oh, and he wanted to know where Brother Ianto was to be found."

"Oh, indeed?" said Arabis, knitting her brows. "And why was that, I wonder? How have he come to hear tell of Brother Ianto?"

"Whisht, girl! Ask more questions that a magistrate, you do! Why this, why that? How should I know? Maybe he needs glasses with him. Pass me my cheese, if you please, and a drop of metheglin to keep out the cold, and I will be writing another two-three verses while you tuck yourself off to bed. Late, it is indeed."

Arabis tidied the caravan, covered up Hawc, and went to bed, but as she drew the curtain of her bunk, she asked,

"Will the foreign gentleman be staying long in these parts, Dada?"

"Eh? What's that you say, cariad?"

"The foreign gentleman. The Seljuk of Rum. Does he stay here long?"

"No, not long," Tom Dando said, taking a mighty bite of cheese. "Goes off to stay at Caer Malyn tomorrow; interested in all the gold treasures there, seemingly, and had an invitation from his lordship to go and study them."

"Ach y fi! If *that* is the sort of company he keeps, I hope we see no more of him."

"There's silly you are, girl! Interested in gold he is, that's all."

But Arabis, curling up in her bunk, was more than ever relieved that the Seljuk had caught no glimpse of Owen at the wagon, if he was a friend of the wicked Marquess. Maybe it was he who had arranged to have the harp stolen for Lord Malyn? And why should he be inquiring after Brother Ianto? It was all odd, and most suspicious.

She was worried, too, about Owen; the miserable, defeated set of shoulders as he walked away after Brother Ianto had made her heart ache with compassion. Restlessly turning on her pallet she resolved to go down to Brother Ianto's cave first thing next morning and talk over what was best for Owen to do next. At last she drifted off into a troubled sleep, and dreamed that the Marquess, smiling with wolves' fangs, was holding the harp just out of Owen's reach while he hit it with a hammer.

"He'll break it!" Arabis muttered, half sitting up in bed; then she realized that the tapping sound she had heard was in fact someone knocking at the door of the wagon. Could it be Owen?

Pulling on her dress she tiptoed past Tom, who had fallen asleep with his head resting on a pile of poetry.

Outside the door she found the same tiny bearded man who had earlier given her the lump of gold.

"What is the trouble with you, now, sir?" Arabis asked, sleepily rubbing her eyes. "Late hours you do keep, indeed! Hush not to wake my Dada, if you please. I will step outside."

Once she was down the steps the little man gave a tug at her arm. In his eyes she caught such an urgent, pleading, beseeching look that she guessed something was badly amiss. It did not seem to be connected with himself; indeed his cough appeared much better for the draught she had given him.

"Wait you one moment then," whispered Arabis gently. Both she and her father were accustomed to be called out at night from time to time; she put on her warm red cloak with the hood, packed up a basket of the remedies most frequently called for, carefully covered Tom with a patchwork quilt, and scribbled a hasty note: "Gone out to patient. Back soon. Yr loving daughter Arabus."

Then she caught up the horn lantern and slipped out again to where the little man was patiently waiting.

To her surprise he led her not in the direction of the town, but up towards the quarry face, along a narrow path among bushes, and at length paused before one of the larger cave openings, giving her a measuring look.

"In there?" said Arabis, somewhat taken aback. "Da chwi, where are you taking me, friend?"

But the man, evidently deciding that she was not too tall to enter the cave, pulled her forward again without answering, and they went inside.

Arabis was not alarmed, but she was greatly interested,

for she began to suspect that her unusual client must be one of the little fairylike beings, the Tylwyth Teg or Fur People who were thought to dwell in the caves of the mountain. Up to now she had been inclined to consider them nothing but a legend, invented by the timid and credulous inhabitants of Nant Agerddau, but the little man certainly answered their description in many particulars. She found it hard to believe, though, that he would suddenly pull her into a bottomless chasm, or disappear leaving her lost in the bowels of the mountain, or turn into a flaming dragon and devour her. His hand, pulling her along, was warm and seemed human enough; though he did not speak she felt instinctively that he was friendly towards her and could be trusted. And, after all, he had swallowed her medicine and it had done him good. That was another proof, Arabis thought, that he was not one of the Bendith eu mamau, the Little Blessed People; if he had been, surely he would have no need of human remedies?

This cave (unlike the one Owen had entered in search of the harp) did not come to an end, but struck downhill, deep into the mountain, growing wider and higher as it descended. The horn lantern threw so small a circle of light that Arabis could catch no more than a glimpse, now and then, of rock walls sparkling with crystals, and occasionally a great cluster of stalactites, like icicles of stone, dangling from the roof overhead. The floor was hard and their steps echoed hollowly as they proceeded; the air, as in all the caves of the Whispering Mountain, was warm and steamy.

Presently her guide came to a halt in what seemed to be a large chamber at the bottom of the tunnel; he put his fingers between his lips and whistled shrilly. Almost at once another man, equally small and hairy, appeared out of the dark, blinking at the lantern as if he were distressed by its light.

The two men conferred together in a musical foreign language, then the second one tugged forward a pair of animals which he had been leading; Arabis nearly dropped her basket at the sight of them, for in the whole of her life she had never laid eyes on such peculiar-looking creatures. They were about the size of donkeys, but had big, flat, shuffling padded feet instead of hoofs; their necks were long and swaying, their backs curiously bumpy, their expressions sardonic, and they were covered with long, shaggy black fur, which was moulting here and there; some of the looser hanks were tied up with bits of string. They smelt strongly and disagreeably of fish.

Her guide gestured her forward; Arabis realized that she was expected to climb on to one of these animals; each wore a sort of saddle, adapted to the strange shape of their backs. The second man thumped them with his fist and they knelt down on the rock making a noise, half snarl, half snuffle, which gave Arabis little confidence in their good intentions. However, she mounted, perching her basket and lantern in front of her (there was a bump, convenient for this purpose, on the animal's back), her guide also mounted, calling out some word of command, and the other man stood back.

The creatures heaved up awkwardly on to their feet and set forward into the dark. Their flat pads made little sound on the rock and Arabis found it hard to judge exactly how fast they were going, but it seemed very fast indeed; their method of progress was to lurch forward until they were almost ready to topple over and then right themselves at the last minute; she soon felt as if all her bones were being pulled apart. She had often bestridden Galahad or the mountain ponies but this was utterly different, and the most uncomfortable ride she had ever taken.

I believe I know what these beasts are like, she presently thought, peering at the long flexible neck and rather sheep-like head in front of her, there is a picture in one of Dada's books about foreign lands. Camels. That is it, they are like camels.

She had pronounced the last word aloud and, to her surprise, for she had given up expecting her companion to speak to her, he suddenly gave a flashing smile, nodding his head up and down.

"Gamal, gamal!" he agreed, thumping his steed.

"They are really camels? But how do camels come to be in by here, under the mountain? That is a strange thing, surely?"

He answered in his own incomprehensible tongue. She would have liked to ask more: why were the camels so small and dwarfish, their bumps flattened out, how was it they could see in the dark? But there seemed little point in asking if she could not understand his answers.

"Owen will know," she thought. "Very likely in his little Book of Knowledge it will be giving the whole explanation. But camels underground in Wales—who would have thought it, indeed!"

Meanwhile the camels had been speeding along an apparently endless, straight, level underground passage which ran alongside an underground river. Arabis, while not exactly alarmed, began to be somewhat anxious because they were covering such a distance; "At this rate," she thought, "it will be daybreak before I so much as reach my patient, and gracious to goodness knows when I shall get back home again; Dada will have to see to his own breakfast."

She was not afraid that Tom would be worried about her; she knew him better than that. If she were to be absent for a week together he would do little more than lift his head from his poetry and murmur, "Dear, dear, Arabis not back yet, then?" before dashing down another verse.

After an interminably long ride, during which Arabis was able to doze a little, holding on to the pommel of her saddle, the tunnel brought them into a vast cavern which was illuminated by clusters of pale phosphorescent lights hanging far above.

They were still following the course of the river which crossed the floor of the cave in a deep channel. The water, running smooth and silent, was a pale milky green, cloudy but most beautiful, and was evidently hot; wreaths of steam rose from its surface. Far ahead Arabis could see a series of massive pipes, like those of some enormous church organ, which ran up the cave wall and were lost to view in the gloom overhead; the river appeared to flow into these pipes, but how the water was persuaded to run perpendicularly upwards, Arabis could not imagine, nor where this great underground hall could be; they must, she was sure, be very far from Nant Agerddau, perhaps beneath the Fforest Mwyaf.

Now they left the river and entered a narrow dark opening concealed among rocks where they came to a halt. The guide made signs that Arabis must dismount here. She was not sorry to do so. No sooner had she slid stiffly down than yet another small dark figure appeared and led the camels away into the shadows while her companion, again respectfully taking her hand, drew her along a narrow track, which, climbing at a steeper and steeper angle, presently changed to a flight of rude stairs cut in the thickness of the rock. One thing soon began to puzzle Arabis very much and alarm her a little: the rock here seemed to vibrate, as if constantly battered by some powerful force, and she could hear a sort of booming hum, which sometimes became very loud.

This noise abated slightly as they climbed and presently a little daylight could be seen ahead; after several turns in the stair they came to a cleft in the rock wall. Arabis stood on tiptoe and looked through this hole, in the hope of discovering where she was.

"Wchw!" she exclaimed in utter astonishment. "No wonder I was thinking it a long way. Fast goers those camels of yours are, indeed to goodness!"

Straight ahead, nothing could be seen but greenish dawn sky, with a couple of silvery seagulls floating across it. But when Arabis craned far out and looked down she could see, at a giddy depth below, great breakers crashing over jagged rocks at the foot of a cliff. And if she turned to look up she could see that the cliff continued towards the sky for many hundreds of feet.

"There's only one place I know of where the cliffs are as high as this," Arabis muttered, "and that's south of Port Malyn, where the castle stands. But, Dewi Sant, who'd have thought we had come so far!"

There was no doubt of their location, though, for when

she leaned out farther still and looked to her left she could see a slender black-and-white finger thrusting from the waves, the Shambles Lighthouse, set there to warn shipping of dangerous shoals.

A gentle tug on her hand reminded her that her own position was none too safe, and also that a patient was waiting; she withdrew cautiously from the window-slit and followed up the stair once more.

They had not much farther to go.

The staircase here branched and divided into many narrow passages running hither and thither inside the cliff; each led to half a dozen or so cell-like chambers. Some of these were fairly large, some very small, but they all resembled one another in three respects; they were not natural caves, but had been quarried out not long ago by the tools of men; each had a tiny window-hole, looking out to sea; and each was furnished simply but with a richness that made Arabis gasp. Jugs, basins, and pails, the commonest utensils, were made, without exception, of pure, shining gold, beautifully worked. But there were no tables or chairs, no cupboards, no doors; the curtains and bedding were all made of thick, black, coarse material—Arabis guessed it to be woven camels' fur. In another sad particular all the dwellings were alike also—each contained one or two sick people, sometimes three or four. Arabis was touched to the heart by the uncomplaining patience of these sufferers as they lay, wracked with coughing, feverish and heavy-eyed on their camel-fur pallets, men, women, and tiny children; their eyes followed her trustfully as she passed from cave to cave, dispensing medicines, pastilles, and powders, rubbing their chests with wintergreen, bathing their foreheads with essence of mint and balm. They were all very alike—small, dark, hairy people, pale-skinned, with lustrous flashing black eyes; very few seemed to have escaped the sickness, but those who were still able eagerly helped Arabis tend the others.

All too soon, of course, her stock of medicines began to run low; she had not brought nearly enough for so many patients.

"What is to be done now, just?" she considered. "If I go home for more, that wastes a terrible deal of time, and I am afeared some of them will die if they do not get help soon. I wonder if someone would take a message back to Dada, and then I could stay here looking after the rest.

"Can any of you understand me?" she asked the three or four who were assisting her, and tried to explain what she wanted. They shook their heads doubtfully; although they seemed to understand a word here and there, they could not grasp the whole message. Stepping aside they conferred together; she caught the name *Yehimelek* repeated several times. Then her original guide (she distinguished him by his cap) seized her hand again and led her along another passage to a cave she had not visited yet. This was larger than the rest, screened off by a camel-fur curtain, and occupied by one man only. He was plainly very old—his long beard and thick bushy hair and whiskers were perfectly white; he looked frail beyond belief, leaning back on a pile of camel-fur cushions. But the eyes in the wasted face were deep and dark and full of intelligence; his tone when he addressed Arabis was faint and hoarse but authoritative.

"On behalf of my people I, Tabut Elulaios Yehimelek,

Architect, Engineer, and Hereditary Foreman of the Children of the Pit, do thank you, lady, for your goodness in coming here to help us. I fear we can give you little in return except gold; of that, useles though it be, as much as our last seven camels can bear, you shall carry away if you wish."

Here he was interrupted by a terrible fit of coughing, which made his slight body shake like a cobweb in the wind.

"There is glad I am to be able to help, sir," Arabis said when he had recovered a little. "Indeed I am not wanting your gold, I thank you, but only to do a bit more. If I do write a message to my da at Nant Agerddau, could one of your people take it back to him? Then he could be bringing our wagon over to Port Malyn, and no need to go all that way for medicines, see?"

"Shishak!" the man on the couch called. The guide, who had waited outside, came in and bowed respectfully.

"Write your message," Yehimelek told Arabis, "and Shishak will ride back with it. But, I beg you, ask your father to be secret, and not to mention this matter, or we shall be in danger of slavery and death."

"No need to worry," Arabis assured him, scribbling a note on the paper that had held a powder of foxgloves. "Not a one to gossip, my dada." But she added the warning, folded the paper, and gave it to Shishak, who bowed again and departed at speed. "I have asked him to give Shishak as much medicine as he can carry, and to start himself for Port Malyn directly. Now, can I be doing something to relieve your worship?" Arabis said.

"Not until you have helped every last one of my people," Yehimelek answered proudly, through another fit of coughing. "Shall it be said that the leader accepted relief while others were in need? Never!"

So Arabis returned to the other sufferers, and had soon exhausted her entire stock of medicine on them.

She had noticed, as she went from one sick-bed to another, that there was pitifully little food in the caves: a small quantity of dried fish, a few gulls eggs, nothing more; plainly, since most of the able-bodied men had fallen ill, stocks had run low; it seemed to her that part of the people's trouble might come simply from starvation and a lack of greenstuff. Struck by an idea she returned to Yehimelek.

"Sir," she said, "do any of your tunnels lead down to the foot of the cliff?"

"Assuredly. How else would my people catch the fish needed to support us and our camels?"

"Could somebody show me the way down?"

"Strato! Tennes!" he called, and when two of the helpers came in he gave them orders to take Arabis where she wanted to go. They led her down hundreds of steps, the noise of the sea outside becoming louder as they went, and finally emerged, through an entrance cunningly masked with seaweed, on to an outcrop of rock at the base of the cliff. There was no beach, and little danger of being seen; the tide, as it fell, merely exposed more and more dangerous rocks; all fishing craft kept well away. The ebbing tide had also left behind great swags and piles of seaweed; this Arabis proceeded to collect, and the two men helped her. They rinsed it in a trickle of fresh water which ran down the cliff, and took it to an empty cave where Arabis kindled a driftwood fire and made signs that she wanted a large pot. A gold one was fetched, large enough to contain a whole sheep. Half filling this with fresh water she boiled up the seaweed into nourishing broth which, when thick and succulent, was distributed in gold cups, gold mugs, and gold pipkins to the entire community. Arabis took a bowlful to Yehimelek who accepted it gratefully when he had made certain that everyone else had some too.

"Ah," the Hereditary Foreman sighed when he had drunk his soup. "I was angry when I discovered that Shishak and Ahiram had gone to seek help without asking my permission (they knew I would never have given it). But I believe they made a wise choice. With the help of this excellent broth, and your good medicines, lady, my people may be saved yet."

"May I ask a question, sir, if it will not trouble you?" Arabis asked, taking the bowl from him.

"Surely."

"Why do you, only, of all your people, speak my language?"

"It has been a rule with us," he said, "ever since we were brought to this country by force a hundred and two generations ago. To prevent our being absorbed into the conquering race and forgetting our ancestry, only one man in each generation is allowed to learn the outlandish tongue."

"A hundred generations! Does dim dwywaith!" Arabis said to herself in amazement. "Even if each man lived only till he was twenty, that is two thousand years!"

"But who brought your excellency's people over here, then?" she asked. "Was it the old Romans, maybe? And where did you come from? And why did they bring you, in the name of goodness?"

"They brought us as slaves, to mine gold for them out of these hills," he said. "They brought us because above all other races we were skilled in the crafts of mining and working gold. And then, when our conquerors went away, we were left behind. So we hid ourselves in the mines that we had dug and resolved that never again would we let ourselves be enslaved. As to the land we came from, it is very beautiful, with blue sky and green trees, and golden sands, and white cities; it lies many months' journey to the south. Alas, alas, for Sa'ir and Taidon, for Jyblos and Zibach and Kashin, and the beautiful mountains of Sur! One day, one day we shall return to them! We lead our lives in darkness and fear, coming out only at night to catch fish and pick the herbs of the hillside; our people dwindle at each new generation and pine in this damp northern climate; even our camels grow small and infirm. But one day a ship will come to carry us nack to the land of our fathers. One day, one day, it will happen."

His voice had fallen into a sort of dreamy chant. Arabis wondered if he really believed it.

"Eh, dear to goodness," she said. "there's sad. Living underground, so damp and nasty, for thousands of years! No wonder you have all got such terrible coughs with you. But," she went on reasonably, after thinking the matter over, "why didn't you all pack up and return home—I mean, why didn't your great-great-great-grandfathers do so—when the old Romans (if it was that trouble-making lot) left this country? Why didn't you do that, then?"

"Because," Yehimelek said simply, "we did not know which way to go."

Pondering this problem, Arabis fell silent. Her eyes wandered round the room for inspiration, and then remained fixed. For embroidered in gold thread on the inside of the door-curtain, where she had not noticed it before, was a beautiful life-sized representation of a golden harp.

7

As Owen moved towards his grandfather a stone whistled past his head and smashed one of the museum windows. Owen, turning swiftly, was just in time to see Hwfa Morgan stoop and pull a cobble out of the ground.

"Stop that!" he shouted indignantly.

"Where's our harp? How much money did Lord Malyn give you for it?" somebody shouted back. Another stone flew, narrowly missing old Mr. Hughes.

Owen was desperate. "Listen, all of you!" he shouted. "Listen!"

To make his voice carry farther he scrambled on to the mounting-block at one side of the museum-porch. Ignoring a rotten leek which came sailing through the air and struck him on the arm, he bawled out at the full pitch of his lungs:

"The harp was *not* sold to the Marquess of Malyn. It was stolen."

"Get down, boy!" hissed old Mr. Hughes, close beside him. "Must you shame me worse that I am shamed already? I *know* you stole the harp—I have already received your abominably spelt and ill-written letter. But not a penny need you expect to receive for it—be sure of that. Wretched, abandoned lad—I do not know how you have the face to return to the scene of your crime?"

"*I* did not steal the harp!" Owen declared. "It was taken by two men called Bilk and Prigman, who forced me to go with them.

"All in it together, like as not," somebody commented.

"Do not attempt to deceive me, boy; I know your writing," Mr. Hughes said.

"Of course it was my writing—they made me write at the point of a knife! It is Bilk and Prigman who have the harp, and I believe they stole it for the Marquess of Malyn, because my grandfather would not give it to him."

This last was plainly news to the crowd.

Mr. Morgan the innkeeper said thoughtfully,

"Well now, there is maybe a grain of truth in what the boy tell us. Certain it is that those two were very thick with his lordship when he stayed at the Dragon, and why would that be, I am wondering? Jailbirds they were, for sure."

"Parcel of thieves, the whole crew of them," called Mrs. Evans the grocery. "Duck these two in the river now, just, and the others when we lay hands on them is it?"

The section of the crowd who wanted action muttered agreement. More missiles were flung. One of them—a rotten apple—struck Owen and spattered him with cider-smelling mush.

"My grandfather has nothing to do with it!" he shouted. "Listen—you *must* listen to me. Grandfather refused to let

Lord Malyn have the harp—those two men said so. That was why they stole it!"

"Lies! Lies! Tell to the marines!" somebody shouted.

"Quiet, neighbours! Give the boy a fair hearing, *I* say!" the burly Mr. Morgan called out. "Courage he has at least, no denying. Not sorry I'd be to see the day when *you* spoke up so bold," he added sharply to his son Hwfa, who laid down the cobble he had been about to hurl, and looked sheepish.

"Right, boy! Tell your story, then, is it? And if anyone care to interrupt, he have me to deal with!"

Mr. Morgan stepped forward to the mounting-block and turned to face his neighbours, who muttered and grumbled, but forbore to throw any more stones or vegetables.

As briefly as possible, Owen related how he had been overpowered and kidnapped by Bilk and Prigman, how he had been taken to Nant Agerddau and imprisoned, how he had escaped, only to find that the men had left the place, presumably taking the harp with them. His vehement, earnest manner began to convince the crowd.

"Would you believe it, then?"

"There's scandalous—imagine a great, rich lord hiring two scoundrels like that to make off with our precious harp! Or maybe it was that foreign fellow that was staying at Mr. Morgan's—I wouldn't trust *him* further than the length of his moustaches!"

"And planning to murder the poor boy—it do make your blood run cold!"

Only Mr. Hughes refused to be persuaded; he listened to Owen's tale with his face set like flint; at the end he declared loudly,

"I do not believe a word of it. Never in my life did I hear such a pack of lies!"

Owen turned even paler than he was already.

"But Grandfather—" he began.

"Do not address me as *Grandfather*, boy! I disown you! Understand me clearly—from now on I will have no more dealings with you! I will not feed you or house you—I do not acknowledge you as my flesh and blood. You have put shame on the ancient name of Hughes!"

"Shame yourself, old man!" shouted Dai, the potman from the Dragon of Gwaun. "The boy have done his best, isn't it? There's nasty, casting off your own kin!"

"Yes!"

"Hear, hear!"

"Heart of granite, the old ceidwad do have!"

Exasperated, Mr. Hughes turned to face the accusing crowd. "Clear off, every one of you!" he shouted. "I've no patience with you. For the last three years, since I retired from active service, I've tried to run your museum in a decent, shipshape manner, and what thanks do I get for it? First you accuse me of stealing the harp, now you call me names and interfere in my family affairs. Well, from tomorrow you can look after your own museum, because I am resigning my post; some other fool can have your ten shillings a year! Now, kindly take yourselves off, because I wish to go to bed."

He moved back towards the porch.

"Grandfather—" Owen began again. But the old man, stonily ignoring him, stepped inside and slammed the museum door.

There was a moment's shocked silence. Then, soberly, the crowd began to disperse.

"Duw!" Luggins Cadwaller said in an awestruck tone. "There is an old tartar you have for a granda, Owen Hughes! Sorry I am if ever I was a bit nasty to you—reckon you had enough at home to put up with."

In spite of an angry glance thrown at him by Hwfa Morgan, the large, good-natured Luggins ambled over to where Owen stood, still numbed by his grandfather's rejection of him, and thumped him on the back.

"Cheer up, boy! Lot of silly fuss, I say, over an old harp with one string, eh, Mog?"

Mog nodded. He was eating a large handful of laver-bread, but stopped chewing long enough to say,

"Glad I am *my* granda hasn't thrown me out of doors! What'll you do now, Owen Hughes?"

His tone was inquisitive, rather than unkind.

"Do?" Owen was still somewhat dazed. He rubbed his forehead perplexedly, rather taken aback at the apparent good will of these boys who had hitherto been his enemies. But Hwfa and Dick, Soth and Follentine and Dove still scowled at him with dislike and hostility; only, he now realized, their enmity did not worry him as it had done before. "Do?" he repeated. "Why, I must try to get the harp back. Yes," he went on, as what seemed his only possible course of action occurred to him. "I must go to Caer Malyn and tell the Marquess that Bilk and Prigman have gone off with the harp and that, as he is suspected of hiring them to steal it, he should help us to get it back."

"Bachgen dda! That's right!" exclaimed Mr. Morgan approvingly. "Coward, did you say this boy was, Hwfa? Why he have twice your spirit. Going to see Lord Malyn! There's many a full-grown man in this town would not dare!"

Hwfa Morgan scowled at his father and muttered unwillingly, "Nothing so wonderful about him that *I* can see. But I'll go along with you if you like, Owen Hughes."

For he perceived that Owen's behaviour had won him respect, even popularity, and that it would be as well for his own position at least to make a pretence of sharing the general opinion.

"And I'll go too!" called out Luggins joyfully. "Like to see his lordship's castleful of golden furniture, I would!"

"I'll come too." "And I!" volunteered Dick and Follentine and Dove, following their leader's example.

"Don't leave poor old Mog behind, boys!"

Soth glanced questioningly at Hwfa, who muttered behind his hand, "Just wait till we have him out in the woods on the way to Caer Malyn. Mincemeat we'll make of the little adwr!"

Upon which Soth, smiling his sickly smile, lisped, "Glad I thall be to come along too, Owen Hugheth!"

Hwfa and his associates stepped out of the rapidly dwindling crowd and joined Owen round the mounting-block.

"Start right off, will you then, Owen Hughes?" Mog said.

Owen would have liked to set out that instant, but Mr. Morgan advised waiting till next morning.

"No sense trying to get through the Fforest Mwyaf at night, boy; eaten alive every last one of you would be, even my Hwfa, and he's as tough a mouthful as ever gave the colic to a hungry wolf. Better come down to the

Dragon for a bite of supper and a nap; welcome with us you are, since your old granda have turned so prickly. Plenty of room there, since all the gentry have left. The foreign gentleman didn't stay long after Lord Malyn went; up to visit the museum first, and then off with him to Nant Agerddau in a hired chaise; wanted to see the Devil's Leap was what he *said*."

It was agreed that the boys should start at daybreak with food for the journey and whatever weapons each could provide. Owen ventured to tap on the museum door and ask his grandfather if he might borrow the ancient crossbow from the collection of his arms, but his request was greeted by an implacable silence from inside.

"No matter," Mr. Morgan said. "Plenty of leather we have, down at the Dragon; make yourself a slingshot, you can."

However, next morning, much to Owen's surprise, Luggins arrived carrying the museum crossbow (which was in good working order, thanks to the way Owen had been obliged to polish it every night) and a handful of bolts.

"How did you persuade my grandfather to part with it?" Owen asked Luggins as the party of eight set out down the rocky, forested glen of the Gaff river, armed with sticks, knives, pikes, and the crossbow.

"No trouble at all!" Luggins said, smiling his wide, simple smile. "Thought I'd call in, just, as I was passing the museum. At the door, I was, when a carriage stopped there, and a fellow all done up in gold lace says to your granda, "Mr. Hughes, is it? I have orders to bring you at once before his worship the Marquess of Malyn. He desires to see you without loss of time." Well, while your granda was grumbling and arguing the toss, the way he has with him, what did I do but nip in the door behind him, whip up the crossbow, and out the window. Simple, see!"

Owen congratulated him absently, his mind much occupied with this news. It sounded as if the Marquess had not got the harp, but had received his letter and sent for Mr. Hughes to demand an explanation. So that made two. The Seljuk's letter had missed him; Owen had been relieved to find it waiting at the Dragon of Gwaun and had quietly taken the first opportunity of putting it in the kitchen stove. But where was the fourth—that addressed to His Highness Prince David of Wales?

The route the boys were following lay along the course of the Gaff river and through the forest; this way was the most direct but more dangerous than the turnpike road, first because of wild beasts, and secondly because part of the track lay in a dry watercourse where the river had sunk underground, and the way was subject to sudden dangerous flooding after a storm. However at present the day was fair and they hoped it would remain so.

The party had strung out in twos along the rocky riverbed; first Hwfa and Soth, who walked some distance ahead of the rest, mutering together in low voices and occasionally casting back glances full of ill-will at Owen.

Next came Dick and Follentine, slashing with their sticks at every plant they passed, and throwing stones at every bird and animal.

Luggins, Dove, Mog, and Owen brought up the rear, walking in a square, three of them openmouthed in wonder while Owen, out of the lore acquired from his little book, instructed them as to the natural wonders that lay on every side.

"The Hedgehog will patiently fubmit to every provocation for its own fecurity—do give over poking the poor thing, though, Dove; it will never unroll while you do that! The giant oaks you observe overhead belong to the genus Quercus. The Mushrooms, Mosses, Ferns, and Liver-worts, all of which you see here abundantly displayed, belong to the twenty-fourth order of that excellent botanist Linnaeus."

"Hwchw!" said Mog, who was chewing a large mushroom. "I thought all this land belonged to his lordship? Will old Linnaeus be annoyed, think you, if I pick his mushrooms?"

At this moment Follentine, hurling a rock at what he supposed to be a large grey boulder, had the misfortune to strike an elderly she-wolf who was curled up sleeping in the morning sun. She woke and flew at him with a snarl; yelling with fright he took to his heels, but she overhauled him in half a dozen bounds and seized the skirt of his jacket in her long fangs. While the rest of the boys stood paralysed by fright and indecision, Owen swiftly strung the crossbow and fired a bolt with such dexterity as to knock the wolf head over heels, killing her instantly.

"Y mae ofn arnaf i!" blubbered Follentine. "She nearly had me, the brute! I'm not coming any farther. Back home, me!"

"Rubbish, man! Shame on you! She hardly touched you. Handy shot of yours that was, Owen, boy!" exclaimed Mog, examining the dead wolf.

"I'm wounded! I might die!" Follentine persisted, craning his neck to try and observe the back of his thigh, which the wolf's teeth had grazed. "Look at the blood! Bleed to death I shall for sure."

Wishing that Arabis were there to advise him, Owen bandaged the slight wound with a handful of cobwebs and some dock leaves; notwithstanding all their persuasions, Follentine then made tracks for home, declaring that he was sure mortification would set in unless his mother cleaned the wound. Pursued by cries of "Mam's babby!" from Dick and Hwfa he hastened up the gorge and was soon out of sight.

The rest of the party then proceeded on their way, Luggins, Mog and Dove continuing to congratulate Owen on his marksmanship, which had filled them with astonishment, while Hwfa, Dick, and Soth kept some distance ahead, seeming more disgruntled than delighted at this proof of his ability to defend himself.

"Have to get the bow away from him, we shall, before we nobble him," Hwfa decided. "You do that, Soth; Dick and I'll find an overhanging rock and drop on him from it. That ought to settle him."

"I—I theem to have thprained my ankle," Soth stammered nervously, beginning to limp. I'm not thure that I thall be able—'

But Hwfa turned on him such a menacing glare that he fell silent.

However before the three could put their plan into execution they encountered a hazard in their path by which the whole party was brought to a halt.

The dry watercourse had been descending through the forest in a series of steps, each deeper than the one before;

halfway down the lowest, which dropped some thirty feet, the river again appeared, cascading out of a hole in the rock below the point the boys had reached. They were faced with the problem of how to make their way down this cliff, crossing over the waterfall, so as to rejoin their path, which continued along a narrow ledge on the opposite side of the gorge. Plainly at some recent time a fall of rock had removed a section of the path.

"Bit awkward that is," Luggins grunted, looking at the sheer drop below, and the spout of water which boiled into foam as it hit the rocks at the bottom.

"Oh, what thall we do?" lamented Soth. "I wish we'd thtuck to the turnpike!"

"Got any notions, Owen, boy?" asked Mog, swallowing a handful of blackberries which he had snatched from the brambles as they came along.

Owen glanced up. Above them a small, but ancient and powerful yew tree grew out from the left-hand cliff, leaning more than halfway across the gorge.

"If we could climb that tree—" he murmured thoughtfully.

"And then what? Have a heart, man! Jump thirty feet, do you expect us?"

"No, but if only we were provided with a rope—Stay! I have it!" And Owen was gone, running back the way they had come. In five minutes or so he reappeared, trailing behind him some long strands of tough, fibrous creeper-stem.

"*Clematis vitalba*, or *virginiana*," he explained. " 'This beautiful plant, covered with white bloffoms, or furry fruit clufters, makes indeed a fitting bower for any maid or traveller who may chance to seek shelter. Leaflets are three-nerved from the bafe, entire or with a few coarfe teeth, hairy on the nerves—' "

"Hairy on the nerves?" Dick muttered. "It's *murder* on the nerves, look you! Pound me into picws, you can, before I will be trusting myself to that bit of grass!"

"It is very strong," Owen assured him. "In the Caucasus these stems are frequently used for making light baskets—'

"Os gwelwch yn dda! I am not an egg!"

"I will go first and show how," Owen said confidently. He paced the width of the gorge, measured the descent to the ledge with his eye, and did a quick calculation, then knotted two of the creeper stems together.

"To find the strength of a rope," he informed his companions, "you should square the circumference in inches, and divide by three, for the breaking strain in tons. I am joining these two pieces together with a *rolling hitch*, as they are of slightly different sizes; I shall secure one end to the tree by means of a *timber hitch*, thus—'

Winding a spare strand of creeper round his waist, and slinging the crossbow on his back, he shinned up the tree with great agility and tied the end of his rope to a suitable branch; then he laid hold of the rope and slid down it to within four feet of the lower end.

"Letth cut the rope, now, eh, Hwfa?" whispered Soth, but Hwfa, watching Owen's actions with the utmost interest, took no notice of his henchman.

"What'll he do now, he can never drop from there?—Ah, I see, he is going to swing."

Indeed, Owen, by working his body backwards and forwards, soon had the rope swinging vigorously, right across the gorge, and when it was at the extent of its swing he was able to drop easily on to the ledge.

Mog and Luggins watched with their mouths open.

"Duw!" said Luggins. "Have we to do that? Dammo! I don't fancy it above half. Suppose the rope breaks? I'm a lot heavier than you, boy!"

"It's all right," Owen called. "I have calculated that the rope will take at least a hundred and eighty-seven pounds."

"That's just about what I weigh, man! Oh well, if it'll hold me, it will take the rest, no danger, so I might as well try first."

With which cheerful words big fat Luggins clambered up the yew tree, knocking off twigs right and left and bending the boughs almost double. Owen did feel a qualm of anxiety as Luggins entrusted himself to the creeper stem; however it bore his weight admirably, and once he was fairly launched on it he found the whole experience highly delightful and swung back and forth several times with loud cries of "Un, dau, tri, pedwar, pump, chewch, saith, wyth, naw, deg!"

"That's enough!" cried Owen, when he had reached number ten. "This is not a game!"

"Grand sport it is, though!" panted Luggins, landing so heavily beside Owen that he nearly knocked him off the ledge. "Come back here we must, when we have called on the old Marquess."

Having seen how much Luggins enjoyed the crossing, Mog and Hwfa were eager to try, and soon followed his example. It was quite another matter, though, with Soth Gard, who, white as ashes, utterly refused to trust himself to it.

"It ithn't that I'm thcared," he said several times over, through chattering teeth. "Ith jutht that I haven't got a head for heighth. I think I'd better go home."

"Coward! Sheepheart!" shouted Hwfa furiously, but his words made no impression on Soth, who turned and walked rapidly up the gorge in the direction of Pennygaff.

"I—I had better go with him, maybe," Dick Abrystowe said hastily—he too was rather pale. "A long way from town we are now, see? Fall into some trouble on his own, he might—meet another wolf, who knows? Go with him, I will, to see he gets safe home."

And without more ado Dick set off in pursuit of Soth and the pair were soon out of sight.

"Pity they wouldn't try," Owen said rather regretfully as the rest of the party proceeded in the opposite direction. "We could have doubled the rope and parbuckled them down like barrels, once there was somebody on this side to hold the other end."

"Where did you learn such a mortal lot about ropes and knots?" Mog asked.

"On my father's ship, when I was small."

And Owen proceeded to enliven the journey with tales of childhood spent aboard His Majesty's sloop *Thrush*, before the Poohoo Province uprising had rendered it necessary for Captain Hughes to send his wife and child back to England on a tea-clipper. Luggins, Dove, and Mog listened spellbound to these stories, but Hwfa still remained aloof, a gloomy, thoughtful expression upon his face.

For several hours now they travelled without incident along the dry bed of the river, which once again had sunk through a hole and out of sight underground. Towards noon, however, the wind began to rise, and dark clouds obscured the sky. Autumn leaves in great showers came rattling down from the forest trees above the gorge, and Owen looked back along their course, knitting his brows. The mountains around Pennygaff could just be seen in the distance, black against a purple sky.

"Looks like rain back there, eh?" Dove said nervously. Owen nodded.

"How much farther before we come out of the gorge?" he asked Mog, the only member of the party who had been that way before.

Mog was not very sure; it might be a matter of five or six miles, he thought.

Owen lay down and pressed his ear against the ground.

"I think we should get out of the gorge now," he said quietly.

"Scared to have your feet wet, is it?" jeered Hwfa.

But Dove, Luggins, and Mog were only too ready to follow Owen's advice as fast as possible.

"Only, how shall we set about it, man? Bit steep, these cliffs, and higher than the new Habakkuk chapel!"

Owen proceeded to unroll from his waist the long rope of creeper he had carried with him.

"Only need a little bird, now, to fly up with the end in its beak!" Hwfa said acidly.

But Owen replied, "We do not even need that." Pulling a reel of thread from his pocket, he fastened one end of the thread to an arrow, and fired it in such a way as to make it pass over the trunk of an oak which grew halfway up the cliff. Luggins ran to retrieve the arrow, while Owen attached the other end of the thread to a length of twine, with which he was also provided. The twine in its turn was tied to the end of the creeper which by this means they were enabled to pull up over the leaning tree-trunk until half its length dangled down on either side.

"Might as well have brought along a proper rope while he were at it!" muttered Hwfa.

The two creeper-stems were then twisted and knotted together; Owen demonstrated how to climb up them, and Mog, Luggins and Dove clumsily but eagerly scrambled up the improvised ladder and out of danger. With Hwfa it was not so simple. Heavy, awkward, and extremely reluctant to display his lack of skill, he stood with arms folded and a scornful expression on his face.

"Needn't think you can get *me* to make a monkey of myself," he mocked. "Proper lot of fools you all look, sitting up in that old oak!"

"Come on, Hwfa, man!" Luggins urged. "Famous it is up here—snug as a belfry!"

Owen slid down the rope again, full of anxiety.

"Do climb up, Hwfa," he urged. "I am sure there is not much time left."

Indeed, heavy drops of rain were beginning to fall as the storm moved down the valley and, more ominous still, a kind of muttering rumble could be heard coming from the direction of Pennygaff.

"Cowards!" Hwfa sneered. "My old granny would laugh to see you perching yourselves up there."

But the rumble increased in volume to a roar; even Hwfa turned somewhat pale.

"Hwfa, please, you *must* climb the rope!" Owen begged. "Indeed, there is no time to waste! Feel the ground shake!"

"Dammo! Do not loiter! Climb, for your life, man!" shouted Mog, who, high in the tree, had a view round a bend in the gorge. "The old river's coming down on you like Noah's flood!"

Haggard-faced, Hwfa took hold of the rope.

"What do I do, then?" he asked angrily.

"Reach up as high as you can, then pull yourself up. Cross your legs at the knees; press the outsides of your feet tight as you can against the rope."

Hwfa pulled himself up clumsily but his feet, wildly kicking, failed to get a grip of the creeper which threshed about beneath him. Owen grabbed and steadied it.

"Put your feet on my hands. Right! Now pull up again!"

Supporting and shoving from below, Owen assisted Hwfa to climb about halfway up the rope. Then Luggins, leaning down from above, grabbed hold of Hwfa's wrists and gave him a mighty heave upwards.

"Owen! Get on the rope!" yelled Mog. "Make haste, man!"

Seeing that Hwfa was half supported by Luggins, Owen sprang on to the rope himself; only just in time. A massive black wall of water, high as a house, came churning down the gorge, casting great rocks aside, uprooting trees and tossing them about like twigs. The end of the creeper was dragged downstream, the weight of two bodies made it creak ominously and start to give. But Luggins, exerting all his strength, fairly lifted Hwfa into the tree, half skinning him in the process, and Owen flung himself up the rope, climbing faster than he ever had even in the shrouds of the *Thrush* with his father's critical eye on him. Just as he flung himself over the tree-trunk the rope parted and fell into the torrent, where it was instantly swept away.

"Duw!" panted Luggins. "That was a close one then! Are you all right, with you, Owen man?"

Owen nodded. He was still getting his breath. They all gazed down, awestruck, at the tossing, racing water beneath. The flood had risen to within a few feet of the roots of their tree.

"Never have I seen it come down so quick," Mog said, from his higher branch. "Regular cloudburst there must have been up at Pennygaff. Owe all our lives to you, we do, Owen, I reckon!"

"No matter for that," Owen said. "After all you'd never have been here but for offering to come with me. I only hope the other three got safely home before the flood rose."

"My goodness, yes," said Luggins.

Hwfa was silent, gloomily surveying his scrapes and grazes.

For two hours the swollen river roared beneath them, and the rain beat down, stripping the last leaves from the tree where they sat uncomfortably perched. Then by degrees the sky cleared and a watery sun shone out again.

"How are we going to get down out of this hurrah's nest now our rope's gone?" asked Luggins.

Dove and Mog instinctively looked to Owen for suggestions. Hwfa muttered,

"Let's see what Mr. Genius Hughes have to offer."

Owen considered. The flood beneath them was ebbing now, but still looked to be seven or eight feet deep.

"Best we jump down while there's water underneath to break our fall," he said. "Otherwise it's going to be a long drop to the ground."

"I can't swim," objected Luggins.

"Dewi Sant, hold on to me, then, boy," said Mog, who could.

"I can't swim either," said Dove. All eyes turned to Hwfa, who sat biting his nails. He remained silent.

"Best wait a bit longer then, maybe," said Owen doubtfully, though he was itching to get on.

Not long after, though, a large tangled mass of branches and wreckage came sliding along on the flood; there were great boughs, whole young trees, and part of a wooden bridge, all jammed together.

"Quick, lads, now's our chance!" cried Owen, as this mass drew near. "Jump in and hang on to anything that will hold you up."

Mog nodded and, to encourage Hwfa, who was looking mulish, give him a sudden vigorous push that knocked him head-over-heels into the water; Luggins did the same to Dove and then valiantly plunged in himself. Owen, pausing only to pull the strap of his crossbow tighter and button his glasses into his jacket pocket, dived after them, and a splash nearby told him that Mog had followed his example.

Luggins and Dove managed to seize hold of the bridge, which easily supported them; Mog swam down with the current and grabbed the branch of a young birch tree; but Owen, coming to the surface and looking round him, could see no sign of Hwfa. Then, behind him, he heard a kind of bubbling grunt and, turning, was just in time to see Hwfa's agonised face appear above water for an instant, then sink again.

Owen immediately dived towards the spot where he had seen Hwfa vanish, searching as best he could among the half-sunk wreckage which was all being swept downstream. For a moment he thought he had failed and his heart sank in despair; then his groping hand encountered a face; feeling back over it he seized hold of Hwfa's hair and with a few powerful kicks brought him up to the surface. By great good-fortune a felled pine-trunk was floating by; Owen was able to get one arm over it and instructed the choking, water-logged Hwfa to do likewise.

"Are you all right?" he inquired. Hwfa nodded without speaking.

"Heigh-ho, boys! Having a fine old joy-ride then?" called the irrepressible Luggins as they went tossing along between the rocky, tree-grown cliffs. "Join Owen Hughes and all the fun of the fair, is it? Swingboats first, then merry-go-round!"

"More like the Tunnel of Death," muttered Hwfa. "Lucky if we're not all sucked underground."

Owen, too, had been worrying in case the Gaff river did another of its sudden plunges to subterranean regions, but luckily they had not been carried for more than half a mile when the current swirled round a corner and deposited them, soaked, grazed, bruised, but otherwise unhurt, on a spit of land in the middle of the flood. They tottered weakly on to higher ground.

"What's the good o' this? It's an island. We're still marooned," Dove said disgustedly.

"Not for long. Look how fast the water's going down now," Owen pointed out. "I reckon we'll be able to wade across in fifteen minutes."

"Bit of dinner, I could use," Mog said. "Wonder if there's any blackberries on this island."

He roamed off and began to explore; presently they heard him shout.

"Hey, boys! Hey, come here! A drowned corpus there is on this island!"

They rushed through the bushes to the spot where Mog stood pointing. The body of a man, dressed in a tartan kilt and prune-coloured velvet hunting-jacket, lay propped against a chestnut-tree. Nearby was a musket, which had been discharged, and a smaller fowling-pistol. A hunting-knife had fallen from the dead man's hand. Not far off, to the boys' astonishment, they discovered no less than three wild boars which the man had evidently killed.

"Got stuck on the island with them when the flood came, maybe," Dove said. "There's brave he must have been. Pity he got drowned."

"Stupid! He's not drowned, with him," Hwfa pointed out. "Dry, his jacket is."

It was true. This part of the little knoll which formed the island had evidently been high enough to escape flooding.

"Then what killed him?" Luggins wondered.

"Where are you eyes, boy? Nasty great wound he do have on his leg; same place as Follentine, but devil of a lot worse. One of the old pigs must have spiked him."

"Wait a minute," said Owen, who had been carefully examining the apparently lifeless body. "I don't believe he is quite dead; see, his eyelid fluttered just then."

Seizing the man's hat, which lay by him, he ran off to the river for water. While filling it he observed that the hat was richly embroidered with gold thread; three white feathers on it were held in position by a clasp containing a diamond the size of a walnut.

Some great lord, Owen thought vaguely, returning with the water, which he sprinkled carefully over the man's forehead. Meanwhile Luggins rubbed his hands, while Dove and Hwfa collected dry wood and kindled a fire.

"Food he'll be wanting if he's alive," Mog said, and began gathering up the chestnuts which lay plentifully strewn in the grass under the tree.

Hwfa discovered a knapsack and brought it, wide-eyed.

"Look at this, will you! A crown embroidered on it, there is! And a bottle of wine inside. Good thing to give him some of that, eh, Owen boy?"

It was the first time he had spoken to Owen directly, without a sneering or hostile note in his voice.

"Ah, that's capital!" Owen said, taking the flask with a smile of thanks. "Can you hold his head, Hwfa, while I trickle some into his mouth?"

But at this moment the hurt man made a faint movement and opened his eyes, looking up in bewilderment at the ring of faces above him.

"Hech, sirs! What's all this clamjamfry, then?" he asked weakly.

8

The little port of Malyn was huddled in a V-shaped cleft at the point where the Gaff river emerged from underground long enough to grind its way through the black Cliffs of Draig (where once a dragon was said to have nested) and so out into the stormy Atlantic.

No dragon nested on the cliffs nowadays. But there were plenty of fisher-folk in Port Malyn who considered, although they would not have dared even whisper the thought aloud, that the Marquess was just as bad, if not worse. High above the town, approached by one narrow, winding, precipitous road, his castle brooded like a raven perched on the very brink of the cliff; it was said that if the Marquess chose to toss a peach-stone from his bedroom window it would fall a thousand feet before it sank into the waves. And many believed that more things than peach-stones had been hurled from that window; guests who offended the Marquess, prisoners who had the foolhardiness to defy him, were known to have vanished without a trace. But of course it was quite possible that their bones still mouldered somewhere inside the castle, which was very extensive, or down in its dark dungeons which burrowed deep, nobody knew how deep, into the cliff below.

On a wild gusty evening, at about the time of Owen's encounter with the wild boar in the Fforest Mwyaf, another traveller, conveyed in a hired chaise and pair belonging to the Boar's Head Inn at Nant Agerddau, was rapidly passing through Port Malyn.

"Humph," this personage observed, glancing about him as the driver guided his horses carefully along the quayside, between lobster-pots and piles of fishing-nets, "a romantic hamlet, verily, but it appears to be a trifle blighted, down-at-heel, nodding to its fall, would you not say, my good fellow?"

In fact many of the little tumbledown houses stood empty; the tenants had been turned out, due to their inability to pay Lord Malyn's extortionate rents.

"Wb," grunted the driver, who considered that he was paid to drive, not talk, and he got down to lead his horses up the last steep, zigzag ascent to the castle, glancing somewhat resentfully at his passengers. The traveller's small dark-skinned servant, who, like his master, was dressed in furs, quickly took the hint and jumped out, but his master ignored the driver's expression and continued to sit comfortably in the chaise, exclaiming at the wild prospect of mountain and forest that began to open out behind them as they mounted the hill.

"And that will be the Shambles Light, I infer, presume, dare say? Most picturesque, most! And yonder, far off, must be the brow, apex, peak, of Fighat Ben, the famous summit I observed at Nant Agerddau? Summit to write home about, as you would say, ha ha!"

"Hwch," said the coachman.

"And this battlemented edifice ahead is belike the seat, snuggery, diggings of the excellent Marquess of Malyn? A most desirable and commodious residence, indeed!"

"Hwt," said the driver. He pulled his team to a halt—not that they needed much pulling—before a stone archway, inhospitably barred by a pair of massive iron gates.

Finding no sort of bellpull or knocker, the driver picked up a stone from the road and beat on the gate with it; the resulting hollow clangs presently had their effect; a wicket opened, and a liveried porter thrust out his head and eyed them in a surly and forbidding manner. By and by he withdrew his head again and instead stuck out a placard bearing the message:

WHAT DO YOU WANT?

"Gentleman to visit his lordship," said the driver curtly. And he muttered under his breath, "Sooner him than me, indeed to goodness!"

The porter reversed his placard. On the other side it said:

NAME?

"His Excellency the Seljuk of Rum."

The porter clanged his grille shut and vanished; after a longish interval he reappeared and with much grating and grinding began to undo the iron bolts.

"Well, well?" cried the Seljuk impatiently when the gates stood open wide enough to admit the carriage, "what are you waiting for? Drive on, my good chap, fellow, old boy!"

"Two sides to that, I am thinking," said the driver. "Hired to drive you to Caer Malyn, I was, not right into the castle. Sooner put you down here, I would."

"Tush! Pshaw! Odds bodikins! In fact, fudge, my good man. Pray continue!"

Grumbling, the coachman climbed back on the box and drove the chaise across a paved courtyard. But when they came to an inner archway he stopped again.

"Come, come, come?" cried the Seljuk. "Proceed, my dear crony, I beg. There is yet another court, campus, quadrangle, beyond that archway, can you not perceive, remark?"

"Do nicely this one will," the driver said. "Not keen to go any farther, I am, see?"

And in spite of all remonstrances he proceeded, with the help of the small servant, to unload the Seljuk's baggage by the inner gateway, and then assisted his passenger to alight with rather more haste than civility. Since at this moment two powerful men in the livery of footmen—though they rather resembled prizefighters—appeared and silently shouldered the Seljuk's bags, the latter paid off his driver and followed them without further objections. The driver for his part hardly waited a second, so anxious was he to be gone; he swung his horses round and fairly galloped them across the outer court, through the gateway, and down the dangerous hill.

Meanwhile the Seljuk and his servant, following their

two guides, passed through a complicated maze of courts, cloisters, halls, and passages, all on different levels, due to the fact that Castle Malyn was built up the side of a steep hill, until they reached a luxuriously furnished set of apartments which had evidently been made ready for the guest. High-piled fires of sea-wrack blazed in the hearths, giving out green flames, hot water steamed in a gold bath, candles burned in golden sconces, while a polite but silent major-domo (all Lord Malyn's servants seemed either forbidden or unable to speak) handed the Seljuk a note which said: "His Worship the Marquess will be graciously pleased to receive you at six o'clock in the north tower."

"Thanks, my good chum," said the Seljuk when he had read this message. "Five o'clock is it now? Then you may depart, make tracks, hop off; I shall not require your services further."

The major-domo bowed and retired, intimating that he would return just before six and escort the visitor to Lord Malyn's apartment. With the assistance of his own servant the Seljuk then rapidly bathed and exchanged his travelling-garments for satin pantaloons, a cambric shirt, a striped cummerbund and a sort of Eastern smoking-jacket, very gorgeous in plum-coloured brocade. Next he consulted a large timepiece and finding, with satisfaction, that it was still but fifteen minutes after five, he extracted from his valise a small compass. Bidding the small servant remain there, and murmuring, "Upsy daisy! All aboard! Tally ho!" he quitted the apartment and proceeded in a northerly direction, consulting his compass at frequent intervals, whenever he came to a choice of directions. He stopped from time to time, as well, to gaze about him in wonder—and indeed, Castle Malyn was a remarkable place. Although situated a thousand feet above the Atlantic, subject to the full force of the wind, it was so strongly built that scarcely a hint of the gale blowing outside could be felt within its walls; in fact the air was oppressively warm and the Seljuk found himself obliged to give a twitch to his moustaches, which were beginning to droop. On account of this moist heat, the numerous large ferns planted in golden tubs prospered amazingly; many of them were well over six feet high. The granite walls had mostly been left in their natural state, unadorned, but the floors were everywhere carpeted with ankle-deep gold velvet, so that the Seljuk, who wore Turkish slippers of soft leather, was able to advance without making the slightest sound.

At last, after climbing several flights of steps, he arrived in what appeared to be the castle's main hall. This was some forty feet long, ornamented with boar-spears and sets of tusks; the heat here was even greater, and the potted ferns had grown to the size of young palm trees. Thanks to their protective cover the Seljuk, moving silently forward, was able to elude the notice of two or three footmen who were throwing dice by the main entrance, and to arrive unobserved near a doorway from which Lord Malyn's voice could be heard issuing.

This entrance was partially screened by thick, yellow velvet curtains. Moving so that these draperies would conceal him both from the footmen and from the sight of anyone inside the room, the Seljuk proceeded to gaze abstractedly at a grinning boar's head on the wall, while he listened with the closest attention.

"And you expect to be paid for *that*?" Lord Malyn was saying.

"Well, we done the prig, didn't we? We run the risk o' being cotched by the macemongers. Wasn't our fault the twangler was gone a'ready."

"Indeed, a most remarkable tale," the Marquess said silkily. "So, on the very night that you were to perform my errand, you will have me believe that by some bizarre coincidence, the curator's grandson had already made off with the object?"

"That's about it, gaffer. Beats cock-fighting, dunnit, how these things comes about? The young kinchin had left a note for his granfer, scribed very neat: "Dear Granda, sorry to prig your property but I'm off." And that's the probal truth, your worship, sure as my name's Elijah Prigman, ain't it so, Bilk? Prigged the bandore, he had, before ever we got there."

"By gar, that's so," agreed Bilk. "Stole a march, he did, the miching young co. I'll lay the miserable sand-blind little foister is halfway to London by now."

"Sand-blind?" the Marquess said sharply. "You have met this boy then? You know what he looks like?"

There came a suppressed grunt from Bilk; it sounded as if his partner had kicked him.

"Why yes, your worship, we seen him in Pennygaff while we was a-waiting for your worship to come along and tip us the office," Prigman's voice said.

"And his name is Owen Hughes?"

"That's so, your honour; a little twiggy, black-haired kinchin, knee-high to a spadger-bird. He wears glazing cheats—'

"Spectacles, yampy-head! His ludship don't gammon our way o' talking," Prigman cut in.

"It did not occur to you to bring along this letter he had left for his grandfather so that I could see it for myself?" the Marquess said abruptly.

"Why—why no, your ludship." Bilk sounded taken aback. "Asides," he added righteously, "if we'd a done that, the poor old gager wouldn't a had no notion what had come to the boy!"

"But you say the note was neatly written?"

"Ah, to be sure! Uncommon tidy character, a Reverend couldn't a scribed it out neater, eh, Prig?"

"Then you would not say it was the same writing as this?"

The Seljuk, stretching his ears, thought he caught the crackle of paper. Then followed a silence. Then Prigman, clearing his throat in a embarrassed way, said,

"Why, yes, surely, gaffer. Reckon 'tis the same hand, eh, Bilk?"

"Aye," said Bilk. "Odds bods, it fair makes you hurkle, dunnit, to think o' the young co lighting out wi" the bandore and then writing off so bold to his ludship and all the other worships, asking for a thousand mint clinkers—ach—arrrgh!"

Evidently Prigman had kicked him again.

"You are quite sure it is the same writing?" Lord Malyn repeated. "Although the other, you say, was so neat, and this is so untidy and ill spelt?"

"Maybe he was in a hurry when he writ this one," mumbled Bilk.

"As you say. But it seems singular, does it not, that his

writing should be shaky and hurried *after* he had made off with the harp, when he had all the time in the world, and yet the note written *before*, when he must have been in haste to be gone, was so tidy and careful?"

"Maybe he writ t'other one in school."

"A likely theory! You are sure *you* did not write the notes?" Lord Malyn suddenly rapped out.

"Us? Why—why no, gaffer! How could us? Your ludship knows neither on us can scribe!"

"How did you know that the boy had written to other people as well as to myself?"

"H—how d-d-d . . . ?"

Bilk was by now evidently almost paralytic with fright under this questioning. But Prigman said stoutly,

"Who don't? The tale's all over the countryside, your ludship, that he writ to you, and to the foreign worship, and to his royal highness."

"Indeed? Are you so certain?"

"I—I think so, your worship."

"You think so, do you? It is strange, is it not, that I have a letter here in the same handwriting, awaiting the arrival of his highness the Prince of Wales, which has not even been *opened* yet? How do you know what is in it? Shall I tell you what *I* think?" the Marquess said menacingly. "*I* think you are in league with this young boy, who is no doubt a seasoned thief. You bade him write the letters, you have him hidden away somewhere with the harp"—"No, no, gaffer, you got it all wrong!"—"and as well as coming to me with an impudent request for money you have not earned, you expected to make a handsome profit from the ransom as well. But you are wrong, my fine friends—very,

very wrong! I think you had better produce that harp without loss of time before I lose patience—it would be a pity if, by the time you agreed to remember where you have it hidden, you were unable to fetch it because you had not the use of your arms or legs."

There was a sort of squawk from Prigman.

"But, your worship, we doesn't know where the blessed bandore is! That's Ticklepenny's truth!"

A long, unpleasant silence followed. Then the Marquess said in a cold voice,

"Enough. You shall have till Wednesday to lay hands on it. Provided you bring it by then, safely and secretly, you will receive the same fee I promised before—not that you deserve it. But if not, you need expect no mercy. I shall find you, wherever you are. I found you in London, did I not?"

"Y-y-yes, your honour!"

"Remember it, then. Now get out of my sight. Garble, see these men leave the castle without delay. Oh, and Garble—send for Mr. Owen Hughes, the curator of the Pennygaff Museum, will you? And his grandson too, if the boy is to be found. Also make sure that two or three dungeons are empty by Wednesday, be so good, and that the thumbscrews are oiled, and so forth."

Prigman let out another terrified whimper; then the two men appeared in the doorway, pale and trembling, escorted by the impassive Garble. Bilk was heard to mutter. "I *told* you it were puggle-headed to play May-games with his lordship. Now you'll *have* to tell me where you put the bandore!"

The Seljuk remained motionless, half screened by curtains, and they passed without observing him; then he moved forward as if, having stepped aside for a moment to admire a fine pair of boars' tusks, he was just continuing on his way.

At that moment the harassed major-domo came hurrying along the hall in search of him, evidently horrified at the thought of a guest left to roam the castle unescorted.

With a smile that almost curled his moustaches to his ears, the Seljuk allowed himself to be led into the presence of the Marquess, who was walking up and down a large apartment, languidly fanning himself. He did not look exactly ruffled, but there was a tightening about the corners of his fine, thin mouth, a yellow gleam in his eyes, and his long fingers held the gold-and-parchment fan as if, had it been a knife, they would gladly have stuck it into somebody. He was dressed very elegantly in velvet, black as night, but with a citron taffeta waistcoat.

Looking stout and gaudy by comparison, the Seljuk advanced to meet him.

"My dear sir! It is most affable of you to grant me the treat of visiting your stately nest, dwelling, domicile! And after such a short acquaintance, too!"

"On the contrary," rejoined the Marquess with equal politeness, "it is kind of you, my dear Seljuk, to give me the pleasure of your company. Without it I should have been sadly dull, for his highness the Prince of Wales, whom I am also expecting, seems to have been unaccountably delayed."

After several more civilities Lord Malyn led his guest into a dining-room which, like all the inhabited part of the castle, was furnished in black, gold, and velvet. A small but sumptuous repast had been laid out on an ebony dining-table.

"And now, my dear sir," said Lord Malyn presently, when they had eaten guinea-fowl glazed with honey, saffron rice, parsnips, pineapples, nectarines, and peaches, "let us take our coffee into the library, and pray tell me how I can entertain you? Would you like to see my tiger-fish? My golden orioles? Or my reptile collection? It is small but choice; for instance, I have just acquired two tiger-snakes, charming creatures, which are, as you know, reputed to have a stronger venom than any other species."

"Thank you, thank you," replied the Seljuk, hurriedly gulping the coffee from his tiny gold demitasse, "but pray don't trouble, put yourself out, turn topsy-turvy on my account; wild creatures do not tickle my fancy (not to spin you a yarn or put too fine a point upon it); indeed we have rather too many of them in my homeland. No, what would really solace, cheer, rejoice, warm the cockles, drive dull care away, would be to see your lordship's collection of gold articles."

"Ah yes, of course," Lord Malyn said carelessly. "You are quite an expert on gold, are you not; I was forgetting you had told me so at Pennygaff. Come then, by all means."

And he led the way through his library, past long shelves of heavily gilt volumes, into another room furnished entirely with glass cases. These were all filled with gold objects; every conceivable thing that could be made from gold seemed to have its place there: gold tools, gold weapons, ornaments, and utensils; there was a gold spinning-wheel, a gold musket, even a gold dictionary, with the words printed on sheets of gold-leaf.

The Marquess called for more candles, and when these were brought the effect among all the treasures there was strangely magical; a kind of shimmer filled the room as if the very air had become imbued with gold particles.

"Ah, how truly gladsome, pleasing, felicitous," exclaimed the Seljuk, and he strolled between the cases, looking very intently first at one object, then at another. While he thus examined the exhibits Lord Malyn, in his turn, watched the Seljuk very sharply, concealing his scrutiny under a pretence of weariness.

"My dear host, what a store, what prizes you have! And so resplendently polished! And such a charmingly warm room!"

"Oh, my servants attend to the polishing," Lord Malyn said, gracefully stifling a yawn. "And as for the warmth, I can claim no credit for that, it is natural; I have merely had pipes laid from Nant Agerddau to my castle; they carry hot vapour underground from the Whispering Mountain. So I have a never-failing supply of heat. The pipes come up underneath the castle; even my dungeons are warm." And he smiled benevolently, pouring the links of his gold snake-chain from one hand to the other.

"Indeed, how very ingenious and de luxe," the Seljuk said absently. He was studying a set of gold fish-hooks. "Tell me, pray, my amiable friend, where did you procure these?"

"Strangely enough, they were picked up on the shore not far from here. Such gold articles are sometimes found on the shore hereabouts; it is thought that perhaps an old treasure-ship may lie wrecked somewhere off our coast."

"Ah, so? And this gold flute?"

"I had it from an old lady in Nant Agerddau; she had inherited it from her father who always declared he had picked it up in a quarry on the side of Fig-hat Ben. More probably he stole it."

There were golden cymbals, too, and a small gold trumpet.

"You do not have a harp?" the Seljuk inquired, glancing about the room.

". . . No, not at present," Lord Malyn answered after a slight pause. "Are you interested in harps?"

"It might be easiest to tell from a harp," the Seljuk murmured, half to himself. Peering closely at a gold kettle, he added, "I recall some legend of a gold harp told me by a friend of mine, a Brother Ianto."

Lord Malyn started, as if his gold-linked toy had turned into a tiger-snake and bitten him. His eyes dilated.

"*Brother Ianto*? You *know* Brother Ianto? Of the Order of St. Ennodawg?"

"Indeed, yes!" Puffing a little, the Seljuk leaned forward to examine a gold bridle. "If it were not for the good brother I should now be demised, bumped off, dead as a doornail, my dear sir! I have much cause to be obliged to Brother Ianto; last year he was so obliging as to pull me out of the far distant Oxus river."

"Oh—last year—" Lord Malyn's excitement died down again as quickly as it had sprung up.

"So," pursued the Seljuk chattily, inspecting a pair of gold bellows, "it was perforce one of my first concerns to meet, make contact, forgather with this lovable ecclesiastic as soon as the affairs of the Kingdom of Rum permitted me to visit your country."

"Brother Ianto is in *Wales*?" Now the Marquess's eyes fairly blazed: the Seljuk appeared mildly startled by the interest his words had excited.

"Dear me, yes; I had the pleasure of calling on him yesterday in his homely grotto."

The Marquess had turned and was tugging at a bell-pull; when Garble, ever alert for a summons, came silently in, his master said sharply,

"Garble! Send somebody at once to search for a monk, a Brother Ianto, who is to be found inhabiting a grotto— where did you say you found him?" he demanded of the Seljuk. "At Nant Agerddau? very well. Don't delay, Garble. If there should be a harp with him, that is to be brought also."

"Yes, your lordship."

The door closed softly behind Garble.

"What a kind thought to bring him here!" the Seljuk said. "Then I too shall have the pleasure of seeing my obliging preserver again. But Brother Ianto has no harp I can assure you, pledge credit, warrant, etc. If he had, I should have been greatly interested to see it."

"Oh? And why would that have been, my dear guest?"

Lord Malyn was making an attempt to mask his excitement under an appearance of calm; he led the way into a smaller apartment fitted up as a withdrawing room with sofas and tanks of tiger-fish. The Marquess flung himself on a sofa and gestured to his visitor to do likewise; the Seljuk, giving a glance full of dislike at the tiger-fish, turned his plump back on them and gazed instead at an eight-foot maidenhair fern.

"Why are you so interested in harps? What can you learn from a harp?" Lord Malyn repeated.

"Why, who made it, of course, naturally, to be sure," the Seljuk said simply.

"And what is that to the purpose?"

"In order to explain that, I must needs relate you a portion of history, my dear host, ally, and patron. Some three years ago a message in a bottle was picked up in the harbour of Sa'ir, which, as you may know, is the chief port of my country. Naturally this message was brought to me, as the Seljuk."

"And what did it say?"

"It was written in a very ancient form of our Rummish language. It said, "Alas, alas, far from our warm homeland we, the Tribe of Yehimelek, languish in darkness and sorrow, hidden beneath the Whispering Mountain."

"Indeed?" commented the Marquess. "And what did you understand from this mysterious message?"

"Why, sir, it so happens that some generations ago a portion of my subjects were lost, mislaid, let slip; naturally I am most anxious to restore these poor creatures to their homeland. Since the message was picked up I have sent out missions to investigate mountains reported to be whispering in any parts of the world. Then, happening to encounter Brother Ianto last year and hearing from him of your renowned Fig-hat Ben *and* your famous legendary harp, I leapt to a conclusion, smelt a rat, resolved to leave no stone unturned, decided to visit this salubrious area myself as soon as affairs of state permitted."

Lord Malyn's eyes had begun to gleam again.

"But what has the harp to do with this tribe? I confess I am still somewhat in the dark," he inquired.

"The tribe of Yehimelek, my dear sir, were always famous among my people for their skill in gold-mining and gold-working. And chief among their skills in the ancient time was that of fashioning gold harps. For instance we have in our National Museum of Rum a gold harp more than two thousand years old—'

Lord Malyn's eyes gleamed even brighter. "You think the Harp of Teirtu may have been made by your lost tribe?"

"Perhaps, maybe, possibly, indeed, who knows? Certainly I was sorry to hear from the worthy curator of the Pennygaff Museum on whom I had the honour to call that his harp had just been stolen. The unfortunate gentleman seemed quite distraught indeed. Naturally I had hoped that a sight of it might allay my doubts, scruples, waverings; alack, what a slip 'twixt cup and lip!"

"But the Harp of Teirtu, after all, is also extremely old," Lord Malyn said smoothly. "Even if it had been made by a member of the lost tribe, that does not prove that they are still in existence now."

"No, my dear old Marquess, but then consider the message in the bottle, picked up only three years ago."

"A message in a bottle may toss about the ocean for hundreds of years before some chance wave casts it ashore."

"But—aha! my dear sir—this was a glass bottle embossed with the inscription 'Llewellyn's Ginger Stingo, Cardiff, 1802'."

"So," Lord Malyn said slowly, "you really believe that a lost tribe of craftsmen in gold may be hidden to this very day somewhere beneath the Whispering Mountain, beneath Fig-hat Ben? My dear Seljuk, what an extraordinarily interesting guest you have proved to be! I do hope, indeed I shall endeavour to *arrange*, that you will prolong your stay beneath my roof for a long, long time."

"Why, thank you sir, I shall be pleased, overjoyed to avail myself of your kind offer; indeed I am sure your castle will make an excellent, tophole base for exploring the neighbouring vicinity.—And now I trust you will not consider me unbred if I retire to my chamber, my good friend? I have had a somewhat travelsome day."

"Naturally, my dear Seljuk; I wish you to consider yourself *quite* at home. Do just as you please; this, you must know, is Liberty Hall." And the Marquess rang twice for the major-domo. But as soon as the Seljuk had been escorted to bed, amid smiles and affability, Lord Malyn rang again.

"Garble," he said when for the third time his secretary appeared, "I want you to keep a strict watch on the Seljuk. Be discreet, don't let him see you, but follow him wherever he goes. Don't let him out of your sight for a single minute."

9

By now Hwfa's fire was burning briskly.

"Do not try to stir yourself yet, sir," Owen said to the hurt man. "In a moment you shall have some warm wine."

Making certain that this was the correct treatment he pulled out his little book and consulted it, to the admiration of Luggins and Mog, neither of whom could read.

" 'Treatment for Wounds, Shock, Hyfteria: Adminifter a little Warm Stimulant, lay the patient in a Recumbent Pofition. Hot Fomentations applied to affected part. Allow fmall quantities of Gruel. The Patient should be kept cheerful, spoken to kindly yet firmly, and told to ftop any eccentricities. If necefsary adminifter a teafpoonful of Sal volatile and dafh cold water in the face.' "

"Hout, ma wean," protested the patient, struggling to sit up. "Whit gars ye ca" me eccentric? I'm nae mair eccentric than only ither body—but I shouldna say nay to a wee drappie of yon warm stimulant."

A little wine had now been heated in the silver cuplid of the stranger's wine-flask; this was administered; meanwhile Dove and Hwfa, under Owen's direction, pounded up a handful of chestnuts in some more of the wine and cooked the mixture into a kind of porridge.

"I'm afraid it's all we can do in the way of gruel, sir," Owen apologized, but when a spoonful of it was offered to the hurt man he smacked his lips and declared it to be the best claut of parritch that he had tasted since coming south of the Roman wall. When it was all swallowed they tried to apply fomentations of hot wine to the stranger's wound, but at the very first attempt he let out such a yell of indignation that they were obliged to desist.

"Deil rax your thrapples, lads, are ye clean daft? Ne'er pit gude Bordeaux to sic a villainous ploy as yon! Na, na, it will gang mair glegly inside than out—" and he took the cup from Owen and drained it, muttering to himself in an undertone, "But there, whit can be expected from a wheen pock-pudding Welsh caterans?"

Owen was puzzled; he had begun to suspect that the wounded man might be the missing Prince of Wales, particularly when Dove, giving him a nudge, pointed out a crown and feathers engraved on the stranger's silver wine-flask, cup, spoon, and hunting-knife.

But why should the Prince of Wales wear a kilt and speak with a Scots accent?

This riddle was presently solved, however. The chestnut porridge did their patient so much good that he was able to sit up, declaring in a stronger tone than he had yet used that he was muckle obleeged to them and that they were as gleg and handy a set of lads as a hunter could hope to meet. He then tried to stand, but found this beyond his power; his wounded leg had stiffened and he was unable to set it to the ground.

"Ech, oich, neighbours! Sair as I mislike tae trouble ye mair, I believe I'm obleeged to ask if ye will be sae gude as to convoy me to the nearest town. Dooms me! tae think that Davie Jamie Charlie Neddie Geordie Harry Dick Tudor-Stuart should land himself in sic a fashous fizzenlous pass!"

"Oh, sir!" Owen exclaimed. "Then you *are* his highness the Prince of Wales!"

The other boys gaped in surprise at this, for they had not heard Mr. Smith's proclamation, having been outside the museum at the time, and so had no notion that the prince was in the neighbourhood.

"Och, aye, sirs, I'm Wales, but nae case tae mak" a plisky-plasky abeut it"—as they began awkwardly bowing and tugging at their forelocks—"in the forest, ye ken, we're a" friends thegither."

And while the boys were collecting fallen boughs and weaving them into a rude litter to carry the prince he entertained them, in the most natural, cordial, sociable manner, with tales about his childhood in the castle of Balmoral, and the hunting he had enjoyed in the Scottish forests.

"But, Gude save us," he concluded, "our Scots boars are douce and meek as lambs compared wi" yon flitesome Welsh tuskers! Three of the hallions set on me like Bulls o Bashan this morn in the tempest and I had muckle ado to dispatch them.—Ah, thank ye my lads, I'm fair beholden to ye"—as they assisted him on to the stretcher—

"though it fashes me to take ye out of your road."

The flood had now diminished so that it was possible to wade across from the island, and the boys set off southwards through the forest, four taking turns as stretcher-bearers while one rested and kept a lookout. The weather was much colder now; a keen wind whistled through the trees, almost stripped of leaves by the storm; to keep the hurt man warm they covered him with dry moss scraped from the undersides of rocks.

Owen, privately, was somewhat disappointed by the commonplace appearance of the prince, a slight, active-looking man in his early thirties, with a long nose, reddish hair, and a weather-beaten complexion due to his insatiable passion for hunting. However, his sparkling dark-grey eyes and air of command made the boys treat Prince David with instinctive respect, though he continued to chat to them cheerfully as they bore him along.

Presently Owen decided that the prince seemed recovered enough to hear some intelligence of a distressing nature, and so broke it to him that his father King James III was ill and calling for him. To their astonishment the prince burst out laughing.

"Aweel, aweel," he said at length, "it's ill tae mak" mock o' the puir auld gentleman; doubtless I maun humour him and gang back tae London; ilka path has its puddle. But I'll wager a guinea that nae mair than lanesomeness ails him; he's aye of a shilpit and dow-spirited humour when I'm awa" hunting."

Owen then ventured to ask the prince if he had yet received the letter dictated by Bilk and Prigman and addressed to him, demanding money for the stolen harp; but the prince had not; he had been alone, he said, hunting in the forest for the past five days, and no doubt a large bundle of mail was waiting for him at Caer Malyn, whither it had been his intention to proceed.

"Oh, sir! Then, please, when you receive the letter, tear it up and take no notice of it; indeed I was forced to write it, but I did not steal the Harp of Teirtu and do not want money for it; all I want is for it to be restored to the Pennygaff Museum."

"Hout, mannie, what't all this hirdum-dirdum about a harp? Ne'er speir at me sae lang-nebbit, but tell me a round tale about it frae the beginning."

Thus encouraged, Owen once more told the whole story of the harp, and the other members of the party also added their comments and amplifications to the tale as they carried the prince along. He listened with the greatest interest.

"Whisht, whisht, did ye ever hear sic a puckle pirn?" he commented. "And so who do ye jalouse has yon harp the noo, then?"

Owen did not quite like to voice his suspicions of Lord Malyn; Prince David was presumably a friend of his if he had been proposing to stay at Caer Malyn. But the other boys were more outspoken.

"No danger, sir, it's the Marquess himself! Promised to pull down the town of Pennygaff stone by stone, he did, and let the forest grow over it, if he did not get his hands on our harp. Black shame it is!" Mog said earnestly.

"Rubbish! All wrong you have it, boy!" contradicted Luggins. "Not his lordship but the foreign gentleman wanted the harp, so I was hearing."

"There's a fool you are! It was the Marquess, look you, without a doubt!" asserted Hwfa.

"Nonsense, then! It was the foreign gentleman, indeed!" cried Dove.

"Humph!" said Prince David. "Whichever ane o' them it was, it's plain that those twa souple scoundrels Bilk and Prigman maun be sneckit into jail; ance they are tied up in iron garters they'll soon enough betray the cheat-the-wuddy villain who hired them tae mak" off wi" yon harp. The faurst burgh we reach, I'll e'en command the justices tae carry oot a search for them. Where are ye bound, lads?"

The boys had agreed, hastily discussing the matter, that since he was obliged to return to London it would be folly to carry the prince all the way to Caer Malyn; they had therefore turned aside in the direction of Nant Agerddau, which, Mog reckoned, would not be more than ten or eleven miles south of them. Here the prince could obtain treatment for his wound, and would be able to hire post-horses and a carriage from Mr. Thomas at the Boar's Head for his journey home. Owen chafed somewhat at this interruption to his errand, but he admitted to himself that the prince's convenience must come first. Also, there might be a chance to see Arabis again. And—another consideration—with the Prince of Wales prepared to help him, surely his own fortunes must now take a more favourable turn?

They had left the gorge and were making their way through a level stretch of forest, checking their course by means of Owen's compass. In order not to jolt the hurt man too painfully they were obliged to go at a fairly slow pace; after an hour or so the prince announced that he was faint with hunger. At this time Hwfa, armed with the crossbow, was going ahead as lookout; not long afterwards he was lucky enough to shoot a hare, which they cut up and toasted on sticks over a hastily kindled fire.

The prince, nibbling a leg of hare washed down with the last of the wine, declared that Hwfa was a bonny shot and, given a little practice, would make as brisk a hunter as any lad north of the highland line. Having eaten, his highness soon became drowsy and Owen, a little anxious about him, urged the others to make as much haste as possible. The day had become even colder and the sky was thickening and darkening; a recurrence of the storm seemed probable. They went on fast and silently, saving their breath for walking, since the track they had taken now began to climb the lower slopes of Fig-hat Ben.

"Snow, it do look like," said Mog after an hour or so, squinting up at the murky clouds overhead. Sure enough, in half an hour or so, a scurry of white flakes began to blow past them, borne on the north wind that whistled fiercely at their backs.

Dove, who had been taking his turn as lookout, came back to the main party and beckoned Owen aside during a pause when they were getting their breath at the top of a steep ascent.

"Hey, Owen boy," he whispered, "what did those two crwydadiau look like? The two that took the old harp?"

"Bilk and Prigman? I hadn't my glasses on for most of the time I was with them, but one was short and stout and sandy-haired, and the other was tall and dark with a flat face. Why?"

"Whisht, you," Dove said. "If you will come this way I

will show you two men the very spit-image of that, sheltering under a rock."

Owen's heart beat fast. He followed Dove, who led him cautiously round a rocky outcrop grown over with young firs, which gave fairly good cover.

"They have moved on again," Dove muttered. "There they are, see, Owen, climbing the slope."

Owen peered through the snow, rubbing his glasses, and saw two figures, one short and stocky, the other tall, going up the hill; could they be Bilk and Prigman? It was hard to decide in the poor light. The two men stopped and seemed to dispute, shaking their fists at one another; then went on again.

"I do think it might be them," Owen said, frowning with the effort to see through the flutter of snow. "Indeed I am almost certain. But I can hardly leave the prince to follow them."

"See what the others have to say, is it?" suggested Dove. "Going the same way as us, anyhow, those two seem to be."

So they returned to the stretcher party, who were busy adding another layer of moss to the prince's covering.

"Not too good, the old prince, I am thinking," Hwfa said, "Brick-red his face is, and breath coming very quick; best we get him to shelter fast, eh, boys?"

"Wait, you," Dove said. "We have seen those two thieves, Bilk and Prigman, climbing the hill yonder; first give them a taste of their own medicine, is it?"

Hopeful grins spread over the faces of Luggins and Mog, who dearly loved a fight, but Hwfa shook his head.

"Best not to waste time," he said, and Owen, who had

been looking at the prince, entirely agreed with him.

"We must hope they are going to Nant Agerddau too," he said regretfully. "But Hwfa is right; we ought to take his highness on as fast as possible; I'm afraid he is falling into a fever. Maybe the toasted hare disagreed with him."

The prince was indeed very flushed and restless; he seemed asleep but occasionally muttered or called out a few incomprehensible phrases.

"O honari! Ochone! I hae missit the capercailzie! Sorrow fa" the brood. Gie ower yer daft reiks, man!"

"There is a pity, though, not to dust the jackets of that pair while we have them out in the forest," sighed Mog wistfully. "Just a bit of a chat, sociable, and maybe they will be telling us who set them on to steal the harp and where they have taken it. Eh, Hwfa? Just you and me to go, and the other three carry the old prince to town, is it? Not more than a couple of miles now."

"No," Hwfa said, "I am for sticking by the prince. What do you say, Owen, boy?"

"That is not a bad notion of Mog's," Owen said. "Supposing you, Mog, and Dove, follow those two men; steal close if you can, try to hear what they say, and see where they go; then meet us in Nant Agerddau at the Boar's Head."

"Right, you," Mog said happily. "Tie them up in knots, we will. A worm would find it hard to imitate. Come on, Dove."

"No, just make sure they are the right men," Owen cautioned. "They have knives, they are dangerous; especially Bilk, the tall one."

"No matter for that," huge Mog said comfortably. "A

pair of Welsh lads can soon mash them into hotch-potch. You will see."

Mog and Dove made off, running, up the hill, while the remaining three shouldered the litter once more and, being well rested, swung along at a rapid pace. Soon Owen began to recognize landmarks on the route he had taken with Mr. Smith the king's messenger; they climbed out of the forest, up grassy slopes now greyed over with a thin layer of snow, and came at last into the narrow gorge leading to Nant Agerddau.

"No sign of the others yet," Hwfa said, peering through the snow, which came thicker and thicker. "Roundabout way the thieves must have taken, not to be spotted by honest folk. But Mog and Dove will have them marked down, no danger. Old Dove is as good as a bloodhound when it do come to tracking."

"I hope they will be all right," said Owen, who was now having doubts as to the wisdom of his plan.

"No call to fret, boy," Hwfa said. "I will back Mog and Dove against the whole British army, with boots on."

"Perhaps the thieves are going back to the empty house," Owen thought. "Perhaps they left something behind there, or decided to let me loose after all." He wished he had thought to warn Mog and Dove not to go in there, supposing the house was still standing. But then he recalled how anxious Bilk and Prigman had been to leave it; they would hardly be likely to return.

Soon they passed the abandoned row, and reached the entrance to Father Ianto's cave.

"Wait just a moment," Owen said. "If anybody has skill

to care for his highness, it is the good brother who is living in here."

He put his head through the opening and called, "Brother Ianto! Are you there?"

But no answer came out. Owen went inside and found the cave dark and unoccupied; the tapers had burned out. He tripped over something and, stooping to feel about, discovered Brother Ianto's little wooden toolbox. It lay open and, as his eyes became accustomed to the gloom, he saw that the tools were scattered untidily over the floor.

"That is queer," he thought, rather troubled. "It isn't like Brother Ianto to leave his things all strewn about so. What can have happened?"

Hastily he gathered the tools into the box and then made his way back to the others.

"Brother Ianto does not seem to be there," he said. "I will ask about him in the town. He can't be far, or he would have taken his tools. Luckily I have another friend in the neighbourhood who will be able to help the prince."

They took the litter straight to the Boar's Head Inn, where Mr. Thomas the landlord and his wife nearly fell into a distraction with anxiety about their royal visitor, and gratification at the honour done to their roof, and dismay over the need to send somebody somewhere with a message about the prince's mishap, and worry about how they were going to get enough provisions to feed his highness as a highness should be fed.

Sheets were aired, fires lit, cauldrons put on to boil for poultices, and a stable-boy sent running for the doctor.

"Lucky it is we have good Dr. Jenkins in the town," Mr. Thomas said. "A fine skilled physician he is, and does wonders for the folk that come here to take the waters."

"Fine high fees he do charge too," sniffed Mrs. Thomas. "Pull a tooth and he will come near to ruin you, indeed! Sooner take my troubles to the pretty young lady and her da up at the fair, I would. Beautiful oil of goutweed and angelica she has given me for my housemaid's knee, and only a groat to pay."

Owen, when he saw the pompous, consequential little doctor, was inclined to side with the landlady; escaping from the fuss and uproar as the prince was put to bed, he ran off through the snowstorm to the top of the town.

He had been anxious in case the unseasonably early winter weather might have made the fairground people decide to pack up and move on elsewhere; however when he reached the quarry he was relieved to find that most of the tents and wagons were still there, though it was plain that they were not doing very good business. He flew to the spot where the Dandos' caravan had been located—and drew up short in dismay. The wagon was no longer there. Thinking that he might have gone astray in the snow, he turned back and searched more carefully, but without success.

"Have the Dandos left?" he asked an elderly lady in a red cloak, frilled bonnet, and steeple-hat, who was smoking a pipe in the doorway of her tent under a notice that said "Synamon Byns."

"Eh?" She leaned forward, cupping her hand over her ear.

"MR. DANDO AND HIS DAUGHTER? Where are they?" Owen shouted.

"Eh, dear boy, How should I know? Went from by here,

they did, yesterday, but I am not knowing where. Not a one to chatter, Tom Dando, and his daughter I was not seeing at all before they left. Will you be buying a cinnamon bun, my little one? Fresh baked, they are, and so crusty to melt on the tongue!"

Owen's mouth watered at the thought, and at the warm scent of baking which came from the old lady's tent, but he had no money, and regretfully declined. On his way back to the inn he asked all the people he met if they had seen Brother Ianto, but nobody had. However the potman at the Boar's Head, when asked, said he believed a messenger had come from the Marquess inquiring for Brother Ianto, and had later been seen driving him off towards Caer Malyn in a gig.

"But why should his lordship want Brother Ianto?" Owen demanded, rather troubled.

"How do I know, boy? Leave bothering me—dear knows, enough work I have for three men, looking after the customers in the bar and mixing up this devil's brew for Dr. Jenkins. Lucky it is that old Seljuk and his servant left and went off to stay with Lord Malyn; pity all this lot wouldn't go as well."

The potman was beating eggs, turpentine, vinegar, and ammonia together in a pewter beermug; the doctor, leaning over the stair-rail, called,

"Make haste, man! Am I to stand all day empty-handed?"

"O dammo! Here, you give it to the old gorynnog," the potman said, pushing the mug at Owen, who carried it upstairs into the prince's chamber. Hwfa was here blowing up a newly lit fire, Luggins carefully supported the prince's reclining form on the bed, while Dr. Jenkins tried to persuade him to drink a treacle posset made from figs, barley, and liquorice. But the patient was far from willing. He threw himself from side to side, uttering strange cries,

"Oigh! Oigh! Ceade millia diaoul! Troutsho!"

"Your highness! Please!" Dr. Jenkins wiped some treacle from his beard.

"Awa, ye blethering goose, ye gabbling skyte!"

"The man is mad, with him!" said Dr. Jenkins vexedly.

Prince David seemed to come to himself a little.

"Dinna gang sae ram-stan, ma man!" he croaked. "Have ye nae a dram o' the usquebaugh? A tass o' aquavitae?"

"Oh, gracious to goodness," fretted the doctor. "What will his highness be talking about, I do wonder? Indeed it is beyond me to understand his ravings."

"I think I know," said Hwfa, who often helped his father in the Dragon of Gwaun. He ran downstairs and soon returned bearing a glass of colourless liquid, which the prince received with a seraphic smile and immediately swallowed down.

"Ah, ye're a canny lad, a lad after ma ain hairt," he said to Hwfa. "Ance the inner man is satisfied, ye can do whit ye damn please wi" the outer!" And turning over, he sank into a sleep so profound that the doctor was able to spread turpentine salve over the wound without in any way disturbing his patient.

Then they all tiptoed downstairs, but as they were doing so, they heard a strange thump in the air, like a soft clap of thunder, and the building trembled.

"What was that?" Owen said.

"Dear, dear! Can his highness have fallen out of bed?"

worried the doctor, and bustled upstairs again, but Hwfa said,

"Outside, that noise was. More like a big gun it sounded."

"Or a fall of rock in the pit," Luggins said.

"No pits round here," said Hwfa.

Owen's knees suddenly felt weak beneath him.

"Come with me, quick!" he said. "I believe I know what it was."

Followed by the other boys he began running down the street towards the empty row of houses. But before they reached the end of the town they met Mog and Dove, who were pale and wild-eyed.

"Please to say what has been going on?" Hwfa demanded. "Wondering what you were up to, we were. No need to push the old mountain over, is it?" He spoke sarcastically, but he was plainly relieved to see his friends safe.

Dove was shaking all over.

"Awful it was!" he said. "Awful!"

"What happened, then, man?"

"Here," suggested Owen, "let's get out of the crowd, and the snow."

Half the population of Nant Agerddau was scurrying down the road, through the snowstorm, to see what had happened; the boys turned aside and walked through the great porticoed cave entrance beside the town hall. A sign on a board said:

NANT AGERDDAU TOWN COUNCIL
DEVIL'S LEAP CAVE

ADMISSION 6D
IMMERSION IN WATERS 2S 6D
WATER PER GLASSS 1S

But the man who usually sat at a table in the entrance cave taking sixpences had dashed off down the town like everybody else.

The boys walked into the cave unchallenged, and made their way through a passage and a series of linked chambers to an inner cavern with a hot pool in it, where old ladies came to bathe their rheumatic ankle-joints.

"Now," said Hwfa, "tell, then, is it?"

They all sat down on rocks.

"We followed those two men," Mog said. "Easy it was. They went up the hill cornerways like crabs, leaving tracks behind them in the snow, no trouble to keep in sight. But where the trees thinned out, hard to get close enough to hear their talk. So we kept on, follow, follow, though the path they took would break a snake's back, so roundabout. By and by they came near Nant Agerddau, us still a good distance behind. Nasty old path thereabouts, too, all loose stones; kick one down, start the whole hillside falling."

"I remember," Owen said. "They took me that way too."

"Then we came into the gorge, and easier to creep near because the road do bend about; stole along we did, quiet to hear one snowflake grind on another, and came on the pair of them sudden, standing still to argue in the middle of the road. Old Dove here squatted down behind a rock and I squeezed into a little bit of bramble-scrub—full of prickles I am yet—and crawled closer and closer.

" 'Will you swear you haven't got it hid away?' I heard one of them say.

" 'Swear till Turpentine Sunday, I will,' says the other, very angry. 'What difference do that make? All I care is that Old Stigmatical will have our necks in three days if we don't get it for him. I'll lay *you've* got it all along!'

" 'If I had it, would I still be keeping company with you, you foister?' says the other, angrier still. ' 'Twas all *your* peevy notions got us into this imbranglement—now you get us out!'

" 'Well I say we'd best go back to the stalling-ken and see what's come to the young co; maybe 'twas he fetched out someways, and prigged back the bandore.'

" 'The stalling-ken ain't safe,' says the second one. 'Anyways, suppose he's still there, and alive, what then?'

" 'Why then,' says the first, nasty to make your blood run cold, 'we'd best stick a shiv in him, so's he won't cry rope on us; then we'll make tracks for France; that's the only part where Old Stigmatical won't find us now he's got his glaziers on us. He'd never credit it if we told him we couldn't find the blessed owch—not after what's gone before.'

" 'Oh, all right,' says the first, 'but let's be quick, then.'

" 'I'll go on my own if you like, if you're afeered,' says the second.

" 'No,' says the first, giving him a look to slice up a side of beef, 'acos I don't trust you farther than I can throw you. Maybe you got up to some skimble-skamble trickery with the young kinchin, arranging for him to win free and prig the bandore from where you hid it. I'm a-coming too.' "

"By now it was snowing so thick that I'd been able to wriggle close as I am to you; I could hear well enough all they were saying. But hard to understand, with the queer words they used, and still not certain sure, I was, if they were the right pair, though it seemed like enough. When they started off towards those empty houses I felt fair and sure, so I gave Dove a bit of a beckon to come on."

"I came on," Dove broke in, "but I came on slow. Not keen, see, because I was remembering what you said about those empty houses, Owen, and how the whole mountain was likely to drop on them. 'Wait, you, boy,' I said to Mog, 'wait till they come out again, be so kind, and then we'll have our little chat.' "

"I was agreeable," Mog said, "so we waited. And we saw the old mountain up above begin to fold itself and slide. The snow it was, see, too heavy on the lip of the cliff. More and more kept coming down from above in an awful, slow, crawling rush; hung on the edge for a minute, it did, and Dove yelling his head off for the men to come out before it fell. Dove yelled, I yelled, till the voice was clean gone from us; but too late, see?"

"It fell on the house?" Hwfa said.

Mog nodded. "If there is a bit of wood or stone in that whole row of houses bigger than a pea now, may I never cross another bridge!"

There was a silence, while the boys thought about the awful fate of Bilk and Prigman. Then Hwfa, always practical, said,

"Pity it was you didn't find out who they stole it for, or what they did with it. No wiser than before we are, now."

"All we know is they seemed to have lost it," Owen said glumly.

"Fine help *that* is," Luggins muttered.

"Oh well." Hwfa stood up. "Back to the Boar's Head, me, and see how our old prince is getting on. Decent old prince he is, fair play; best not to leave that bleed-you-to-death sawbones alone with him too long."

Dove, Mog, and Luggins soberly followed Hwfa, but Owen, suddenly remembering that Bilk and Prigman, in the letters they dictated, had named the Devil's Leap cave as the place where the ransom money was to be left, found himself curious to explore a little more while he was there.

"I'll follow you," he said to the others.

"Think we should stay with him?" said Mog in the street. "Queer boyo, that Owen. Knocked him about, those men did, left him in that house to die, but proper upset about them he seems, just the same. Bit cracked, maybe?"

"Thinking, that's all he is doing, boy," Hwfa said impatiently, giving his friend a clump. "More brains in his little finger, he do have, than you keep in the whole of that great empty head of yours. Come on, and not to bother about Owen, is it? Follow in his own good time, he will. I'll be asking old Davy Thomas at the inn if he can give us a bit of supper; second cousin once removed of my Auntie Olwen Lloyd-Jones, he is."

10

While the Seljuk, in Mr. Davy Thomas's hired chaise, cantered briskly towards Caer Malyn, another vehicle was also proceeding, much more slowly in the same direction. This was Tom Dando's wagon, drawn by the massive Galahad.

When Tom awoke to find a note from his daughter requesting him not to mention his intentions to anybody, but to leave a basketful of listed medicines in a cave near the caravan, and then set out at once for Port Malyn, he was not in the least surprised (nothing ever surprised Tom Dando); he left the basket as directed, paused only to swallow a mug of herb tea, harnessed Galahad, and started forthwith. But he had woken late, and by now the day was well advanced.

Moreover Tom had now reached Canto CCXC of "The King at Caerleon" and had little though to spare for anything else; without a glance at the splendid mountainous and forested landscape opening around him, he sat on the driver's seat scribbling away as if he paid for his fingers by the minute and must get the utmost use out of them; as soon as he covered it, every sheet of paper was tossed back through a small window into the interior of the wagon where, as the hours went by, a huge pile grew up; meanwhile Galahad was left to make his own way to Caer Malyn. This he did, slow and steady, plodding along and minding his own business, stopping from time to time in order to snatch a mouthful of breakfast from bank or hedge. Galahad knew all the roads in Wales as well as the inside of his nose-bag; since Arabis usually chose their course, picking the least-known, little-used tracks where she would be likely to find rare herbs growing, Galahad followed the same route. In his accustomed manner he paused, as they passed clumps of wild rhywbarb and wynwyn, the trailing strands of the perfagl, or the large leathery leaves of the marchruddygl; he came to a halt under oak trees carrying tussocks of uchelwydd, the holy herb used by the druids, or by bright green patches of suran; but today nobody jumped down and went to pluck the leaves and berries.

Travelling leisurely at this pace they were overtaken by dusk before they had reached Caer Malyn, so, finding that he could no longer see the lines as he wrote them, Tom pulled up, loosed the horse, and went inside to continue his poem by lantern-light.

All through the hours of dark he continued to write as if somebody were shouting the words into his ear and he only just able to get them down in time; at last, just as the first green sprouts of dawn began to uncurl in the eastern sky, he drew a line at the foot of the final page and wrote *Finis* under it.

"Well, there is a tidy night's work, Arabis, my little one," he said then, yawning and stretching his cramped fingers. "Now, a good cup of tea, is it, and put all those old sheets in order for your dada?"

Nobody answered and, looking round in perplexity, he remembered that Arabis was not in the wagon; that he was somewhere in the middle of the Fforest Mwyaf, on his way to Port Malyn.

"Hai, how," he sighed, "make the tea myself then, I must."

Although tired out, he was very happy, and now terribly anxious to read the poem aloud to somebody; he bustled about, making tea and feeding Galahad, he read stray sheets of the poem that lay strewn all over the wagon; every line seemed to him marvellously beautiful, the best he had ever written.

"Ach y fi, Gwalchafed, my fat friend!" he shouted, shaking up the reins as they moved off under the trees. "Can't you go any faster than that, and you pulling the finest poet from Bull Bay to Worm's Head?"

Much astonished at this change in his master, Galahad broke into a thunderous trot; so the last part of their journey was swiftly accomplished, and when they arrived at Port Malyn the little town, huddled along the river's narrow gap through the cliffs, was still deep in shadow and nobody stirring.

The tide was low; moored boats squatted on the mud by the small stone pier and a strong salty fishy smell came from the weed-covered harbour walls. A rock shoal lay uncovered out beyond the breakwater; Arabis was down there gathering seaweed, but when she heard the wagon wheels and the clip-clop of Galahad's hoofs she turned and ran swiftly up a flight of slippery steps on to the quayside.

"Hwt there, Dada!" she called softly. "Where have you been, with you? Waiting all night I was! Eaten by the bleiddiau I thought you must have been, and a tough old morsel to chew down, eh, Galahad, my little sunflower? Whoa, now, while I lead you up by here."

And, taking the bridle, she guided horse and wagon out along a narrow track leading away from the harbour and round the base of the cliff to a quarry which made a sheltered and secluded place to halt.

"Now, a good bite of breakfast, for I am famished with me!"

Arabis jumped nimbly into the wagon and set about doing three things at once: soothing Hawc, who was very affronted at having had no attention paid him for so long; putting on a kettle and some rashers to fry; collecting a large basketful of remedies together with as much food as they could spare.

"My word, Dada! Writing a fair old streak you must have been," she exclaimed, shovelling reams of paper together (but very carefully, for she was a good daughter).

"Arabis! It is finished! My poem about King Arthur is finished! Wait till I read it to you—so beautiful to make you weep whole barrelsful of tears, it is!" And plumping himself down in a nest of paper, Tom grabbed bunches of pages and read her all the best bits. "Here, listen to this! Or no, even better this beginning of Canto CCLX is—aha, and here is my favourite part of all, just see if this would not melt a heart of granite!"

Arabis, gulping down bacon and herb tea and bara brith, listened and praised.

"Like the sound of a trumpet that verse is, Dada! Please to read again. Truly, if this poem does not win you the bard's crown at the Eisteddfod, I will not be believing that people have ears any more. Wonderful it is, indeed. But don't let your breakfast get cold with you; plain it is you never touched a crumb of food all day yesterday."

Tom, discovering how hungry he was, began to eat; while he did so Arabis told him about the tribe of Yehimelek, and their desperate need for help, food, and medicine.

At first hardly aware of her words, Tom presently found his attention caught, in spite of his fatigue, and started listening with interest.

"Children of the Pit, eh?" he commented, washing down a bowlful of picws with a swig of tea. "Living underground for thousands of years? No wonder they are a bit on the small side. Shame it is. But," he went on, his imagination kindling, "noble subject for a poem that would be, yes indeed! The Children of the Pit, living in darkness, till their deliverer come. Let me see, now . . ." And he began scrabbling vaguely about among all the loose paper for his quill.

"Now, Dada! One poem at a time, is it?" Arabis chided. "Besides, Yehimelek made me promise, most particular, that we would not mention to a living soul."

"True, that is so. But no harm to write a poem, maybe? Keep in the poetry box, I could, till they were all back home, *then* publish?"

"But, Dada, they do not know how to *get* home!"

"Hwchw," Tom Dando said, yawning. "Wasteful sort of arrangement that is. Have to tidy them up somehow. Let me think, now, then. Notion I have there is something I know about this? Workers in gold brought over by the old Romans? Ring a bell down in the cellars of my mind, that do. Somebody was saying something, it seems to me—'

Arabis waited hopefully. But after a minute Tom rubbed his head, with another enormous yawn, and said,

"Wait till tonight it must, though, the old brain is all cobwebs. Asleep on my feet I shall be in another minute. Maybe I will be remembering in dreams."

"Off to sleep, then, Dada; and I'll be back to make your dinner, is it?" Arabis said, giving him a hug and steering him towards his bunk.

"Never mind for that; breakfast enough to last till Friday you have given me, girl!" He yawned again so widely that it looked as if the top of his head might fall off; his eyes closed as he sank back on the patchwork quilt, and by the time Arabis had descended the steps he was asleep, and snoring so loud that the whole wagon heaved and the seagulls were obliged to quit the roof.

Arabis would have liked to ask if he had seen Owen before leaving Nant Agerddau, but her question, like the origins of the Pit People, would have to keep till evening. "At least Owen has Brother Ianto to keep an eye on him" she thought. Meanwhile it was more important to return to the tribe before anybody in Port Malyn woke up and saw where she was going, or before the tide came in and cut off her access.

Carrying the baskets of provisions she climbed down on

to the rocks at the base of the cliff and scrambled along as swiftly as she could to the seaweed-hung entrance; here she gave a low whistle and was at once greeted by Tennes and Strato, who popped their heads out, pressed her hands to their whiskery cheeks, and relieved her of the baskets.

She spent a busy morning among her patients. By degrees she was beginning to understand a few phrases of their language; quite a number of the words seemed strangely familiar and recalled old, half-forgotten rhymes that her mother had sung to her, long ago. It also became plain to her that, though Yehimelek did not know it, some of the people, probably by lurking on the outskirts of Port Malyn or Nant Agerddau by night, had managed to pick up a little Welsh.

As the day drew on Arabis had the satisfaction of seeing most of the sick people begin to mend, either from her medicines or the nourishing and sustaining qualities of seaweed broth. When she had visited all the patients, and another cauldron of broth was heating, she returned to Yehimelek and found that he, too, seemed stronger; he was up, sitting by his tiny window, wrapped in a camel-fur robe. His black eyes were once more full of fire; Arabis thought that he looked like a little old eagle, hook-nosed and white-haired, slightly moulting, perhaps, but still fierce and proud.

He gave her a cordial welcome.

"Greetings, and may your nets never lack for fish, our noble deliverer! How shall I call you, maiden? What is your name?"

"Arabis, sir, my name is."

"Arabis?" he repeated. "That sounds like a word from

our language. Where did you have such a name?"

"It is a Welsh word, sir, meaning witty. Also it was my mother's name before me."

"And your mother? Was she Welsh?"

"Why no, sir," Arabis said. "She was a travelling singer, who came from the island of Melita."

"Melita?" Yehimelek became quite excited. "But how strange! That name is woven into the history of

"He is an elder of our tribe, a man with a bottomless memory for the old histories. Although it is so long since our forefathers came from there he can describe the streets of Sa'ir and Taidon as if he himself had set foot in them."

Maybe it was the land of Italy your ancestors came from then? Not far from Melita, I am thinking?"

But, try as he would, Yehimelek could not recall if Melita lay east or west, or, he presently began to wonder, north or south of his homeland.

"If only Abipaal were here," he sighed.

"Who is Abipaal, sir?"

"He is an elder of our tribe, a man with a bottomless memory for the old histories. Although it is so long since our forefathers came from there he can describe the streets of Sa'ir and Taidon as if he himself had set foot in them."

"Where is he to be found, sir? Can I be fetching him along for your excellency?"

But Yehimelek shook his head.

"Abipaal is a solitary—a hermit. When the town of Nant Agerddau began to grow in size and many people came there to take the waters, and outsiders entered the caves which had been our undisturbed home for so many hundreds of years, we feared discovery. We had long been used to navigating the Malyn river in our camel-skin boats, coming down the underground ways to the shore to catch fish by night. So we migrated, and made dwellings in this cliff, for ourselves and our few remaining camels. But Abipaal would not leave; he loves the mountain and prefers to stay there in hiding, playing his music and remembering the old tales. And because of his surly temper, the others were not sorry to part from him."

Arabis was interested. "He plays music, sir? What kind of music would that be, I am wondering? I see you have a picture of a harp hanging over your door."

"In the old days," he explained, "my tribe were renowned for their skill in making harps; the conquerors used to buy them. At one time there used to be quite a number of old harps lying about but, these days, since we cannot dispose of them, they have mostly been melted down into more useful articles, such as fish hooks or cooking-pots."

"Eh, dear, there's sad!" exclaimed Arabis warmly. "Dearly would I have liked to buy one, if I had had enough money. Always wanted a harp, I have."

Yehemelek looked at her gravely and kindly.

"Then indeed I wish we had one left to give you, lady, but I fear there is not now a harp to be found among us, except that of Abipaal—if indeed he has not broken his in a passion. For it is a curious thing that, although we can make musical instruments and love music, the power of making music itself is not found among us. We can make things with our hands, from gold and ivory, but weaving beauty out of the air is not our gift, and it is a grief to us.

Abipaal has more skill than most, but it is not great; often in a rage he would hurl his harp down; the sounds he made were more likely to set your teeth on edge than to lift your heart up."

On a sudden impulse Arabis unslung the little crwth, which she had brought with her, and began tuning it. Yehimelek listened with delight, even to the first odd and wandering notes; Tennes and Strato poked their heads through the doorway, and then stole in; soon several more convalescent patients came tiptoeing along, as if they could not resist the sound. Arabis, having tuned the crwth, began to play a simple lullaby. As she did so, more and more people came quietly into Yehimelek's cave and squatted down; by the time she was through there might have been fifteen or twenty of them there, lost in silent enjoyment, their eyes dreamy with recollections of things that had happened before they were born.

It almost seemed as if the music were doing them more good than food and medicine.

"Sir," said Arabis to Yehimelek, after she had played all the airs she could remember, "has your excellency ever heard of the Harp of Teirtu?"

He shook his head. "Not by that name, Lady Arabis."

So she told him the tale of how Prince Kilhwch, helped by King Arthur, had stolen the harp for Princess Olwen, and how it had later passed into the ownership of St. Ennodawg.

"Do you think that might have been one of the harps made by your people, sir?"

"It seems very probable, my child. Can you describe this harp of Teirtu?"

"I have not seen it with my own eyes," Arabis said, "but I know the frame is of gold, and there is ancient writing on it."

"That does indeed sound like one of our make. Where is this harp now?"

"Stolen, it has been, sir." She told of the theft, and Owen's quest. "And I am thinking," she ended, "that it was stolen for the Marquess of Malyn, who lives in the castle at the top of this cliff."

"That is an evil fate for it," said Yehimelek. "Even we, living hidden, know of his wickedness. Sometimes we can hear the cries of his prisoners; our topmost dwellings are not far removed from his lowest dungeons; only a thick wall of rock lies between."

"Dangerous, that sounds, sir? There is a wonder some of his people will not have seen any of your tribe."

"We are careful, my child. We keep a strict watch at all times. Our lives depend on it."

Arabis shuddered at the thought of what would happen to the Children of the Pit if Lord Malyn learned of their existence; without doubt they would be enslaved and forced to work for him; she did not think they would last very long under his rule.

"Would old Abipaal know about this Harp of Teirtu?" somebody suggested.

"That is a good thought," Yehimelek said. "Tennes and Strato, if you are not needed to help with the sick tomorrow, go in search of him and bring him hither."

Another round of soup was now served out and then Arabis decided that she had better leave; the slit of sky beyond Yehimelek's window had darkened ominously. A few flakes of snow found their way in.

"Tomorrow I will come back before it is light," she said. "I will leave my crwth here."

"A good night to you then, Lady Arabis. Our thanks go with you. May the bird of serenity perch on your roof."

Arabis ran down the stairs to the cliff entrance. The tide had come in and gone out again; making sure that no one was in view she slipped through the curtain of weed and away along the foot of the cliff.

Dusk fell fast, and the first few flakes of snow were thickening to a blizzard; Tom's wagon, snug in its quarry, looked warm and cheerful with a light showing in the window. As she approached she could hear the sound of voices; she supposed that somebody must have seen the wagon and come out from Port Malyn for a haircut or a dram of medicine.

She was about to mount the steps when she paused and looked behind her, thinking she heard a footstep in the quarry.

"Is somebody there?" she said. No answer came back; only the sigh of the wind and the flutter of the snow blowing in her face. Deciding she must have been mistaken she opened the door, and was startled almost out of her wits to find the Seljuk of Rum comfortably established in her bunk, smiling from ear to ear and smoking a hookah, while Tom Dando read aloud "The King at Caerleon."

Arabis was vexed. Why does that fat old bird of ill omen have to follow us about? she thought. Isn't the hospitality of his fine friend the Marquess good enough for him? It is too bad, just when I wanted Dada's advice about the tribe.

To her embarrassment the Seljuk seemed to read her thoughts.

"Heydey! It is the obliging young lady, person, spinster, who told me the way to the Devil's Leap," he said with a low bow. "Doubtless you are tired from your day's labours and wishing me at Jericho, Timbuktu, the ends of the earth, so I shall hasten to be off, take my departure, make myself few and far between, ho, ho! I have had a most pleasant, famous natter, gossip, conversazione with your good papa."

"No call to go yet," said Tom Dando, who was dying to read some more of his poem. "My daughter will find us a bite of supper, isn't it, Arabis, my little one?"

The Seljuk looked as if he would be glad to be persuaded so Arabis, unwillingly mustering what civility she could, invited him to stay, and began crossly cutting up wynwyns and making a stew with wystrys and persli.

"By Jove, that smells most mouthwateringly delicious," sighed the Seljuk by and by. "I must confess that I find the table, diet, provender of his lordship the Marquess—who serves nothing but yellow food—somewhat monotonous fare; which was why I slipped down to this rustic seaport to see if I could buy a tomato or a cucumber. But, alackaday, your Welsh sabbath! Not a shop open do I find! And the dismal cold! Imagine then my joy, felicity, bewitchment, to discover again my dear acquaintance Mr. Dando!"

Arabis began ladling the stew into bowls, devoutly hoping that Tom had not let fall any hint concerning the Children of the Pit. But she did not think that he would.

Starting to lay the table she was disconcerted to find the

Seljuk's small brown-skinned servant huddled on the floor beneath it; she had not noticed him before.

He shook his head uncomprehendingly when she offered him oyster stew; however when the Seljuk translated her question he changed to a series of grateful nods. Although he was wrapped in furs and the wagon warm as an oven he seemed shivery, and sneezed as he accepted his bowl.

"Caught cold he has, sir," Arabis said reprovingly to the Seljuk. "There is wrong to bring him out in such weather, look you!"

"I know, indeed I know, my dear young person, but to tell truth he would not be left behind in Castle Malyn by himself; yonder abode puts him in a mortal funk! So I told him he could come along with me, eh, Ribaddi?"

Ribaddi nodded gratefully and broke into a flashing grin; it was plain that he was fond of his master, and Arabis began to think a little better of the Seljuk, who was spooning up the last drops of gravy from his pipkin with a perplexed expression. "In effect," he went on, addressing Tom, "I am troubled about that establishment myself, and I will be glad to ask your counsel my dear confidant, friend in need, fairy godfather."

"Glad I will be to give advice," said Tom. "We are not thinking too highly of the Marquess ourselves, I might mention."

"In fact, to lay bare my heart, between you and me and the doorpost," the Seljuk went on, "I partly came out in search of the police, gendarmerie, constabulary, Bow Street Runners, or what have you? But none do I find!"

"Good gracious me, I should think not, indeed, in a respectable Welsh village!" said Arabis tartly. "A lot of robbers, do you take us for?"

"Hwt, girl," said her father. "Well, indeed, sir, but why are you wanting the police, with you?"

"Two, or three, several, various divers persons have come to the castle of late," explained the Seljuk. "His lordship, as you know, takes a great interest in things made of gold. I, for reasons of my own, also take an interest in such articles, so—ahem!—I take an interest in his lordship's dealings. Some of these visitors he interviewed behind a closed door so I was not able to overhear exactly what he said to them"—the Seljuk looked rather provoked about this—"but I formed the opinion, inference, conclusion, that he was not being quite *kind* to some of them." Arabis and Tom exchanged a quick, anxious look. "One of these people, I have reason to believe, was the venerable and respected Mr. Hughes, by whom I had the brief honour of being shown round the Pennygaff Museum"—"Eh, dear!" exclaimed Arabis—"another, I have only too much cause to fear, was my old friend and benefactor, Brother Ianto."

"Brother *Ianto*?" Arabis was more and more alarmed. "Mercy! Why would his lordship be wanting Brother Ianto?"

"It is to do with a harp, some Harp of Teirtu, I apprehended, conceive, hit the nail on the head," explained the Seljuk. "I understand he wishes to locate, procure, lay his paws on the harp, and is unable to do so."

"Indeed?" Arabis gave the Seljuk a suspicious glance. "Thought he had already made off with the harp, I did. But why send for Brother Ianto?"

"It is because Brother Ianto will be the guardian of the Harp of Teirtu, of course," Tom Dando put in testily, very much surprising his daughter. When she had told him of the harp's discovery he had been still so wrapped up in his poem that he had not seemed to take in the news. "Brother Ianto will be the last of the monks of St. Ennodawg, in whose keeping the harp was left."

"Fancy that! How do you come to know such a thing, Dada?"

"Read it in a poem, I did, fach."

"But, hwchw, in that case Brother Ianto's life is not worth a twopenny pinch of snuff, up in that nasty place!" Arabis exclaimed in great distress. "And what about the poor old gentleman, Mr. Hughes? Very strong in his notion that the harp should go to its right owner, Owen said he was. And a brisk tongue he has; I am thinking he might easily give offence to Lord Malyn. And, oh, sir, was his grandson there? A boy my age, very thin, with him, and black hair, and a short-sighted look?"

"I am not sure, my dear young friend," the Seljuk said apologetically. "I did not view, espy, lay eyes on the arrival of Mr. Hughes, but only listened to Lord Malyn's conversation with him through the door. And, my word, good gracious, gadzooks! They sounded in a huff, in a ferment, in high dudgeon! And I do not believe most of these persons have left the castle yet; I believe they are clapped up there in durance vile!"

"Da," said Arabis, standing up resolutely. "Do something about this, we must!"

"Indeed I am thinking so too," agreed Tom, "but what do you suggest, my little one?"

"You must go to fetch the Prince of Wales, Dada. Time somebody gave that wicked Marquess his deserts, and Prince Deio the only one with power to do it."

"O, possibly so, but where am I to find the old prince?" Tom said, rather startled. "Long way to London it is, look you."

"If you hadn't been so deep buried in your poem these last days, Dada, you would have heard he is coming to visit his lordship for the boar-hunting. Talking of little else, the folk of Nant Agerddau, when we were there. Go back along the high road and there is sure you are to meet him on the way. And then you must tell him to come after Lord Malyn with the militia and put a stop to his nasty ways."

"Right, you," said Tom, standing up and preparing to set forth at once. "But, now, what about those people up at the castle? Short in the temper, Lord Malyn, so I am hearing; suppose he takes a notion to toss them out of his bedroom window?"

"I do not think he will do that until he has the harp safe," said Arabis. "But in any case we shall go back to the castle."

"We?" said the Seljuk. "Us?"

"Right, you!"

The Seljuk's mouth fell open in dismay. "Really, my dear young creature, juvenile, miss," he protested. "I am a lover of justice, verily, but is that wise or needful? If I were in my own country with my janizaries about me it would indeed be another kettle of fish, a horse of a different colour; here I am but a private citizen! In the primary place, how do you propose to enter? The Marquess, you may know, has a rooted dislike of all your charming sex, due, I apprehend, to feelings of spite against a young lady by whom he was jilted, given the go-by, sent about his business, when at a younger age."

"I shall dress up in your servant's clothes, of course. Anyone can see *he* should not go out again tonight. He can go to bed in Dada's bunk, and then Da can drive the wagon towards Nant Agerddau till he meets the prince."

"My stars!"

The Seljuk was not at all happy about this scheme, but when Arabis was determined upon a course of action other people usually found, in the end, that it was easiest to fall in with her plans.

So, not long afterwards, the wagon set off for Nant Agerddau, driven by Tom, pulled through the snowstorm by the valiant Galahad, with the Seljuk's servant, full of aconite, belladonna, hellebore, and ipecacuanha, sleeping comfortably inside under a mound of quilts.

And the Seljuk, a-twitter with apprehension, climbed puffing up the steep hill to the castle, accompanied by Arabis, who had browned her face with walnut juice and dressed herself in Ribaddi's fur jacket and trousers, tucking her black hair inside his astrakhan fez.

When they were halfway up the hill a winged form came flapping heavily through the snowy dark and settled with a martyred croak upon Arabis's hat.

"There now! I was afraid he might do that, so cross as he's been because I left him behind when—" Guiltily she bit off her words and addressed the bird. "Why did you have to come out in all this nasty snow? Go home, bad Hawc!"

But Hawc refused to budge.

"You will have to tell the Marquess that you bought him in the village, I am afraid, sir."

The Seljuk seemed to feel that Hawc was the least of their troubles.

"But what are we going to *do* when we get to the castle, my dear young colleague, partisan, crony? What course do you propose we pursue?"

"Oh," Arabis said airily, "I have several plans. We shall have to see. But first we must discover whether all those people are still there—Owen, Brother Ianto, Mr. Hughes'—thank goodness the Marquess doesn't know about the Children of the Pit, she thought to herself—"and then we must make sure he doesn't harm them until Prince Deio arrives with Dada."

"Indeed, I see," replied the Seljuk rather faintly.

"It is quite simple."

"Plain sailing, mere child's play, no great shakes, in fact?"

"Right, just," said Arabis, and then they both had to concentrate on the steep slope, iced over now, and dangerously slippery.

Just before they reached the iron-barred entrance gate Hawc, evidently disliking the look of the place, rose from Ribaddi's fur hat and sheered off into the storm.

"That fowl has some intelligence in his brain-pan, noddle, headpiece, upper storey," muttered the Seljuk gloomily, raising his hand to knock on the gate.

Twenty yards in the rear a dark figure followed, unseen amid the driving snow, keeping exact pace with them as they approached the castle.

11

As Arabis and the Seljuk entered Castle Malyn the hour of dinner was announced by a footman who beat upon an enormous golden gong.

"Alack, more yellow comestibles," sighed the Seljuk.

Arabis thought he would hardly be able to eat much, anyway, considering the quantity of oyster stew he had just consumed, but when the majordomo ushered them into the dining-room and she stationed herself correctly behind his chair, she was astonished to see him tuck into curried eggs, chicken with saffron, smoked haddock with mustard sauce, peaches, bananas, and yellow plums, as if he had never eaten in his life before.

Arabis, for her part, was almost fully absorbed in studying the Marquess of Malyn. Brought up to think of him as a kind of ogre, she had expected an uglier man than, on first inspection, she found him; but when she looked again at his strange deep yellow eyes a shudder of repulsion and fear nearly made her drop the cloth-of-gold napkin which she was trying to fasten under the Seljuk's double chin. The Marquess did not so much as notice her; his eyes passed her without the faintest interest, and for this she was thankful.

The two men talked about Lord Malyn's collection of gold articles until the peach course had been reached; then the Marquess, coiling his little gold-linked snake round the glass of wine in front of him, languidly inquired,

"And your own researches, my dear guest? How do they proceed? I—ah—believe you took a stroll this afternoon, that you honoured my humble village with a visit? Did you there learn anything of interest about your lost tribe of craftsmen in gold—what was their name? The tribe of Yehimelek? Dear me, a most romantic tale! I quite long to have them reunited with their rightful prince!"

Arabis, who, instructed by the butler, had been about to place a gold finger-bowl by the Seljuk, let it slip; it fell to the ground, splashing its contents over the velvet carpet. At the sound of her indrawn breath Lord Malyn gave her a brief, cold look; then studied her more sharply, his eyes narrowing.

But the Seljuk, unaware of this, continued peeling a peach and answered in a placid voice,

"Why, no, my dear sir! Confidentially, joking apart, to tell truth, I cut short, put a period to my researches—your weather is so inclement!—and instead paid a call on an acquaintance of mine."

"Oh indeed? And who might that be? I was not aware that you had any acquaintance in these parts—apart, of course, from that charming Brother Ianto," Lord Malyn said suavely, still studying Arabis in a manner that was beginning to make her very uneasy, as if her appearance stirred some recollection in him.

"Oh, a most talented, estimable person, a travelling poet, bard, versifier, by name Tom Dando," the Seljuk said enthusiastically. Lord Malyn started, but still kept his eyes on Arabis. "This agreeable troubadour—besides reading many of his excellent works—has been telling me some local lore of Nant Agerddau which, perchance, I appear to have missed, let slip, turned a deaf ear to when I was in that vicinity. I can tell you, it is not like me to be caught napping! But Mr. Dando informs me there is a tradition that small dark persons, known as Fur Niskies, were once wont to roam those parts by night. Now, do not these sound like my lost Phoenicians? Indeed, my dear host, if you will not think it too discourteously precipitate of me, I believe that tomorrow I shall betake myself back to the noble slopes of Fig-hat Ben and trespass on your hospitality no longer!"

"Why, my good friend," replied Lord Malyn, never for an instant removing his eyes from Arabis, "you do not trespass on my hospitality at all! Indeed your presence is so delightful to me that I will be only too pleased to accompany you on your excursion to Nant Agerddau! If your lost tribe are indeed to be found in the caves there, I can hardly wait to be present at the touching scene when you encounter them!"

No, *that* I'll wager you can't, Arabis thought. She was in agony, unavailingly trying to escape the Marquess's eye, unable to attract the Seljuk's attention. Why, why, didn't I ever think of him, she wondered, but who would, so fat and foolish as he seemed? Nobody would be likely to reckon on *him* as a deliverer. Now what's to be done? Perhaps if Lord Malyn and the Seljuk go off to Nant Agerddau tomorrow I can somehow get a message to Yehimelek to keep his people well hidden until the Prince of Wales has come and dealt with the Marquess; but first I must warn the Seljuk not to go letting out any more information; and there's still those poor prisoners to be rescued. Eh, dear! Here is a fine old state of affairs.

At this moment a lean, dark man slipped in, sidled up to Lord Malyn, and began to murmur in his ear. The Marquess listened attentively; his eyes moved from Arabis to the Seljuk and back again; his face did not change, except that the nostrils fluttered, twice. At the end he said, "Thank you, Garble," in a cold voice. The man turned to leave. "No, stay—I may have need of you." Garble moved two paces to the rear.

"So!" Lord Malyn began at last, hissingly. "So you betray my hospitality, do you, my fat friend? All this fine talk is but a cover, under which you plot and plan against me?"

With a slashing stroke he brought his gold snake down across the wine glass in front of him and it broke into fragments.

"Eh?" The Seljuk was so startled that he almost swallowed a peach stone. "I beg your pardon, may I have the pleasure? I don't quite understand, get your drift, grasp your meaning, my dear fellow?"

"I think you understand very well," Lord Malyn replied menacingly. "My secretary here informs me that this afternoon while you were calling on Dando—an intransigent, subversive good-for-nothing with whom I have had trouble before—he heard you plotting together to set the militia to hinder my perfectly respectable activities, to turn the Prince of Wales against me! What do you say to that, my treacherous friend?"

"Why," said the Seljuk stoutly, "I say that it is all a pack of moonshine, tomfoolery, stuff and nonsense, gammon and spinach, pish, tush, fiddle-dedee! There is only your secretary's word for it, after all—and what was he doing, eavesdropping on a private conversation, be so good as to tell me, pray?"

"He was watching my interests, as he is paid to," replied the Marquess. "Moreover he tells me that he heard you plot to release various persons confined in my cells—persons whom I have every right to imprison if I so choose!—further, that to assist you in this underhand scheme you smuggled some female accomplice of the miscreant Dando into my castle, tricked out as your servant! And what have you to say to *that*?"

As the Seljuk opened his mouth to reply, Garble, who had slipped stealthily round behind Arabis, suddenly whipped off her fez, revealing her long hair.

"O deuce take it!" exclaimed the Seljuk to Arabis crossly. "Now we are properly rumbled, in the cart, the cat is let out of the bag with a vengeance! What did I tell you, and so forth?"

"What is your name?" Lord Malyn asked Arabis in a cold, deadly tone. "And how dare you sneak into my castle in disguise?"

But she, now that all was discovered, felt, for some reason, less afraid; she answered with spirit,

"My name is Arabis Dando, and I will be pleased to

hear what I am doing that is wrong! No law there is against wearing a fur hat, that I know of? As for the rest, it is all hearsay, nothing to go on but the word of that shovel-faced fellow!"

"Arabis Dando," repeated the Marquess musingly. "Yes indeed, and now that I come to consider, you have quite a look of your mother, as she used to be when she sang her outlandish Mediterranean songs on the stage at Pontyprydd! Arabis Camilleri! To be sure, how that name does conjure up old times."

Not very pleasant old times, it was evident; the expression in his eyes as he studied Arabis was far from friendly. And, curiously, when he thus addressed her, the tones of his voice stirred up in her, too, a long-buried memory. Although up to that moment she had had no recollection of ever seeing him before, now a distant scene began to come back to her—in the snow—long ago—when she was very small: of themselves, as it appeared, words rose to her lips. Some force from outside seemed to raise her hand until it was pointing at him.

"Woe to you, Malyn! Woe to the despoiler of the fatherless, woe to the roof and all those beneath it! May you hurtle for ever into a bottomless pit! May your inheritance be scattered to the four winds!"

"Enough!" snapped Lord Malyn, white with rage. "Garble! Take her away! Put her in the bottom dungeon with that mealy-mouthed, mumchance monk—let them live on air together.—Has he let out any word, yet, as to the whereabouts of the harp?"

"Not a word, your lordship. I can get nothing from him but a lot of Latin."

"Very well. In that case we may as well dispatch them both with the least possible delay. Put Gog and Magog in with them; that should settle them fast enough."

"But, my lord—" Garble began rather doubtfully.

"Quiet, you! When I wish for your advice I will ask for it. If the old monk has anything to say, maybe the sight of Gog and Magog will fetch it out of him."

"Yes, my lord."

"As for this fat imposter—'

"Upon my halidom!" gasped the Seljuk, outraged.

"—I shall interrogate him myself, and then he can be stuffed in with the curator."

"Now do you see what your schemings and stratagems have let me in for!" the Seljuk cried reproachfully to Arabis as Garble, who was far stronger than he looked, dragged her from the room, helped by a burly footman. But she was too pleased to learn that Mr. Hughes and Brother Ianto were still alive to be entirely downcast; in any case she thought that the Seljuk was being rather unfair; he was merely to be imprisoned with old Mr. Hughes, whereas she and Brother Ianto were also landed with Gog and Magog; she had no idea who the latter might be but felt sure that their company was not intended as a treat.

Down flights and flights of winding stone stairs they went, stairs worn out of the naked rock, shallow with age and slippery with damp; at last they came to a low, wide, irregular chamber, sloping somewhat downhill, and with a curiously wrinkled, fluted ceiling, which resembled nothing so much as the channellings of a great ear. Iron-barred doors were set all round this space; from behind some of them came groans. Garble led Arabis to the door just above the lowest corner, selected a key from a bunch at his belt, thrust it into the lock, and turned it with some difficulty; it seemed very rusty.

"Don't try climbing out the window unless you fancy a six-hundred foot drop into the sea," he said curtly, and gave Arabis a shove which sent her staggering down a short flight of steps. Behind her the door clanged shut.

"Brother Ianto!" cried Arabis, picking herself up—she had landed on hands and knees. "Are you really here? Are you all right, with you?"

"Dear to goodness, is that you, Arabis, my child? Well indeed, how did you come by here?"

Arabis, her eyes beginning to get used to the dim light from the narrow window, made out Brother Ianto rising stiffly to his feet from a corner where he had been sitting or kneeling. She ran to him and hugged him.

"Oh, Brother Ianto, there's glad I am you are still alive! If that fiend have hurt you I will have the eyes out of him personally!"

"Hush, child!" he warned. "Mind your tongue here, you must. Every word we say travels back to them upstairs," and he gestured to the roof.

"Much I care!" said Arabis. "Hope I do that the ears are sizzling on him this minute! Anyway, my dada and the Prince of Wales will soon have us out from here. But are you all right, Brother Ianto?"

"Fine and grand," he said. "Good spot for a quiet think it is here; No complaints, indeed, only for a twinge of the rheumatics in my old bones."

"Soon have that out of you, I will," Arabis said, "while we are waiting for Gog and Magog. Oil of wintergreen I have in my pocket, see, and no trouble to rub on."

So Brother Ianto unbuttoned his hair shirt and she gave him a vigorous rub until, as he said, he was as lissom as a young firefly, and the cell smelt wholesomely of warm wintergreen.

"And who may Gog and Magog be, my child?" he inquired, when Arabis had finished with him.

"I am not knowing yet," said Arabis, putting the stopper back in the wintergreen bottle. Then she cocked her head sideways and added, "But I am thinking we shall not be long finding out."

She could hear footsteps, and the Seljuk's voice raised in indignant protest as he was hustled down the stairs. A door slammed somewhere near by. Then their own door was briefly opened again, just long enough for a basket to be dumped inside. It fell over, tipping out a dazzling tangle of black and yellow, which resolved itself into two large, angry tiger-snakes.

"Not very nice quarters for them down here," Brother Ianto said disapprovingly. "Hard old rock and nothing to eat; no wonder they will be a bit put out. Best to stand quite still, Arabis, my child. A tiger-snake has a nasty temper on him, and no use to say sorry, no offence, once he has lost it."

"Are you all right, your excellency?" Arabis called to the Seljuk, while she stood quite still and watched the tiger-snakes, who were darting in a furious and frustrated way about the cell, and quarrelling whenever they became entangled, which was often.

"No, I am not all right, not at all, far from it, anything but!" the Seljuk called back aggrievedly from a neighbouring cell. "That wolf in sheep's clothing, fiend in human form has cut off my moustaches!"

"Oh, my dear goodness! There's sorry I am!" Arabis was torn between horror and a wish to laugh; she could not help wondering what the Seljuk looked like now, and whether the moustaches had been cut or shaved.

"Let me out of here, you miscreants!" called another voice—that of Mr. Hughes.

"There is lucky you will be!" one of Lord Malyn's men replied mockingly.

"I wish to put on record a very strong objection to the way in which I have been treated."

"Object away!" replied his jailors, their voices retreating up the stairs. "No extra charge for objecting, round here."

Mr. Hughes continued to seethe. "Infamous! Disgraceful! Most improper!" And he added, apparently to the Seljuk, "I am sorry to see you in the same predicament, my dear sir! Upon what grounds has that insolent nobleman imprisoned you, may I inquire?"

"Indeed, I am hardly aware, sure, cognizant, except that he seemed to have some notion that my researches might lead him to the Harp of Teirtu that he is so set upon. But when he discovered that I proposed reporting him to the Bow Street Runners he flew into a passion, fell into a taking, ran amuck; and had me imprisoned, laid by the heels, clapped under hatches, as you see."

"Despotism!" fumed Mr. Hughes. "Why, the man's a fool! My grandson had made off with the harp before you so much as set foot in Pennygaff, what could you know about the matter?"

"Eh, to be sure, if that is not my old schoolfellow Owen

Hughes!" remarked Brother Ianto. "Long time it is since we used to swing conkers together, and sorry I am to learn you are down by here too, Mr. Hughes, my little one!"

"Why, Ianto Richards, is that you? I thought you were in China."

"Reckoned I would just step home, see, and take a look at the old country," Brother Ianto replied.

"But you are the proper custodian of the harp! Small wonder that bird of prey has got his talons on you!"

"Oh, as to that," Brother Ianto said comfortably, "he might have spared to trouble himself, indeed, for it is well known among the monks of the Order of St. Ennodawg that the harp was handed back to the last descendant of the original Teirtu, and very proper too."

"What? The harp handed back?" gasped Mr. Hughes. "When did such a transaction take place, pray, and who was this descendant?"

"Why, about fifty years ago, it happened. A Miss Tegwyn Jones, she was, and in gratitude for the return of the harp she presented the monks of St. Ennodawg with enough liniment to cure their chilblains for two generations."

"But if the harp was returned to her, how did it come to be discovered still in the ruins of the monastery?" Mr. Hughes inquired.

"O, that will be because Miss Tegwyn Jones was of a travelling disposition. Preferred to leave the harp lodged at the monastery she will have, very likely, it being a valuable article."

"Well, that is most interesting, to be sure, and news to me, but I presume Miss Tegwyn Jones is dead, as she has not returned to claim the harp, and it makes no difference to the fact that my worthless grandson has now stolen the instrument," Mr. Hughes said bitterly.

"Oh, no, Mr. Hughes, bach, indeed you are mistaken there," Brother Ianto assured him, shaking his head at Arabis, who was on the point of bursting out. "Quite otherwise the matter was; two thieves by the name of Bilk and Prigman stole the harp, kidnapping your grandson so as to put the blame on him. Seen by a young friend of mine, they were, stowing the harp in a cave at Nant Agerddau, and left your grandson tied up as tight as a whiting to be killed by a landslide; since then no one has clapped eyes on either the harp or the thieves."

"Duw," muttered Mr. Hughes, half convinced by hearing the story come from Brother Ianto. "But in that case, where's my grandson now? And who's to be sure he was not in league with the thieves in the first place?"

Here Arabis could restrain herself no longer. "Why, you silly old man!" she cried indignantly. "Black disgrace it is to have such doubts of your own flesh and blood, and the poor boy half breaking his heart, trying to get the harp back for you! Serve you right it would indeed if Miss Tegwyn Jones turned up and asked what right had you to keep it in your old museum, covered in dust and all its strings broken!"

An awful silence fell. Then Mr. Hughes inquired in an icy tone,

"May I have the honour to ask who it was that just spoke?"

Arabis, already repenting her outburst, did not, however, immediately reply, for in her excitement she had taken a couple of steps forward and both tiger-snakes, roused by this movement, were making their way purposefully towards her.

In his chamber above, the Marquess, listening at the earpiece which carried all the voices of the prisoners up to him, nodded thoughtfully and said to Garble,

"So!" I thought we should learn something if they were all left to tattle together. Miss Tegwyn Jones, eh? Still, I expect she is dead long ago. And, after all, it was that rascally pair, Bilk and Prigman, who played me false! If they reappear, Garble, with or without the harp, have them clapped straight in a cell. I'll use no tools that turn in the hand."

"What about the old man's grandson?" inquired Garble.

"He's of no consequence—unless, indeed, he should lead us to Bilk and Prigman. Still, if he turns up while I'm gone, throw him in a cell too, to await my return."

"Gone, my lord? Where would your lordship be going?"

"Why, to Nant Agerddau, of course, fool, where else? First, to lay that meddlesome Tom Dando by the heels, before he makes mischief between me and the Prince of Wales. I should be able to overtake him soon enough; second, to search for Bilk and Prigman, since that is where the scoundrels were last seen with the harp; and lastly, I have a curiosity to see if I can not unearth some of the fat Ottoman's little underground citizens. That would be a rare convenience indeed—a whole tribe of expert gold craftsmen at my bidding! Order my carriage round, Garble."

"But your lordship! It snows!"

"And so? What of it?" inquired Lord Malyn coldly. "Should I be held up for a little snow?"

"But, my lord, it is increasing to a regular blizzard!"

"Garble, I find you are becoming wearisomely interfering. Pray do as you are bid without further argument!" And the Marquess, twirling his gold snake, shot Garble a look which made him turn pale yellow. "Order fifteen relays of horses to accompany the carriage," Lord Malyn called after him through the door, "and a footman to run ahead and clear the drifts. Let them be ready in seven minutes."

12

Owen walked slowly through the series of entrance chambers to the large cavern which contained the feature from which Devil's Leap took its name. As he advanced the whisper of Fig-hat Ben became more and more distinct; the whole place seemed full of a soft, throbbing mutter; it was hardly a sound so much as a shiver in the air about him.

The cave was illuminated by gas flambeaux which threw a greenish but clear light; Owen therefore extinguished the sixpenny taper he had caught up from the admission table and gazed about him with interest.

The floor in this big cave was not flat, but bowl-shaped; the cave was, in fact, a huge round hole inside the mountain, as if it had been left by a bubble which had swelled and then burst. There were numerous entrances, from which flights of steps had been cut, winding round the circular sides and down to the bottom; here, like the plughole to a basin, yawned a dark, circular opening, perhaps thirty feet across and of an unknown depth; some people said that it descended to the very roots of the mountain, others that it was bottomless. Up this gigantic shaft, borne on a current of air, cloudy wreaths of steam perpetually rose; they broke and changed and took strange forms like the clouds in a stormy sky; Owen saw the shapes of horses and chariots, dragons and dolphins, forming and dissolving silently in the vault of the cavern above him.

Slowly and with caution he descended one of the winding flights of steps; he felt like a fly crawling over the inside of a pudding bowl. Sounds reverberated strangely in the huge place, and he kept looking back, thinking there was somebody behind him, when it was only the echoes of his own feet clattering on the rock.

At length he reached the rim of the great well. To prevent sightseers from falling in, the Nant Agerddau Town Council had fenced it round with a rope, slung between stout posts. At one point these crossed a spur or tongue of rock, about four feet wide at the base and eight feet long, which extended outwards from the side of the well, like some fearsome diving board. Standing near this spur, Owen looked downwards into the dim, vapour-filled depths below. At first the height made him dizzy and he was obliged to close his eyes. Presently, to his astonishment, he began to think that he could hear music—or, at any rate, a series of half musical sounds—long, wavering, twanging notes. To begin with, he thought he must be imagining the sounds, but they grew clearer, as if they moved towards him; then he began to think they were coming from the depths of the well, unlikely though this seemed. Puzzled, wondering if the sounds could be another peculiar effect of the cave's circular shape, he wiped his glasses and stared down, keeping a firm grasp of the rope. By degrees his eyes became accustomed to the murky dimness below and he saw that twenty feet down, directly opposite him, another spur of rock protruded from the side of the shaft. He remembered then a tale which Arabis had once told him: a legend of how the devil had stolen the candlesticks from Nant Agerddau church, was pursued by St. Ennodawg, and jumped from one spur of rock to the other, in his haste letting fall the candlesticks, which the saint skilfully caught in mid-air.

Owen shivered as he imagined leaping over that fearful depth from one narrow prong of rock to the other; surely no one but the devil would attempt such a feat.

Then, to his utter astonishment, he perceived something move on the lower spur—something that seemed alive. Hardly able to believe that he was not dreaming, he saw a tiny grey figure advance, through coiling wreaths of mist, to the very tip of the spur, and stand there, apparently quite regardless of the gulf beneath. Moreover, Owen now realized, the music was proceeding from this figure—if indeed the melancholy noise could be called music.

After a while a harsh, grating voice began to sing, at first in some incomprehensible language; then, suddenly, Owen found that he could distinguish words, and presently whole phrases, though the accent was odd and unfamiliar:

All I need is a harp
For my content:
A talkative harp,
A sociable harp,

A harp of my own.
One time I had a harp
But it is gone.
In an hour of deep despair
Which I repent,
Because its song was harsh
I broke it on a stone.
I cast it into dark,
I heard it fall
And weeping went
For many days alone,
Having murdered my harp.
Unhappy Abipaal!

But now, from dark
Another harp is sent!
I have set new strings
And will teach them to sing
A new song excellent,
A new song meant
For Abipaal alone,
Sweeter than all,
Second to none,
O talkative harp,
Sure and tender is your tone.
O happy Abipaal,
All I need is a harp
For my content . . .

Owen listened with great surprise to this wild and uncouth chant, which seemed to float up to him out of the rocky hollow on waves of mist. Although the singer professed great love for his harp and satisfaction with it, in fact it seemed to Owen that he treated it very carelessly, even roughly, thumping and thwacking it, shaking and almost tearing it apart; when, due to his clumsy handling, it gave out a particularly dissonant sound he flew into a positive passion and several times looked to be on the point of hurling it down the well, only just managing to restrain himself at the last moment.

Anxious to view the harp at closer quarters, Owen resolved to try and find some means of coming nearer to the player. Plainly it was necessary to be careful; if, as appeared probable from his song, Abipaal had already flung one harp away, there was too much danger of his repeating the deed to take any liberties with him.

There were several openings in the sloping wall behind Owen; he chose the one nearest him and followed the winding passage into which it led, guided by the strains of Abipaal's curious music which were audible even here. Where the passage divided he took the more downward course, and after some five minutes of groping in the dark, he emerged on to a kind of natural terrace which encircled the great vertical shaft at the level of the lower spur. Abipaal's song could be heard much more clearly here, though, on account of the windings of the passage Owen had followed, he was almost directly opposite, on the far side of the well.

Owen, although he took care to keep himself concealed in shadow, now had a fairly good view of this strange little character, for the greenish light filtered down the well from above and illuminated the spur of rock on which he stood.

He was extremely short, not much over three foot six; his garments, which were indescribably tattered and disorderly, appeared to be made of some grey fur; from under his grey fur cap a mass of wild, dark, unkempt locks protruded; his horny feet were bare and his face, gnarled and withered as an old elm-root, suggested that he must be a great age, probably well over eighty.

The harp he held contrasted strangely with his appearance, for it was fully strung, brilliant gold, and shining; it might have just left the maker's hands. Yet its appearance was surely familiar? Owen had dusted the harp of Teirtu so many times in the Pennygaff Museum that he felt almost certain he was not mistaken; there, in the utmost peril, as it seemed, of being dashed to destruction at any moment by its impatient player, was the lost treasure.

"He ought to be able to play the harp better at his age," Owen thought, as a particularly discordant and jangling clump of notes came staggering through the air and Abipaal, in a perfect frenzy of frustration, stamped his foot furiously on the rock, and then hopped up and down in agony. His position, capering about on the very edge of the abyss, seemed extraordinary perilous; several times Owen held his breath in terror as he seemed bound to fall, but it was plain that he must be amazingly sure-footed and muscular, for although he frequently leaned right over the edge, he always drew back without the slightest trouble, and continued singing and playing with unabated energy. Part of his difficulty in playing, Owen realized, came from the unusual shortness of his arms and the fact that the harp, though not a large one, was far too big for him; his left arm could not reach all the way across the strings unless he turned the instrument sideways on and then, of course, his right hand could hardly reach the strings at all.

And the harp? Creeping closer still, Owen felt his hope grow to a certainty; he recognized the leaves and fruit ornamenting the frame, and the strange, beautiful, upward-staring face carved at the tip of the bow. Little Abipaal had certainly made a magnificent success of cleaning and repairing the formerly stringless, dirty, dilapidated instrument; it seemed sad that his skill as a player lagged so far behind.

Abipaal had launched into a new chant:

"Sing flat, not sharp,
You disobedient harp,
Why can't you do as are told,
You miserable bit of gold?"

Twang went the strings as he struck them a vicious blow, screeching with rage at the resulting jangle.

"Poop me!" whispered a voice from somewhere to Owen's left. "What a rumpus the little cove do make—ain't he wreakful, eh Bilk?"

"Regular rug-headed little abram," agreed another voice. "Right tricksy we'll need to be to get the bandore away from him, so frampold as he is; if we aren't right sprag he'll toss it down old Bogey-boo's hole afore we can get it off him."

Owen nearly fainted with astonishment and dismay at the sound of these two voices, which he had thought silenced for ever. Prigman and Bilk! But how in the world did they come to be here in the cave, how had they escaped from an awful death in the buried cottage?

"Warn't it a bale o' luck, though, chancing on the little cullion down in these here vaultages, eh, Bilk? Who'd a reckoned, when that there doddering hillside came down on the roof, that the floor'ud give way and we'd fall through on our pantofles like this, live and skipping, *and* find the little queer-bird as must have prigged our bandore? Look how he's cleaned it up, too, and new catlings, neat as ninepence, naffy as new! I daresay Old Stigmatical will fork over twice the lour for it now."

"You still reckon on handing it over, then?"

"Burn my galleyslops, yes! I've no fancy to pass the rest of my days without any fambles or stamps! Ask me, his lordship is own brother to Horny himself—no matter where we huggered he'd search us out in the end. I reckon trying to play him false was a mug's game."

"It was *your* notion," Bilk said sourly.

"Oh, quit brabbling. All we need to do now is to get the tinkleplunk away from little Caliban there, and we're up to our gorges in velvet. Now: you slide round thataway and then let out a shout to startle him, I'll stand yonder to cut him off when he scampers. Agreed?"

"Ay, let's get at him."

"Don't you dare!" Owen bawled, as loud as he could. "You leave him alone! Keep your hands off that harp!"

He could not endure the thought of Bilk and Prigman getting possession of the harp for the second time; rather than that, it would be far better for Abipaal to keep it. At least he had put it to rights and appeared to love it in his peppery way.

A silence of utter astonishment followed Owen's shout. Then Bilk muttered,

"Trine me, it's the young bumble-cock! How in mandrake's name did *he* get here?"

"Never mind him!" said Prigman urgently. "Get after t'other one. *Quick*, you monument!"

For Abipaal, alarmed by the voices, had not paused an instant but, with one agile goat-like bound, had quitted his pinnacle of rock and vanished into a cranny behind him. Prigman, who was nearest, gave chase, Bilk followed Prigman, and Owen brought up the rear at top speed, running blind in the dark, feeling his way along the rock walls with his hands.

It was a frantic, headlong scramble. Owen was not even sure whether Abipaal had not already given his pursuers the slip and gone off into some undetectable crevice; but if not, Owen was determined to help fight off the thieves at whatever cost.

Luckily the way they were going lay all downhill. Owen, having passed two hours in a tree and spent much of the day helping to carry the Prince of Wales, was already somewhat fatigued; had he been obliged to run uphill he would soon have fallen behind. As it was, being young and light on his feet, he was able to keep up tolerably well in the rear of the heavy, blundering Bilk and the stout, short-legged Prigman. How far Abipaal was ahead of them, he could not tell, nor where they were going; the passage they had taken seemed to lead deeper and deeper into the heart of the mountain. Little by little, however, it widened; at last they emerged on to a sort of platform, or quayside, overlooking an underground river. Arabis would have recognized the spot. A pale glimmer of light from far ahead illuminated the scene.

"Gone to ground," said Bilk with an oath. "The little ferret's diddled us."

"No he hasn't, drumblehead. He's taken to water. Don't you see where we are? This here's the Malyn river—goes all the way to Port Malyn, and the hot pipes carrying steam to the castle lays at the bottom of it. I know, acos when I was a kitchen boy at the castle I used to carry their peck to the coves what was a-laying of the pipes."

"And so?" growled Bilk. "How does that advantage us?"

"Why, you nodcock? Our little twangler's taken boat downstream; all we need do is follow him and he'll navigate himself right into the fox's mouth, right to Old Stigmatical's castle. How's that for a gaudy fine shift? We've got him in lipsbury pinfold if we do but follow."

"How about the young whipster? We don't want him on our tail."

"Oh, we lost him a dozen turns back; he'll not fret us again. Come on—there's another boat."

"*That* walnut shell? I'm not trusting my quarrams in *that*."

"Oh, don't be so poor-stomached!"

Bilk, however, insisted that it would be quicker to run along the bank; accordingly they set off into the dark. Owen who had only waited in the shadows until they were out of earshot, immediately leapt into the little skiff that Bilk had mistrusted, undid the mooring rope, and launched off downstream in pursuit.

The boat, which appeared to be made of leather with the fur left on, was very light and rocked wildly until

Owen, who at a young age had been taught seamanship by his father, discovered the knack of kneeling motionless amidships and helping the fragile craft downstream with two triangular wooden flaps evidently intended as paddles.

Gliding along, not far behind, in the shadow of the rock bank, Owen was able to overhear a few snatches of Bilk and Prigman's conversation.

"When we've—prigged the bandore—off the little whiskered cove—" puffed Prigman, pounding along the towpath, "there's a way up into the castle from that hall where the central-heating pipes rises out o' the river. Up a lot o' steps it goes, through the cellars where his worship keeps his barrels o' bouse, and the queer-kens where he stows the prisoners."

"I'll lay you used to find your way into the cellars, if not the dungeons," grunted Bilk, toiling beside him.

"Ah, and I did! I was always a rare hand as a wrester even when I was a boy—could pick my way through any locked-up jigger in the land with a blade of grass and a goose-feather and a drop of oil."

"That's handy, then," panted Bilk. "Us can go up the back way with the bandore when we've slit little Caliban's weasand."

"No call for that," said Prigman, who seemed to have curious objections to out-and-out murder. "Us can tie him and leave him to cool in one o' they vaults where the tide will come in and cover him."

"I say slit his weasand. Look what happened with t'other one. He got away and spoilt our lay. Trouble he may be to us yet, rot him!"

"His lordship might want to see this one—to make sure we're telling a true tale."

"He can see him just as well with a slit weasand."

"Carry him up all those stairs? Not on your Oliphant!"

They were still arguing this point when Owen realized that their voices were drawing farther and farther ahead; peering down to discover the reason for this he saw that he was kneeling in warm water; evidently his boat had struck and holed on some sharp underwater rock, and was slowing down. There were no bales; he was obliged to beach the boat, empty it, and launch off again. It filled once more, this time much faster, there was nothing for it but to take to land. His rest afloat had done him good and he set off with renewed energy, but he had lost a good deal of time and the thieves were now out of sight in the long tunnel which followed the underground course of the Malyn river.

Owen ran on desperately. When at last he suddenly burst into a vast empty cavern, and saw the central-heating pipes climbing the opposite wall like huge silver snakes, Bilk and Prigman had vanished.

Collecting himself, Owen looked around and saw that there were numerous openings leading out of the big cave. His only course was to try each in turn.

He investigated several; some led to smaller, empty caves; one passage, after much turning and winding, led him out on to the snowy hillsides above Port Malyn. Behind him, Malyn Castle frowned on its crag; snow continued to fall and in the east a wild red dawn was breaking.

Should he go up to the castle at once and demand to see the Marquess? No, he thought; while he wasted time, those two scoundrels were probably engaged on murdering poor Abipaal, who had never done anything worse than pick up an apparently discarded harp in a cave on Fig-hat Ben and put it to rights.

Owen turned back resolutely into the tunnel; this time, when he entered the main hall, he thought that he could hear a faint cry coming from an entrance he had not yet tried. Summoning the last of his energy he ran to it and made his way down a steep narrow descent. At the foot of this slope he tumbled, before he could stop himself, over an eight foot drop into a small, sandy cave, lit faintly by a slit high in the wall above him. The sea's roar was plainly to be heard; evidently the slit gave on to the beach. In fact, as he pulled himself to his feet on the damp floor, a spray of icy salt water showered in through the hole; it was clear that this must be the cave mentioned by Prigman which filled when the tide was high.

Owen heard the faint sound again, behind him; he spun round and distinguished a small, trussed figure lying in the gloom. But the Harp of Teirtu was gone.

"Eh, dear, sir!" exclaimed Owen in distress. "Did those brutes leave you like that? Only a minute, and I will get you undone."

It took a bit longer than that, for Owen had lent his knife to Hwfa, when the hare needed skinning, and had never had it back. At length, however, he had the last of Bilk's savagely tied knots undone; the reward he received was that Abipaal flew at him like a fury, biting, kicking, and clawing.

"Hey!" protested Owen, fighting to protect his eyes and spectacles from this uncalled-for attack. "Give over, leave me alone, stop it, stop it! *I* haven't taken the harp! Oh, do stop, for goodness' sake, otherwise we shall never catch up with that pair of scoundrels."

Abipaal either did not understand, or did not choose to; he continued to bite and kick. How long the struggle would have lasted, as Owen was concerned not to hurt his furious little attacker, there was no knowing; but a mass of water suddenly slopped through the opening and soaked them both. When they rose, gasping, Owen realized that the water in the cave was already over his knees and nearly came to Abipaal's chin.

"This is stupid!" Owen exclaimed. "No use staying here to be drowned. Up you go, sir!" And with a final effort he picked up the scratching, struggling Abipaal (who weighed no more than a truss of straw) and thrust him on to the rock shelf which sloped up to the entrance.

Abipaal immediately turned and hissed at him like an angry goose.

"Now, sir, if you will be so kind as to give me a bit of a hand—'

But Abipaal, without the slightest indication of having any such intention, turned and scurried up the slope, leaving Owen submerged up to his chest in seawater, gaping after him.

13

The captives in Lord Malyn's dungeons were not given any supper. Nor, for that matter, did they receive tea, dinner, or breakfast. But about an hour after the time when breakfast ought to have been served, Garble made a round of inspection, peering through the grilles in the dungeon doors.

He was disconcerted, on looking into the cell occupied by Arabis and Brother Ianto, to find them both still alive and well.

"Odd that is," he muttered. "What has come over Gog and Magog? His lordship will not be best pleased."

"Mr. Garble!" Arabis called indignantly. "You must get those tiger-snakes out of here! Most unsuitable accommodation for them, it is, and they are not at all well, with them. No proper medicine I have for them, either. Very poorly indeed, one of them looks, and the other one is lying on her back!"

"Now that is spoken like a girl of sense and feeling,"

Mr. Hughes remarked approvingly from his cell. "Cruelty to animals is most abhorrent, though, to be sure, it is only what one would expect from Lord Malyn, and all of a piece with his repulsive ways!"

Garble, however, was extremely reluctant to enter the cell and inspect the tiger-snakes at close quarters; only the repeated demands of Arabis and the thought of how angry the Marquess would be, should he return to find his pets no more, finally persuaded him. Slowly and unwillingly he detached the bunch of keys from his belt and moved towards the door.

At this moment, however, another door, the one leading from the cellars below into the prison lobby, burst open, and two persons erupted violently through, singing at the tops of their voices:

"The bandore boy to the wars has gone,
In the dews-a-vill you'll find him!
With his fol-de-rol and his om-tiddle-pom
And his—*hiccup*—slung behind him."

"Hey-o, Garboil, me old co," roared Prigman. "What are you doing, a-boggling away down here like a moldwarp? Lead us to his ludship, man, we've summat for him as he'll fair pop his glaziers at sight of!"

"Aye, sprag's the word, my bawcock," agreed Bilk. "We doesn't want to keep old Stigmatical a-waiting, does we? Hiccup knows, we had enough trouble ferreting out the way here, along those tortive, cranksome pash—hic, pardon me—passages of yourn down below."

It seemed plain, from the two men's high spirits and the

strong atmosphere of Canary wine surrounding them, that a major part of their route had lain through Lord Malyn's cellars.

"His lordship is away from home at present," Garble said coldly. "Anything that you have for him you can hand over to me." Then his eyes widened as, through the gloom, he caught the sparkle of the harp, which Prigman proceeded to untie from his back. But he preserved a calm demeanour and merely added,

"Ah, you have done the job properly at last, I see. Let me have it, then. Make haste, pray."

"Ho no, Garboil, me old hodge-pudding," Bilk said. "Not afore we sees the colour of his ludship's mint-sauce."

"Do not be impertinent. Hand over the instrument," Garble said sharply, selecting a key and moving, in an unobtrusive way, towards the door of an empty cell.

But Prigman, instead of passing over the harp, began to pluck in a random manner at the strings bawling out,

"Hey-diddle-diddle, my merry men,
Let's all go to the bousing-ken!"

while Bilk, mumbling, "Ah, you're a lovely old friend, a lovely old cough-drop, Garboil, me old gumboil," lurched forward and enveloped Garble in a most unwelcome embrace, from which he tried in vain to extricate himself.

Meanwhile the prisoners in the cells, who had listened with the utmost interest in this exchange, were not silent.

"Why," Arabis cried out when she first heard the voices of Prigman and Bilk, "those are the two thieves who stole the harp from your museum, Mr. Hughes! And I believe they have it on them now."

"Ah, the scoundrels," muttered Mr. Hughes, listening. "But where, then, is Owen?"

"Does dim dwywaith, without a shadow of doubt that is the Harp of Teirtu," sighed Brother Ianto, listening to the horrid jangle of notes produced by Prigman's inexpert hands. "Golden sound she do have, even when played by such a rheibiwr!"

"Well, well, well?" cried the Seljuk somewhat snappishly, for he had passed a miserable night in the damp little cell, kept awake by the ear-splitting snores of Mr. Hughes. "If that obnoxious peer has now procured the harp he sought, perhaps we may all be allowed to decamp, absquatulate, show a clean pair of heels. Open the door, if you please! I demand to be put in touch with the Rummi consul!"

"Mr. Garble, do something about those tiger-snakes you must!" Arabis exclaimed strongly. "Indeed I will not be surprised if one of them is at its last gasp; should it be here any longer I will not answer for the consequences!—Queer, isn't it," she added reflectively to Brother Ianto, "that the smell of wintergreen disagreed with them so, special since it did you so much good!"

Garble, harassed by all those different demands, was in a quandary, wondering how he could get the harp away from the two thieves and clap them in a cell, as instructed by Lord Malyn. He felt badly in need of assistance, but both turnkeys were upstairs having their dinner. Then it occurred to him that if the tiger-snakes were really in such a poor way, he might use them to frighten Bilk and Prigman without running much risk himself.

"Wait, then, you!" he said, at last disentangling himself from Bilk's Canary-scented hug. "I do not suppose you imagine Lord Malyn keeps his cash in the dungeons? You will have to accompany me upstairs when I have seen to the prisoners."

"Oh, very well, tol-lol," replied Prigman. He had just discovered how to play the first three notes of Three Blind Mice on the Harp of Teirtu, so he burst into song again,

"They all ran after the harman-beck
Who cut off their tails with a famble-sneck—'

"Stop making that atrocious noise!" snapped Garble. He stepped up to Brother Ianto's cell and peered through the grille again, vainly trying to see the snakes, which were just inside the door. Then he called, "I am coming in to inspect the reptiles. Stand well away from the entrance. I have a blunderbuss with me and shall not hesitate to shoot." This was quite untrue, but he hoped that if, cowed by the threat, Arabis and Brother Ianto stood well back, he would have time to whip in, grab the ailing snakes, and out again, before they could either hinder him or try to escape.

As his key rattled in the lock, Arabis, standing by the narrow little window, received one of the greatest shocks of her life: Owen's face appeared outside, with Hawc hovering just beyond him. He laid a finger on his lips and Arabis remained silent, though her mouth and eyes were wide open with amazement. Owen pulled himself up, balanced a moment with his hands on the sill, then pushed a knee over and slipped neatly inside, panting a little. "Would you mind holding my glasses a moment, sir?" he whispered to Brother Ianto, who was chuckling quietly to himself. Hawc, who had flown in after Owen, took frightful exception to the tiger-snakes and began hissing and heckling at them in a manner which they, poor things, were too low-spirited to resent.

"The *harp*!" breathed Arabis. "Bilk and Prigman have it just out there—" She pointed to the door. Owen nodded, and stole over to stand flattened against the wall—not that he needed to be all that quiet, for Prigman was now carolling,

"Hey diddle diddle, up on the pillion,
Who's the old mort in the scarlet mandilion?"

while Bilk did a kind of clumping step-dance all round him.

Garble turned the key, opened the door, and stepped briskly inside; as he did so, and while his attention, after a brief glance at the two captives, was fixed on the snakes, Owen, like a shadow, slipped through the doorway behind him, removing the key from the lock as he passed.

Owen's intention had been to take Bilk and Prigman by surprise, snatch the harp, run back into the cell, and lock the door. But this plan was thrown into confusion by the sudden and unexpected arrival of Abipaal, who shot in through the cell window like something fired from a catapult, dashed past the astounded Garble through the cell door, flung himself at Prigman, kicking, biting, and scratching his face, grabbed the harp, and was away through the open cellar door before either of the two thieves had the presence of mind to stop him.

"Dang me!" gasped Prigman, rubbing his half-blinded eyes. "The little Turk! He's fair clappered me! After him, Bilk—stir your strossers, man!"

But Owen had tackled Bilk from behind, tripping and throwing him to the ground, effectively preventing him from pursuing Abipaal until the fiery little man was well away with the harp.

"What in Beelzebub's name is going on here?" exclaimed Garble, rushing back out of the cell and searching in vain for his keys, which Owen had pocketed. He began trying to drag apart the struggling Owen and Bilk.

"Never mind *them*, fool! The harp!" gasped Prigman, at last getting his eyes open and staggering after Abipaal. Bilk rolled away from Owen's grasp and followed; Garble hesitated a moment, trying to decide which would anger Lord Malyn more, to lose his prisoners or the harp which had seemed so nearly secured; he decided on the harp, and set off after Bilk.

Arabis and Brother Ianto, finding no one there to stop them, came warily from their cell, stepping over the dozy tiger-snakes.

"Thank goodness you are safe! Yehimelek told me you were here and Hawc led me to the right cell," Owen said, giving Arabis a quick hug. "Here are the keys! Let out the others, I can't wait; I must go after that dratted little Abipaal or they'll make mincemeat of him. I had no notion he was behind me! Follow down—oh, thank you, Brother Ianto!"

He received his glasses back and disappeared at top speed.

"Well! There is a thing!" said Arabis. "Who would have expected it?"

"Oh, not a bit surprised, I am!" Brother Ianto said cheerfully. "Always thought there was more in that boy than he knew himself. Eh well; best to get out of here, maybe, before anybody upstairs notices what is going on."

He went methodically round the cell doors, unlocking them all; the prisoners were only too glad to make off down through the cellars without waiting for explanations. All except for old Mr. Hughes.

"What in the name of goodness is going on here?" that gentleman demanded. "Where is the harp *now*? What have those two rascals done with it? Was not that my grandson's voice I heard? Did I not say that he was somehow involved in this murky business?"

"Oh, go and eat flummery!" snapped Arabis, at the end of her patience. Then she collected herself and added politely, "Your grandson, Mr. Hughes, have just rescued us all by climbing a six-hundred-foot cliff, and if you have sense you will not be standing here chewing the rag, but will bustle off out from by here before any more trouble will arrive, is it?"

"Of a certainty, yes," agreed the Seljuk—Arabis had to suppress a gasp of horrified amusement at the sight of his devastated moustaches—"Let us cut our stick, walk our chalks, slip our cable, before that detestable nobleman returns hither."

Without more delay they set off after Owen, though Arabis was conscience-stricken about leaving the tiger-snakes.

"Since it was my oil of wintergreen that upset the poor things," she said. "But surely to goodness somebody will come down before long. There must be *someone* in that great castleful of folks can spare time to care for such a fine pair of snakes."

Mr. Hughes still wanted his explanation.

"You say my *grandson* rescued us?" he demanded, panting, as they ran down endless flights of stairs. "So who has the harp? Where is it now?"

"I am thinking that queer little fellow who climbed in after Owen will have made off with it," Arabis said. "Abipaal, Owen called him." Then she suddenly stood still, put her hands to her head, and exclaimed, "*Abipaal!* Where was the sense with me? He will be the one who stole the harp from where Bilk and Prigman left it! And then somehow the thieves will have got it off him, and now he has snatched it back, good luck to him!"

This was meaningless to Mr. Hughes, but the Seljuk pricked up his ears.

"Abipaal? Who is this person, my dear young friend, companion, fellow-fugitive?"

As he asked, the little party came down the last flight of steps and through an open door into the great cave where the central-heating pipes rose from the Malyn river. But the hall was not empty now. Regardless of the fact that day was now well advanced, about a score of the Children of the Pit were grouped there in a ring. They all clutched golden weapons that would have made Lord Malyn wild with envy; they were being given orders by Yehimelek, who, splendidly dressed in black and gold, looked thin and pale but every inch a Hereditary Foreman.

"Half of you at top speed to the caves of Fig-hat Ben, in defence of our brother Abipaal," he was saying. "Although he has involved himself in this trouble because of his foolish craving for a harp, yet he is our brother and we must assist him if it is within our power. The rest of you, whom I shall command myself, must hasten at once to the help of our healer and deliverer the Lady Arabis, whose voice, I am told by our reliable scouts Shishak and Ipshemi, has been heard coming in cries of distress from the Wicked Lord's dungeons. No wonder she did not return to us at first light, as promised! It may be that the valiant young man, Owen, who saved our brother Abipaal from drowning, has been able to release her, but until we see her safe with our own eyes, it is our duty to go to her support. Never shall it be said that the tribe of—'

"Yehimelek!" cried Arabis, who had gathered the gist of this. "It is all right! I am safe! Go back, go back quickly to your caves before any of Lord Malyn's people come through here and find you!"

At the sight of Arabis the little Pit People raised a shout which, though joyful, was somewhat shaky and weak, as many of them were still hardly more than convalescent from their illness. They began to gather round her, bowing, smiling, and patting her hands.

"Lady," said Yehimelek gravely, "from the bottom of my heart I rejoice that you are safe. I, Tabut Elulaois Yehimelek, Hereditary Foreman and leader of the Children of the Pit—'

"Yehimelek!" cried the Seljuk.

Throughout this exchange he had stood silent in wonder, gazing at the gallant little group shakily flourishing their gold weapons. Two great tears had gathered in his large brown eyes and rolled unnoticed down past his lopped-off moustaches. Now he could restrain himself no longer. He stepped forward.

"Yehimelek!" he cried again in his own tongue. "Brave leader of your exiled tribe, I salute you! Honour be yours, and may your name be written for ever in the annals of our people. Do you know who I am? I am your Seljuk, come to carry you to glory and joy in your long-lost homeland, the Kingdom of Rum!"

At first Yehimelek and his people made no reply. Silent, amazed, and doubtful, they gaped at the Seljuk, while the sense of his words sank in. One reason for their hesitation was the fact that his language, after so many generations apart, was a bit different from theirs. The Seljuk, eager and anxious, gazed back at them, waiting for their reaction.

Slowly it came. Wondering murmurs began to rise, as one and then another worked out the meaning of what they had heard.

"The Seljuk!"

"He says he is our Seljuk!"

"At last he has come!"

"He will carry us home to Rum!"

With a broken cry, Yehimelek tottered forward and fell on his knees before the Seljuk.

"Lord, forgive me! I am an old man and my wits are slow! Oh, what have I ever done, unworthy, that I should have lived to see this day? Happy, happy Yehimelek! I shall tread the streets of Sa'ir and Taidon, I shall see the green mountains of Sur! Lord, we are indeed your people. Never, never did we doubt that one day you would come for us."

Greatly moved, the Seljuk raised him up and embraced him.

Arabis, who had been crying unashamedly while she watched the reunion of the Pit People with their rightful lord, now glanced back the way they had come.

"There's happy I am also, to see this day," she said, blowing her nose, "but I am thinking we had best all clear out of here, and pretty fast too. Sounds up above, I believe I can hear."

She ran back to the door from which they had just emerged, tried all Garble's keys, found one that fitted, and locked it.

"Indeed, lady, you are right," said Yehimelek. And he said to the Seljuk, "Lord, I am proud to offer you and your friends the hospitality of our poverty-stricken quarters."

"There's kind you are!" said Arabis warmly. "But easy in *my* mind I shall not be until I know what has become of Abipaal and Owen and the Harp of Teirtu. No offence, but I think I shall just be following on in the direction of Nant Agerddau."

Since in fact Yehimelek, the Seljuk, old Mr. Hughes, and Brother Ianto were all equally anxious to learn what was going on, they agreed to set forward without further delay, and Yehimelek provided camels for the party. The rest of the Pit People tottered thankfully back to their beds.

During all the preceding scene Mr. Hughes had maintained a silence of astonishment. Still silent, he mounted on the diminutive black camel allotted to him, and urged it into a rapid shamble behind that of Brother Ianto.

"Are you all right, sir, with you?" Arabis asked him solicitously.

"Yes, yes, child!" he replied in his usual somewhat testy manner. "I have bestridden plenty of camels before this, I assure you, when we were taking on water at the port of Alexandria. You need not concern yourself about me."

Arabis, therefore, went ahead to listen to the Seljuk, who, as he rode along, was endeavouring to give his retrieved subject a brief account of what had been happening in the Kingdom of Rum during the past two thousand years.

"Somewhat changed you may find it, I fear," he admitted. "But still, a royal welcome we shall give you, and a special valley is already set aside for you, full of fruit trees, peach and fig and apricot, where your people can rest and grow strong in the sun."

Mr. Hughes looked after Arabis. "That is a most unusual young gal," he remarked to Brother Ianto. "Seems uncommonly well-informed and full of sense on a number of subjects. Must confess I did her an injustice when young Owen brought her and her father to the museum last week; thought they were after the Harp of Teirtu."

Brother Ianto, as was often his wont, chuckled quietly but made no answer.

"Well, you have to be careful with that gypsyish sort of customer," Mr. Hughes added rather defensively. "Gracious knows what sort of man her father is."

"Not the sort of man to take what does not belong to him, I assure you," Brother Ianto said. "Tom is a poet.

Sooner write a good poem than wear the crown of England he would."

"Tsk, tsk! Head-in-the-clouds sort of customer! All very fine, no doubt, but somebody ought to look out for the gal—see she gets a decent eddication," muttered Mr. Hughes disapprovingly.

Arabis, meanwhile, was full of curiosity to hear about Owen's encounter with the Children of the Pit. Yehimelek explained that Tennes and Strato, who were just setting out to go in search of Abipaal at Nant Agerddau, had heard voices coming from the underwater cave, and had seen Abipaal emerge from it, wet and gasping. From his confused, and not at all grateful, account, they deduced that someone had saved him who was still in there; they had pulled out Owen, now in a very exhausted condition, and taken him to Yehimelek. Owen had immediately recognized the beribboned crwth and asked where Arabis was; the fact that he knew her had reassured Yehimelek. Owen was dried off and given seaweed broth; what he really needed was sleep but there had been no time for that; Shishak and Ipshemi arrived in great alarm, crying out that while on watch duty in the upper caves they had heard the voice of Arabis coming from Lord Malyn's dungeons. Since the Pit People had taken care that no tunnel directly connected their abode with the dungeons, Owen had decided that his quickest way to go to the rescue would be to climb up the cliff face; he had been followed by Abipaal, intent on recovering his cherished harp.

"Fancy his having had it all the time!" Arabis said. "Now he has taken such a liking to the harp, I am wondering how we can persuade him to give it up."

"Worry about those three scoundrels of Lord Malyn's first, is it?" Brother Ianto suggested. "Not to mention Lord Malyn himself."

"Oh, my dada will have come up with the Prince of Wales by this time," Arabis said confidently. "And sure it is, old Prince Deio will be able to deal with that pack of adynod!"

14

Tom Dando, silent, absent, and broody from the poem that was growing inside him, and Tom Dando with the weight of that poem safely transferred to paper were two very different people. Now that he had slept and woken again and knew that his poem was still just as good as he had thought it when he wrote down the last line, he would not have changed places with the Tsar of all the Russias.

"Stir your shaggy stumps, Galahad, my little one!" he shouted joyfully, when he had clipped all the pages of his poem together with mountain-ash clothespegs, and made sure that Ribaddi was securely tucked into one of the bunks. "Terrible old night it is, indeed, but at least the wind is behind us; see if you can't go a bit faster than that wind, eh, my old ceffyl?"

Galahad, fresh from a day's rest, required no urging; striking sparks from stones with his great hairy hoofs he thundered along, powerful as the locomotive engine *Puff-*

ing Billy, and a great deal faster. His mane streamed behind like cirrus cloud, he neighed and snorted and blew out long jets of steam, while the wagon swayed, rattling, from side to side; luckily Ribaddi had fallen into a deep sleep or he might have been alarmed at this helter-skelter method of covering the ground. Tom Dando, seated on the box with an old blanket flung round him, sang at the top of his powerful tenor voice every song and hymn he could remember; the "March of the Men of Harlech," "Cwm Rhondda," "Hyfrydol," and "All Through the Night"; when his memory gave out he started over again, or set words from his poem to tunes of his own invention, while Galahad whinnied in response and galloped even faster. And all the time the wind howled furiously behind them and ribbons of snow flew after them, but the way ahead was still clear enough; they were just keeping abreast of the blizzard.

"Not so nice for anybody travelling behind us, though, I am thinking," said Tom cheerfully, and he sang,

"The cold wind doth blow, and we have got snow,
And what will the robin do now, poor thing?
He'll sit in the cwpwrdd until he's discovered,
And tie up his trousers with string, poor thing!"

"Careful with the feet, Galahad, my little gafr, and keep a bit of a lookout for the old snowdrifts, just the same, is it?"

Now that Tom was guiding Galahad they went by the most direct route, and so covered the distance to Nant Agerddau in less than one-third of the time it had taken them in the opposite direction; about an hour before dawn they had reached the Boar's Head Inn and Tom was banging on its shutters and demanding to know if the Prince of Wales was staying in the town.

"Dear, dear! What a time to come rousing honest folk!" said Mr. Davy Thomas, crossly opening up. "Gracious to goodness, is it you, then, Mr. Dando, and what can I be doing for you?"

"Is Prince Deio under your roof, friend, or if not, can you tell me where I can be laying my hands on him? Urgent it is to have speech with him, see!"

"Staying here he *was*," said Mr. Thomas fretfully, "but delirious from a wound, and most peculiar behaviour with it! Asked for a bowl of picws with a dram of wine in it about midnight, and then nothing would serve but he must go out, he and that gaggle of young rapscallions from Pennygaff, to look for one of them that was lost. Lame as a three-legged chair, he was, with his wound, and the boys obliged to carry him on two benches, and Dr. Jenkins most put out. "No responsibility do I take if your highness will be having your death by this," he says. "O go dive in one of your own possets, man," says the prince and off he goes, though dear knows you'd think he'd not miss one boy out of the lot that's been eating me out of house and home!"

"Lost boy?" said Tom. "Fancy that! Where would he be lost, then, and why hunt for him at such an hour of night?"

"Off to the Devil's Leap cave they were going, but what I say is, no sense in looking for young scamps that wish to cheat the town of its money by sneaking in at night without paying their sixpence; leave them find their own way out and a lesson in honest behaviour, I hope!"

"Devil's Leap cave? Much obliged to you, Mr. Thomas

my little one, and I will just be stepping along that way, then."

"O, no trouble," said Mr. Thomas, for poets bring good custom to inns and one must be civil to them. Then, as it was no use going back to bed, he stomped indoors to scrub the tankards. Tom drove on through the town, and straight into the Devil's Leap ante-cave, which he found lit by dozens of candles but empty. Dismounting—for the next cave was lower and would not accommodate the wagon—he rubbed Galahad dry and gave him his blanket and nosebag; glanced inside to make sure Ribaddi was asleep and the precious poem safe; then proceeded on foot to the inner cave, where he could hear somebody whistling.

When Tom reached the Devil's Leap cave itself, and looked down into its great bowl, he perceived a solitary man lying on a sort of couch composed of two benches, near the edge of the central well. From the benches, and the fact that his leg was bandaged, Tom guessed this person to be the Prince of Wales, so he made his way down until he was close enough to bid him a civil good morning.

"And a gude morn tae ye too, sir, whoe'er ye be," the prince replied, ceasing to whistle. "Have ye by any chance obsairved a wheen laddies roaming ayont this ill-faured cavern?"

Tom regretted that he had not, but added, "Glad I will be to go in search of them if your worship wishes?"

"Oh, no, no," replied the prince peevishly, " 'tis best they should gae on sairching for the lad that's lost, but 'tis unco" wearifu" work waiting here for ane or tither to turn up, sin" I can only stoit aboot sae dot-and-gae-one. I suppose ye would not hae the time to sit down and have a crack wi" me?"

Nothing could have suited Tom's purpose better. He sat down on the rock and, without pausing a moment, launched into the whole tale of the Harp of Teirtu, from its earliest origins up to the present day. Some of this tale, of course, Prince David had heard before from Owen, but much of it was new to him, and such was Tom's skill as a narrator, that he listened to the whole in silent amazement, only occasionally murmuring, "Losh!" or "Weel, who'd ha" thocht it?"

"So you see, your highness," Tom ended, "there is a proper scoundrel that Marquess of Malyn, and causing a lot of trouble and inconvenience to many innocent persons."

"Och, maircy, yes, the fause loon!" exclaimed Prince David. "I'm fashed to think I ever agreed to veesit the wretch, but hoo was I tae ken he was sic a black-hairted freebooter? But he and his joes shall be clappit in prison as soon as ever the morn's morn has dawnit, on the word of Davie Jamie Charlie Neddie Geordie Harry Dick Tudor-Stuart! I'll order the procurator-fiscal tae mak" the arrest afore breakfast. Maybe ye'd wish tae gang back wi" yon offeecial tae Castle Malyn directly?"

"I am thinking that might be no bad notion," Tom agreed. "But not too good the old weather just now, see? Go and have a look I will."

He came back shaking his head.

"Blowing harder than Gabriel's trumpet, it is, and enough snow already down to bury a whale, and as much more to follow! No one will get back to Caer Malyn yet awhile, I am thinking."

"Hout-tout, there's a peety," said the prince. "I hope your lassie wisna come to harm at the hands o' yon villain in the meantime."

"O, as to that," said Tom Dando comfortably, "fine sense my daughter Arabis has, and I am thinking she can take care of herself."

"Then," said the prince, "sit ye doon again, man, and mak" yerself comfortable. Tell me mair anent yon Harp o' Teirtu. Gin it disna belong tae Lord Malyn (may the deil fly awa" wi" him) nor to yon Brither Ianto, i" maircy's name, who maun be the richt owner?"

"Indeed," said Tom Dando modestly, "I am thinking that I am."

'Dear sakes ava!" cried the prince, thoroughly startled. "Say ye so? Expound yon riddle, man?"

"Simple, it is," Tom Dando said. "Miss Tegwyn Jones, to whom the monks returned the harp in exchange for a couple of tons of chilblain liniment, was the direct descendant of Teirtu, and she was my grandmother. Mrs. Davy Dando, she became. Fine old lady she was, when I knew her, and could cure a sheep of the scrapes quick as kiss your hand."

"Ech, oich!" said the prince. "But if the harp was yours all along, man, wae's me, why did ye no" lay claim to it?"

"Better things I had to do," Tom Dando said, "than join in a lot of clack over an old harp, and me with my poem to write."

"Poem? Are ye e'en a poet? Fine I'd like to hear some of your verses, for I love a gude poem a'most as much as a gude hunt!" exclaimed Prince David, his eyes lighting up with enthusiasm.

Tom needed no further encouragement; he began reciting "The King at Caerleon," which Prince David heard with extreme delight.

"Man!" he cried, when Tom paused for breath. "Yon are the noblest lines I hae heard this twel" month and more!"

"Indeed, I am thinking so too," agreed Tom. "If I do never pen another line, there is something the world will have to remember Tom Dando by."

From talking poetry the two men presently moved on to swapping songs, and then it was not long before they were singing, or rather shouting duets, for the prince had a baritone as powerful as Tom's tenor, and the resonance of the cave made it irresistible to sing as loud as they possibly could. A considerable amount of time passed in this manner.

They had just worked their way right through "Chevy Chase" when Tom Dando observed with some surprise that they were not alone. The prince, who sang with eyes tight shut, had not noticed, so Tom respectfully plucked his velvet sleeve to acquaint him of the fact that a small, fur-capped, grey-bearded, untidily dressed stranger was perched near them on the lip of rock, listening to their song with an expression of the most rapt and lively pleasure.

"O, excuse me, your highness," Tom said, "but would this be the person that your highness's people are searching for by here?"

Prince David opened his eyes.

"Losh, no!" he said in surprise. "I never laid eyes on yon wee callant in my life before. But, man! That harp he's lugging on his back! Couldna yon be the harp that all the clamjamfry's been aboot?"

"Indeed, that might be," said Tom. Very civilly he addressed the small man. "Please to forgive the liberty, friend, but might I cast an eye over that harp of yours for a short moment?" And he held out his hand.

Owen and the tribe of Yehimelek would have been amazed, for Abipaal, instead of biting, kicking, and gnashing his teeth, made not the least resistance or objection, but sat watching, eager and attentive, while Tom took the harp and ran his hand across the strings with the touch of a master.

"Certain sure that's Telyn Teirtu herself, though she have been tuned and fettled up sweeter than ever she was in Granny's day," Tom said. "Was it you put her in such good order?" Abipaal nodded. "Then I do bow to you, friend," said Tom, and did. His fingers wandered over the strings again and found a sweet, chiming tune, the "Bells of Aberystwyth."

"Eh, that's bonnie," said the prince, simply.

Little Abipaal seemed dumbstruck that such music could exist; he had fallen into a dream, rocking slowly to and fro. Every now and then he heaved a huge sigh, as if his heart were too big to be contained inside him.

"Dinna gie o'er, man! Play us anither tune while we wait for the lads tae return wi" yon lost one," urged the prince. But Tom, who had almost forgotten, under the influence of poetry and music, that someone was missing, jumped up and said, "Better it would be, indeed, if I were to help hunt. Who might this lost boy be, and how did he come to enter the cave by night?"

"Why," said the prince, "it is a canny, braw lad by name Owen Hughes, who helped carry me a" the road here from yon Fforest Mwyaf. Why he had tae gang stravaging off into this unchancy spot then, gude kens, but I guess 'twas someway connectit wi" yon Harp o' Teirtu whilk has thrown ye a" into sic a dickery-dookery. And I maun say," he added handsomely, as Tom's fingers absently pulled out another enchanting strand of melody from the harp, "here's Prince Davie Jamie and-all-the-rest-of-it Tudor-Stuart winna say it wasna waurth the trouble!"

"Owen Hughes? Eh, dear, the poor lad," Tom Dando said, and had just handed the harp carefully back to Abipaal, who still seemed bemused, when several persons arrived upon the scene with dramatic suddenness.

Firstly Bilk and Prigman, closely followed by Garble, burst out of one of the openings in the sloping wall and with a shout of triumph rushed towards Abipaal as he stood still regarding the harp in his hands with a doubtful, melancholy expression. He started at the sound of their voices and retreated to the very edge of the Devil's Leap.

But now another, larger group, consisting of Luggins, Hwfa, Mog, and Dove, appeared from a second opening.

"Haihwchw, lads!" exclaimed Dove. "There's those two scaff that Mog and I followed. How in wonder did they manage to get out of that house when the cliff tumbled in on it? More lives than Auntie Blodwen's old Tomalkin they must have!"

"Never mind how!" said Mog. "Likely they have poor Owen trussed up somewhere. Strangle the pair of them, shall we, till they tell us where?"

"Just let me get at them," said Hwfa.

They flung themselves on Bilk and Prigman, before the latter could reach Abipaal. The cave re-echoed with thuds and yells; Garble came to the assistance of Bilk and Prigman, but even so the three men were far outmatched by the four massive boys. Mog and Dove together tackled Bilk, Hwfa hurled Prigman to the ground with an expert cross-buttock throw, while Luggins pulled Garble down by sheer weight, and then sat on his chest, nearly crushing him.

The prince, in the meantime, was watching with the keenest interest.

"Gude lads! Gude lads! Gie the rogues a bonnie loundering!" he cried joyfully. "Gin I hadna this lammit leg I'd be in there aiding ye!"

Presently the fight abated.

"Stunned, my boyo is," Hwfa said with satisfaction. "Bit of cord, have you, Mog, man? Tie him up tidy, I will, before he do come round."

The boys pooled their string resources. Mog had quite a long piece, which did for Prigman; Dove contributed a neckerchief, which was used to tie Garble's hands behind him; Luggins, rather shamefacedly, produced from his pockets a number of short lengths of cord to which horse chestnuts had been attached, and began removing the chestnuts and tieing the lengths together.

"Hurry up," said Hwfa crossly, "before I will give you a good clip on the ear. Conkers, indeed! Shame you have brought on us, boy."

In guilty haste, Luggins dropped the last two conkers and handed over the joined strings; Bilk was tied up.

"Tidy job, to be sure," Tom Dando said, with approval. "But where is young Owen Hughes?"

"Not a sign of him have we seen," Hwfa said. "Maybe these scum can be telling." Threateningly he turned on Bilk, and asked him, "What have you done with our mate, and do not try to tell me a lie, or there is clear down your throat I will push your nasty teeth."

"B-b-blest if I know where the little micher has got to," stammered Bilk, looking scared to death. "We h-heered him a-letting out a whoobub down yonder, but that was hours agone; since then we haven't seen him, and that's Ticklepenny's truth!"

In spite of all threats he stuck to this story, and his listeners began to believe that it must be true.

"Perhaps he have fallen down a hole? Maybe we should fetch the fire-brigade," Luggins said, looking worried.

But at this moment Owen himself rushed out from one of the passages, pale with haste and exhaustion.

"Where is Abipaal? Is he all right? And the harp? Ah, thank goodness!" he cried with a gasp of relief, observing first the boys and then the small figure, huddled with the harp on the rocky brink. "I thought for sure he would come back here! But where have Bilk and Prigman got to, and that other fellow?"

Luggins stepped back to exhibit the captives.

"Tied up we have got them like a lot of old mailbags," he said proudly.

"No thanks to you," Hwfa muttered.

Prigman was beginning to stir in his bonds; Bilk and Garble eyed their captors balefully.

"Aweel, aweel," exclaimed Prince David, "now we're

a" thegither ance more, and the bonnie harp findit that's been the cause of sic a muckle clamjamfry, let's e'en gan awa" oot this murky hole. Fetch up the harp and the wee mannie, but ye can leave yon ruffians bide; we'll syne send the justices for them. Perdition on this doited leg; I fear ye'll hae tae carry me yet again, lads."

Accordingly, the boys approached Prince David to pick up his improvised litter, but before they could reach him a voice from above cried, "Stand!"

Halfway up the side of the cave, at the head of one of the flights of steps, stood the Marquess of Malyn.

He presented a wild and sinister figure. His face was deathly pale, paler even than the snow which encrusted the many capes of his greatcoat, and in either hand he held a cocked pistol. His strange yellow eyes burned with a feverish light when they beheld the Harp of Teirtu, and Luggins trembled superstitiously, making the sign to avert the Evil Eye, as the Marquess began to descend the steps.

"Diafol, Mog, he do look like old Bogey-Boo himself!"

"Let nobody move," warned Lord Malyn. "The first to do so will receive a breakfast of lead!"

"Gude save us!" exclaimed Prince David. "Malyn! Whit gars ye act sae daft, man? 'Tis treason o' the blackest tae point yon brace o' barkers at your ain anointit prince!"

"Oh, are ye there, Wales?" said Lord Malyn, who had not previously observed the prince, his attention being too fixed on the harp. "Well, it makes no odds; neither prince nor commoner will keep me any longer from my objective. I have not driven fourteen horses and a footman to their end through the blizzard to be foiled *now*." His eyes came to rest on Prigman, Bilk, and Garble; his lips curled scornfully. "What, you have let yourselves be trussed up by a handful of ragged pit-boys? Small wonder you made such a wretched mull of trying to get me the harp."

Bilk, red with anger and shame, writhed in his bonds; some of the knotted strings came apart, and he managed to free his hands.

"Good," said Lord Malyn calmly. "Loosen the other two, then bring me the harp. And secure the little creature who holds it. I have a notion that he is one of my friend the Seljuk's people."

"Dammo!" exclaimed Tom, starting forward. "Are we to stand here while this herwhaliwr tramples us like grass?"

But one of Lord Malyn's pistols was trained steadily on the Prince of Wales.

"Move but another inch and the prince dies," the Marquess announced coldly. Tom stood still, muttering curses.

"Are those men free? Right; now fetch me the harp."

Warily, sweating with fear of the drop below, Bilk approached Abipaal, who crouched like some small cornered animal on the tongue of rock; his eyes shot from side to side, then up, then down; he cast a desperate look at Tom Dando, who was moving by imperceptible degrees towards the helpless prince.

"Abipaal! called Owen. "Dodge him!"

Bilk shot out an arm; Abipaal slipped to one side, just avoiding it. With a furious oath, Bilk lunged again but Abipaal, mustering all his tremendous strength and agility, bounded from the rock on which he stood down—down—across the abyss, and landed on the lower spur with a triumphant jangle of harpstrings, as if Teirtu herself were shouting defiance at her pursuers.

"Crambo!" gasped Bilk. "The little boggart! Who'd a thought—*help!*"

His lunge had taken him too far; he tottered, swaying, upon the brink for the space of six heartbeats, clutching at air; then, with a fearful, wailing cry, overbalanced and hurtled downwards into the dark.

"Bilk!" cried Prigman. He started forward towards the verge, and trod on the conkers which Luggins had carelessly dropped there. His feet shot from under him, he fell forward, and, hardly a moment later, followed his comrade to destruction.

"Duw!" said Luggins. "Not such a bad thing to have a few conkers along, Hwfa, I am thinking?"

His voice broke the petrified silence into which everyone had fallen at the fate of the thieves. With a hissing intake of breath, Lord Malyn moved his pistols, menacing the boys, Tom, and Prince David.

"Garble," he ordered, apparently quite unmoved by the sudden and shocking end of his two agents, "go after that imp of the pit and secure the harp. He is now down on the lower spur."

Very pale, apparently not relishing the task, Garble moved towards one of the entrances.

"I doubt he'll not catch the little wasp," Hwfa uttered hopefully.

But Garble was not destined even to try; with a sudden hubbub of voices, Brother Ianto, Mr. Hughes, Arabis, Yehimelek, and the Seljuk rushed out from another opening in the rock.

Owen had been slowly edging his little book from his pocket; seizing the chance of this distraction he hurled it at Garble, who, struck heavily on the back of the neck, dropped as if he had been felled by a life-preserver.

At the same instant Tom Dando flung himself between the Marquess and the Prince of Wales; only just in time; utterly maddened and unhinged by these reverses, Lord Malyn was taking aim at the prince. Tom pushed Prince David aside as the gun went off, but took the shot himself, full in the chest.

Arabis let out a piercing cry," Dada!"

The prince would certainly have gone over the edge had not Owen thrown himself forward and just managed to drag him to safety.

"Ach y fi, that filthy swine have killed Mr. Dando!" swore Hwfa between his teeth. "Come on and get him, boys, is it? Only one shot he have left; he can't do for us all."

Glaring, step by step, the Marquess retreated from them on to the Devil's Leap.

"Come no nearer!" he warned. "I shall blow out the brains of the first to step within four yards."

The boys wavered; meanwhile Lord Malyn cast a glance slantways down, plainly trying to gauge whether he would be able to imitate Abipaal's escape and take the frightful plunge across the pit.

"He shan't give us the slip that way!" Owen cried, bounding forward. The Marquess discharged his other pistol, but the shot went wide, and its noise was drowned by a much louder sound; as they all watched, thunderstruck, they saw a crack open in the ground and widen with fearful speed; the whole portion of rock on which Lord Malyn stood, weakened either by the sound of the shots or the unusual activity upon it, began to tilt slowly away from the edge. Lord Malyn started, and made a snatch at the guard-rope nearest to him, but missed it; the rock tilted farther—snapped clean off—and shot downwards, taking Lord Malyn with it. Two minutes later a great blast of hot vapour surged up, evidently displaced from some hollow in the depths of the mountain by the massive piece of rock. It passed roaring through the cave and burst from the numerous vents and fissures above with a violent yelling whistle, as if the mountain shrieked in agony.

Startling though these occurrences were, three persons had taken but little notice of them. Mr. Hughes and Brother Ianto, kneeling by Tom, were endeavouring to stop the flow of blood from his wound, while Arabis frantically tore strips from her petticoat for bandages.

"Air, he needs. We should carry him out," Mr. Hughes recommended.

"I thank you, but not to trouble, is it?" Tom said with difficulty. "Waste of time, see? Done for, I am, indeed, Arabis, my little one, but no matter; decent old life I have had, and plenty of friends to look after you when I am gone."

Arabis, choked with grief, could not reply, but the Prince of Wales, who had been helped back to his bench by the boys, exclaimed,

"Aye indeed, I'll see the lass is brocht up as brawly as ane o' my own, on the word of Davie Tudor-Stuart, for whom ye shed your honest blude! Wae's me, I'm sair fashed that this should ha" come to pass!"

Mr. Hughes gave the prince a startled look; up to this moment he had not realized that he was in the presence of royalty.

"And as for yon harp that all this ploy has been aboot, I shall make sure it is handit ower to your lass, sin" it is richtfully hers," the prince went on, surprising Mr. Hughes still more, "and, man, ye shall hae the grandest funeral a poet could, wi" the music of a hundred harps and a" the bards of Wales to do ye honour."

"There's nice," Tom said faintly, smiling. "No finer than that grand sing we have had together though, I am thinking! But as for the harp, too much hate and spite it have caused already. If that small fellow wish to keep it, let him do so, eh, Arabis, my little one?"

"Oh yes indeed!" Arabis cried weeping. "What do I care about the old harp? Only to have you stay alive, Dada, please, is it? Make a try, now!"

"No, girl, my time is come. Like to have written a couple more poems, I would indeed, but too late now."

Sighing a little, like a man who is weary after a pleasant day's journey, Tom leaned back against the arm of Brother Ianto. Suddenly his eyes brightened, and, for a moment, opened wide, as if he saw something very beautiful and unexpected directly in front of him.

"O well now, just fancy that!" he exclaimed.

Then his eyes shut and he was gone.

A few minutes later little Abipaal, carrying the Harp of Teirtu, came stealing cautiously out of one of the smaller caves where he had been hiding. Timid as a wild goat but drawn, it seemed, by some powerful urge, he approached the silent group, scanning them, evidently searching for somebody. Perceiving Tom stretched on the rock he hurried forward and held out the harp; then stopped short, stared, crept nearer; with a cry of anguish flung down the harp at Tom's feet and sank beside it, wailing and keening and rocking back and forth as if he, too, had received a mortal wound.

When, some time later, the party at last slowly and sadly made their way out of the cave and into the street of Nant Agerddau, they were amazed to see that a great piece of snow-covered mountainside had broken away and rolled down, narrowly missing the town, and leaving a clear view all the way to Caer Malyn. Even more startling, Castle Malyn, on its crag above the port, appeared to be in ruins, roofless and shattered.

"It will be the central heating pipes," concluded Mr. Hughes. "When that rock fell down the shaft it will have displaced a great mass of steam which escaped along the pipes and blew the castle of bits, and I daresay there is no one who will grieve."

"My little people!" cried the Seljuk anxiously. "Oh my goodness, I trust they have come to no harm, hurt, mischief, ill that flesh is heir to! Come, Yehimelek, we must return to them at once!"

"Not too easy through all this snow," Brother Ianto remarked. "Best to go back underground, maybe, if the way is clear."

Arabis, coming out of her private grief, said that she would accompany the Seljuk; so did Owen and Ribaddi, now recovered, after his night's sleep. They were worried about Abipaal; he had followed the party through the streets of Nant Agerddau and would not leave the Boar's head Inn, where Tom's body lay, but stood at the door, crying, with the harp in his arms, refusing to enter or leave, and snarling at anyone who approached him.

"Best leave him for the moment, maybe," said Brother Ianto.

The underground way was clear; and the Children of the Pit, snug in their caves, had not been harmed by the destruction of the castle up above; though greatly alarmed by the fearful sound of escaping steam and falling masonry. Their illness continued to abate and, much relieved, while Arabis and Owen tended them, the Seljuk went down to Port Malyn to make arrangements for a ship to take them all home to the Kingdom of Rum. By good fortune he was able to secure one which would be ready to sail the following week.

Finding the tribe so much better Arabis did not give them any more medicines but instead, as this was what they seemed to want most, spent the rest of the day playing them tunes on her crwth. Owen, tired out by two days and a night without sleep, dozed on a camel-fur cushion nearby.

At evening they returned to Nant Agerddau where the Prince of Wales had been making arrangements for Tom Dando's funeral. Luckily a messenger had arrived from London in the course of the day to say that King James III had recovered from his toothache and found the key of his desk.

Galahad and the wagon had been moved to the stableyard of the Boar's Head Inn. Owen, anxious to spare Arabis some of the pain of a return to the empty home, accompanied her there; they found that kindly Brother Ianto, with the same idea, had come to light the stove and make a potful of porridge.

"Passenger you have now, too," he said, nodding towards the corner.

Squatting on Tom Dando's bunk, with his arms round his knees, was the woebegone figure of Abipaal. His face brightened, through the whiskers, at sight of Arabis.

"Told him you were Tom's daughter, I did," Brother Ianto explained.

Seeing Arabis unsling the crwth from her back, Abipaal brightened still more. He seemed astonished to be given a bowl of porridge—but ate it with a good deal of enjoyment; the moment it was finished, however, he made his way to the crwth and began plucking at it experimentally; then he brought it to Arabis with such a beseeching expression that even in her sorrow she could not help smiling. She played him two or three tunes and a look of such ineffable satisfaction spread over his face that Brother Ianto said,

"Lodger for life you have, I am thinking. I do not believe he will go back to Rum with the others."

"Why should he, if he does not want to go?" said Arabis. "Welcome he is to stay here."

One or twice Abipaal looked hopefully at the Harp of Teirtu, which he had with him in Tom Dando's bunk. But Arabis shook her head.

"Learn to play it one day I will," she told him. "But too soon it is now, see?" And he seemed to understand.

Then Arabis, looking past him, discovered something missing.

"Dada's poem!" she cried anxiously.

"Not to worry, is it," Brother Ianto said. "His highness have borrowed it. He is going to have it published up fine, all in white, with gold endpapers. Now I will say good night to you; off to Pennygaff I am going in the morning with Hwfa, Luggins, Mog and Dove; fixed up with them to come and help me build up that old monastery again, I have. But I will see you both soon, I am thinking."

A few minutes after Brother Ianto's departure the Seljuk came to call.

"Ahem!" he said politely. "Should you care for it, my esteemed young lady, damsel, miss, I shall be only too delighted to take you back with me to Rum and give you an honourable establishment there, in requital for the signal services you have rendered my little tribesmen."

"I do thank your worship," Arabis replied, "most grateful I am for your offer and I will be glad to visit you one day, but I am not wishful to leave Wales at present."

And she made the same answer to Prince David when a little later he limped across from the inn and cordially invited her to come and live with him in Windsor Castle, where the Princess of Wales would look after her with every care. But she gratefully accepted his offer to have the "The King at Caerleon" published at his own expense.

After he had left, Mr. Hughes knocked on the wagon door and stumped in. He looked somewhat ill-at-ease, and his embarrassment was not lessened by finding Owen there, with Hawc sitting on his head, and Abipaal, happily picking out simple tunes on the crwth.

However Mr. Hughes was not the man to shirk an unpleasant duty.

"Come to apologize, my dear," he said gruffly. "Realize now I did you and your good father an injustice when you called at the museum—specially since it turns out the confoun—blessed harp belonged to you all the time. Harrumph! Heartily sorry for what I said. And"—he boggled a bit but finally brought it out—"same goes for you, too, Owen my boy. Misjudged you. Realize now you acted with great sense and spirit. His highness has said some very pleasant things about you. He is going to send out an expeditionary force to look for your father. What do you think of that, eh?"

Owen's face lit up. But his joy was too deep for speech.

"Hope you'll come back and live with me at the museum," Mr. Hughes went on awkwardly.

"At the museum?" Owen was surprised. "But, Granda, I thought you resigned?"

"Had a message from the Pennygaff Council today asking if I'd go back." Mr. Hughes sniffed. "Can't find anyone else to accept their ten shillings a year, I daresay. But what about it? And you too, Arabis, my dear? Do us good to have you with us, wouldn't it, Owen—brighten the dusty old place up a bit."

His expression was so anxious and pleading that Arabis said warmly, "Indeed, there is kind you are, Mr. Hughes, bach, and I would like nothing better! Then I can be going to school and getting a bit of learning. But in the summertime, mind you, I must be going back on the road, or I will be forgetting where the healing herbs grow, and old Galahad out there will be growing stiff in the joints with him."

"And I'll come with you," Owen said.

"And you won't mind little Abipaal?" Arabis mentioned. "Taken up lodging with me, he do seem to have."

"Oh, not a bit," Mr. Hughes said. "I daresay he will be a famous help in the museum. Right, then, I am glad to have that settled and I will say good night." Greatly relieved, he creaked away through the snow. Arabis smiled faintly, as she stood in the doorway looking after him. Owen came to join her.

"You won't mind living in Pennygaff?" he said anxiously.

"No, I shall be liking it! And Brother Ianto will be there—the Seljuk have given him a great sum of money to rebuild his monastery."

The blizzard had blown itself out. Overhead, a clear moon rode among stars; downhill the roofs of Nant Agerddau gleamed silver, and beyond lay the Fforest Mwyaf like a wide white counterpane. From inside the wagon came a musical plunk, as Abipaal tightened a string and tried it.

They stood silent, listening. And heard above them the gentle sighing murmur of the Whispering Mountain, the voice of Fig-hat Ben talking in his sleep.

Then Fig-hat Ben shall wear a shroud,
Then shall the despoiler, that was so proud,
Plunge headlong down from the Devil's Leap;
Then shall the Children from darkness creep,
And the men of the glen avoid disaster,
And the Harp of Teirtu find her master.